Issued to the Bride: One Marine

Cora Seton

Copyright © 2017 Cora Seton
Print Edition
Published by One Acre Press

ISBN: 9781988896014

Author's Note

Issued to the Bride One Marine is the fourth volume of the Brides of Chance Creek series, set in the fictional town of Chance Creek, Montana. To find out more about Logan, Lena, Cass, Brian, Sadie, Connor, Jo, Hunter, Jack and Alice, look for the rest of the books in the series, including:

Issued to the Bride One Navy SEAL
Issued to the Bride One Airman
Issued to the Bride One Sniper
Issued to the Bride One Soldier

Also, don't miss Cora Seton's other Chance Creek series, the Cowboys of Chance Creek, the Heroes of Chance Creek, and the SEALs of Chance Creek

The Cowboys of Chance Creek Series:

The Cowboy Inherits a Bride (Volume 0)
The Cowboy's E-Mail Order Bride (Volume 1)
The Cowboy Wins a Bride (Volume 2)
The Cowboy Imports a Bride (Volume 3)
The Cowgirl Ropes a Billionaire (Volume 4)
The Sheriff Catches a Bride (Volume 5)
The Cowboy Lassos a Bride (Volume 6)

The Cowboy Rescues a Bride (Volume 7)

The Cowboy Earns a Bride (Volume 8)

The Cowboy's Christmas Bride (Volume 9)

The Heroes of Chance Creek Series:

The Navy SEAL's E-Mail Order Bride (Volume 1)

The Soldier's E-Mail Order Bride (Volume 2)

The Marine's E-Mail Order Bride (Volume 3)

The Navy SEAL's Christmas Bride (Volume 4)

The Airman's E-Mail Order Bride (Volume 5)

The SEALs of Chance Creek Series:

A SEAL's Oath

A SEAL's Vow

A SEAL's Pledge

A SEAL's Consent

A SEAL's Purpose

A SEAL's Resolve

A SEAL's Devotion

A SEAL's Desire

A SEAL's Struggle

A SEAL's Triumph

Visit Cora's website at www.coraseton.com

Find Cora on Facebook at facebook.com/CoraSeton

Sign up for my newsletter HERE.

www.coraseton.com/sign-up-for-my-newsletter

Prologue

"**W**ITH ALL DUE respect, sir—isn't there anyone else you can send to marry your daughter? Logan Hughes is... well... kind of an ass," Corporal Myers said. A serious young man with dark eyes and dark, regulation short hair, he leaned in the doorway of the General's office, as if unsure of his welcome.

General Augustus Reed didn't reprimand him. Myers did good work and kept his mouth shut when many others would have protested the way he'd circumvented every rule in the book to assemble the Joint Special Task Force for Inter-Branch Communication Clarity. Anyone else would have balked at the ragtag group of men the General had gathered—men who'd messed up their military careers so badly they couldn't say no to the proposition he'd put to them. Would have protested the way he'd brought them here to USSOCOM in Tampa, Florida, under false pretenses and sent them one by one to Two Willows in Montana, where his five errant daughters lived.

Would have flipped his lid about the mission the General had given those men: Take back control of his ranch, marry his daughters and keep them out of trouble for good.

Myers hadn't raised an eyebrow. He'd kept his mouth shut while the General managed to marry off three of the five men on his bogus task force and prepared to send the fourth one to Two Willows. The General would hate to lose an asset like the corporal.

"What is it you object to?" he asked Myers, knowing all too well the answer. He'd chosen Logan Hughes as a match for Lena, the most belligerent of his brood. Lena would require a hell of a man to convince her to marry; she'd been against the institution as long as she'd understood it. But then she'd been against almost everything he'd ever suggested. Lena was like a bucking bronco, lashing out at any attempt to rein her in. Convinced Two Willows was hers to run since the day she could ride, she'd been furious when he'd hired overseers after his wife, Amelia, had died. The General understood Lena's attachment to the ranch, but she'd only been fourteen when Amelia passed away, much too young to take on such a job.

The General shook his head at the memories of his girls booting out overseers and guardians, over and over again, during their tumultuous teen years. It had been hell at the time, but he had to admit now some of their tactics were worthy of a chuckle or two. He'd been relieved when his oldest daughter, Cass, turned twenty-one and he could send the last of their female guardians packing. As for the overseers, they stayed.

He'd seen too much of the world to imagine Lena

could manage the job on her own. A young woman couldn't ride herd on a bunch of rough men. The ranch required hired hands to run it, and hands were rarely the sort you wanted around your daughters. He'd tried to pick overseers with connections—wives and families around to keep them sane. He'd trusted them to maintain the peace on the ranch and to keep his daughters out of harm's way. Unfortunately, that had only worked temporarily.

It was his daughters' fault, of course—they'd run so many good men off the ranch, the pool from which to choose had gotten too small. He'd chosen wrong last time and nearly gotten his girls killed. The knowledge still stung.

That's when the General decided he needed a more permanent solution. He'd created the task force, sent Navy SEAL Brian Lake to marry Cass, and that had worked out just fine. He'd sent Para-rescueman Connor O'Riley to marry Sadie, and that had worked out, too. He'd sent Navy SEAL sniper Hunter Powell next, and today Hunter was marrying his youngest, Jo.

Which meant it was Logan's turn to head to Two Willows. Although the General shared some of Corporal Myers's misgivings.

"Well?" he asked when the corporal didn't answer.

"Permission to speak freely, sir?"

"Always." The General sighed. Myers was a little too punctilious for his tastes sometimes.

"Hughes... isn't the kind of man Lena wants."

The General straightened in surprise. "What do you

know about what Lena wants?" Hell, was the man blushing? The General leaned forward. What was wrong with his corporal?

"I don't know much at all. It's just… from what you've said, and her photographs…" He waved a hand at the photos on the wall, which depicted all the female members of the General's family. The General understood. In most of them, Lena's expression ranged from focused to, well, fierce.

"Logan Hughes is more of a man than he lets on." The General hoped he was right. Because God help them all if Logan wasn't. "He's a good man. We've got to give him a chance."

"You think Lena is going to give him a chance? Begging your pardon, sir."

"I said you could speak freely, Corporal." The General rubbed his chin. He looked at the documents on his desk, detailing the itinerary of his upcoming trip to Asia and the Middle East. He was getting too old for these jaunts. They used to energize him, but this time—this time he wished—

The General shook off the traitorous thoughts. He was far from old and far from done with his career. He was simply unsettled by the violence that had plagued Two Willows recently. His daughters—and the men he'd sent to marry them—had faced off with a pack of drug dealers trying to make a move on Two Willows three times now. He'd like to think the matter was settled.

But he doubted it.

And then there was the matter of his grandchild. Cass was pregnant, and the thought of that baby was troubling him. Bad enough his daughters kept getting themselves into dangerous situations. A baby needed to be protected.

And a baby made him think of his wife. Amelia would have loved grandchildren, if she'd lived long enough to see them.

He cleared his throat. "Hughes will convince her to give him a chance," he said to Myers. "Send him in."

Myers looked like he had more to say, but he retreated to the door, disappeared through it and came back followed by a huge, barrel-chested Marine.

"Morning, General," Hughes said.

The General surveyed him. Took in his short-cropped light brown hair, direct blue-eyed gaze, massive biceps, and semi-aggressive stance. Hughes was a man who took up all the space in a room when he entered it. If he'd just shut up once in a while, he might have made a hell of a career in the military. As it was, he'd done fine—up until the day he'd punched the lights out of a Sergeant Major. That was six months ago. Hughes claimed he'd done it to break up a domestic dispute between the major and his wife. The major and his wife had a different take. The whole affair had been hushed up quickly for the sake of the assaulted man, his marriage and his reputation. Hughes found himself looking at a premature end to his military career. The General had seized the opportunity to add another man to his task force.

"Ready to head to Montana?" the General asked.

"All packed, sir."

"And you understand your mission?" Hell, was the fucker grinning? The muscles in the General's jaw tightened.

"Subdue your daughter, sir. Lock her up in chains of matrimony. Hand back your ranch. Proceed to enjoy the hell out of myself. Sir."

Jesus Christ, the man was a ball-buster. The General stood up. A tall man himself, he wasn't as tall as Hughes, and that pissed him off. "From now on you'll speak about my daughter in terms of respect or I'll yank you right back here and make sure you're prosecuted to the full extent of the law for battery and assault of a ranking officer. I'll bust you down to Private First Class and make sure you spend the rest of your career cleaning the head night and day. Lena is twice the man you'll ever be. She's the one who should have been a Marine. She can outthink you, outshoot you, outrun you and outclass you. Do I make myself clear?"

"Sir, yes sir!" Logan shouted, suddenly ramrod straight, his hands by his sides.

Still fucking around, the General thought with exasperation. The man's stance was straight out of a goddamn boot camp movie. This was exactly how Hughes got under your skin. Not with outright insubordination—but by being just irritating enough he made you lose your cool.

Which made him perfect for Lena.

The General bit back a smile. Logan thought he was

so smart, but he'd met his match. The General knew that beneath all that bluster was a man who had heart. A man who tried to hide how much he cared under a thick veneer of snappy comebacks and sarcasm. After conducting an investigation of his own, the General had concluded Hughes really had believed the Sergeant Major's passionate argument with his wife was putting her life in danger.

Hughes talked a good game, but at heart he was a Boy Scout. Or maybe altar boy was a better assessment. The General's investigation had also uncovered his very religious upbringing, his two priest brothers and what looked like a lot of guilt that he'd chosen the sword instead of the collar. Personally, he couldn't begin to imagine Hughes exhorting a congregation to abstain from sin; he was usually too busy conducting his own sins.

"Are you capable of respect?" the General asked Hughes.

"Yes, sir."

"Do you understand that my daughter is worth three of you?"

"Hell, yeah, sir. Most women are."

At least the bastard had the grace to look rueful. "Do you understand your role at the ranch?"

"Not in the slightest, sir. With all due respect, why not just let your daughter run the place herself if she's such hot shit?"

"I've been asking myself that question," the General snapped. "Especially when I see the alternative."

"Sounds like she'd be fine if you left her alone, sir," Hughes said.

Alone? Hell, no. He'd left his wife alone, and she'd died. He'd left his daughters alone with an unsuitable overseer and nearly gotten them killed, too. He was done with that. He'd make sure his girls were protected from here on in. "I don't want her alone. I want her safe. Do I make myself clear? That's where you come in. You're good at *protecting women*, right?"

Hughes winced. "Yes, sir." This time he wasn't so cocky.

The General took in the man's obvious discomfort. Hughes knew he'd messed up badly. "Look, son, your instincts are good; you just happened to be in the wrong place at the wrong time. I'm sending you to the right place. Do you understand what I'm trying to tell you?"

For the first time, when Hughes looked at him, the General thought he caught a glimpse of the real man behind the act.

"Are you?" Hughes asked unexpectedly. "Sending me to the right place, sir?"

"I sure as hell hope so."

The General held his gaze a long moment and was gratified to confirm what he'd hoped was true about Logan. The man did care. He wanted to do the right thing. He wanted a second chance. And just maybe he wanted a woman to love.

Hughes nodded. "I'd better get back to packing, sir. I leave within the hour."

"Good luck. Treat my daughter well, you hear?"

"Yes, sir." With a snappy salute, Hughes was gone.

The General sat down at his desk, opened the lower left-hand drawer and pulled out one of the letters Amelia had left for him when she passed away. She'd always been blessed with hunches and premonitions, but it wasn't until she'd died that he learned the extent of her foresight. All these letters—pre-dated and ready for him to read—they'd gotten him through the years since she'd gone.

There were few of them left, and a low-grade dread had begun to eat away at the pit of his stomach with each letter he opened.

What would he do when he'd read them all?

The General refused to contemplate that. Instead, he pulled out the one dated today, opened it and settled in to see what Amelia had to say.

Dear Augustus,

I won't pretend to think you'll walk Jo down the aisle today. I wish you'd gone to her wedding—to all of our daughters' weddings. I wish you'd been by their sides all this time. They need you. I don't know why you can't see that. Especially Cass—pregnant with our first grand-child! I wish I could be there to see my girl become a mother.

The General winced. How must it have felt to Amelia to know she never would? He read on.

Fate has a way of forcing you to face the things in life you don't want to face. Your fears have a way of catching up to you no matter how far you run.

So stop running, Augustus.

Talk to the girls. Tell them how you feel. Be honest with them. No matter what's happened, they love you.

The General doubted that. Not after all this time. Not after the way he'd abandoned them when Amelia died.

For the first time, he couldn't pretend to himself it was his job that had kept him away. Amelia was right; other men could have filled his shoes here. He should have gone home. Raised his daughters.

Protected them himself.

I know you have doubts about the man you're sending for Lena. I know you have doubts Lena will marry any man.

The General sighed. Amelia had known too darn much if you asked him. And she was right—Lena was so angry at him he was afraid she'd never allow a man to love her.

You've chosen wisely, Augustus. I see that so clearly, I hope you let it encourage you. The man you send will be the making of our daughter—and she'll be the making of him.

He didn't know why his throat felt suddenly thick and tight. It couldn't be emotion. He wasn't an emotional man.

But if she was right—

No, she *had* to be right. For Lena's sake; not his. He didn't deserve any comfort at this point.

Corporal Myers opened the door a crack and leaned in. "General? You about ready? We'll be leaving soon."

"In a minute." He waved the Corporal away again.

Augustus, it's nearly time. Neither you nor I can stop what's coming. You need to go home—before the choice isn't yours anymore.

Your loving wife,
Amelia

Before the choice wasn't his? What did that mean?

"General?" Myers was still in the doorway. "Sorry, General, but we really have to leave."

"I'm coming." The General folded up the letter and put it away with the other opened ones, his chest constricting when he glanced at the small pile of unopened ones he had left. He had no time to decipher Amelia's cryptic message in today's letter.

Someday soon he'd run out of letters altogether.

He wasn't sure how he'd stand it.

Chapter One

LOGAN WALKED INTO the large rectangular office that was the home of the Joint Special Task Force for Inter-Branch Communication Clarity, crossed the room, whistling, and sat down at his desk, dropping his bag on the ground beside him. He thunked a tall take-out cup of coffee near the monitor of his computer, kissed the palm of his hand and slapped it against the photograph of a dark-haired young woman with blue eyes that hung on the wall nearby. "Hello, baby girl!" he said, then pulled a breakfast sandwich out of a paper bag and began to eat.

"Don't let the General see you do that," Jack Sanders said in a voice as monotone as a robot's.

Logan didn't care; it had taken him weeks to wear the man down enough to make him say his line. He'd started this gag the first day he'd arrived at USSOCOM. First Connor O'Riley had played his straight man, then Hunter Powell had taken over when Connor headed to Two Willows. Jack Sanders had hated every damn day of it, so when Hunter had left just over a month ago, Logan made it his mission to force the man to play his part.

Luckily, *relentless* was Logan's middle name. It had taken persistence, though. One day he'd said, "Hello, baby girl" over a hundred times before Sanders broke down and answered correctly. These days, Sanders resorted to the monotone voice to register his protest over the whole thing, but as long as he said the words, Logan was satisfied. Doubly so, since usually Sanders— a soldier with the Special Forces—was as cagey as a ferret.

"Don't let him see me eat?" Logan said, with as much innocence as he had that very first time all those months ago.

"Don't let him see you slap the woman you're sup-posed to marry." Jack looked up for the first time. Pointed toward Lena's photograph. "Haven't you left yet?"

"Not without saying goodbye. And eating break-fast." Logan made short work of the sandwich and took the framed photograph of Lena Reed off the wall, unzipped his bag and shoved it in.

"The General will notice that."

"Let him. He's giving me his daughter, isn't he? He can't be pissed if I take her photo, too. Now, if I took Alice's—"

He ducked when Jack snatched a stapler from his desk and hurled it at him. The stapler bounced off Logan's shoulder and fell to the ground.

Jack went back to work, but Logan knew his words had hit their target with as much accuracy as Jack had pegged him with the stapler. Jack was supposed to marry Alice, but the man would have to wait until Logan fulfilled his mission and married Lena before he could try to make that happen.

"Come on, you're going to miss me. Admit it."

Jack snorted.

Logan picked up the stapler and put it on his desk, suddenly reluctant to leave. He had no idea why the General had picked him to marry Lena. From everything he'd learned about the woman, she was going to hate him on sight. She'd hate any man the General sent on sight. And if he failed—

The consequences wouldn't be pretty.

"Well, keep up the good work here at the Joint Task Force."

This time Jack swiveled around in his chair. They both knew the task force was a waste of time—desk work conjured up by the General to bore them so silly that traveling to Chance Creek and marrying his daughters came as a relief.

"Want to know what I'm wondering?" Jack asked.

"What?" Logan was surprised. He didn't know Jack wondered about anything. The man made it his business to know everything there was to know.

"Three men sent to Two Willows. Three marriages."

"So?"

"What are the odds?"

Logan sat back. What *were* the odds? Shouldn't one of the General's daughters have balked by now? "That's a damn good question," he admitted.

"I looked it up online. Matchmaking services have a horrible record as far as success is concerned. You might as well toss names around in a paper bag and draw them two by two—it would work as well. So how is the General—General Augustus Reed, who wouldn't know a thing about romance if it bit him on the ass— scoring a hundred percent?"

Logan had a feeling the General knew more about romance than Jack was giving him credit for. There were photographs of his late wife everywhere you looked here at USSOCOM. Still, he understood what Jack was trying to say.

"I don't know. Divine order?" Logan supposed those successes made his failure with Lena all the more likely.

Statistically speaking.

Or maybe not. Was it like flipping a coin? Each new coin toss still had a 50 percent chance of coming up heads—no matter how many other coins had been tossed previously.

"Divine order?" Jack repeated incredulously. "Who the hell believes in divine order?"

Logan's parents did, with a conviction that made it hard for him to follow a path of his own. So did his brothers, who were both in the priesthood. Logan had spent a lifetime trying to escape the calling his family saw for him. He'd thought he'd done that when he joined the Marines—trading a religious calling for a patriotic one.

Then he'd screwed up.

"Does the General have some kind of predictive technology we don't know about yet?" Jack mused.

Logan cocked his head, glad for the distraction. He didn't want to think about the past he'd run from. "Are you worried you're out of the loop on some new kind of spook software, Sanders?" It had been a running joke among the rest of them in the task force that the soldier might be Intelligence.

Jack sighed. "Just trying to make sense of something that doesn't make sense."

"I've stopped trying to make sense of anything." Logan got to his feet. Unlike his parents and brothers, he'd rebelled against the idea you could be directed toward your fate by something outside yourself. He'd left home. Joined the Marines. Escaped any divine order that might be leveled at him.

And then, eight months ago, the dreams had started.

He touched the medallion he wore on a cord around his neck, then shook his head at the gesture. He wasn't going to be a priest, no matter what his parents wanted. Not even if St. Michael himself kept charging into his dreams at night.

When he'd messed up, he'd thought he was on a one-way ticket back to Idaho. Back to the pressure to conform to a calling he'd never had. Now he'd been saved again by the General. Here he was, on his way to Chance Creek to get married and put to rest forevermore his parents' wish for him to become a priest. To hell with the dreams.

"There's something else," Jack said, interrupting his

thoughts. He pulled a document out of a file folder and handed it to Logan. A photograph, but of what Logan couldn't make out.

"What is it?"

"Drone footage. Of Two Willows. I finally got one there this morning to do a flyover. See, here's the house and the carriage house."

"Oh, yeah. There are the outbuildings." Logan could see it now. Everything lined up with the maps on the walls of their office. It had taken them a while to realize why the General had surrounded them with intelligence about his own ranch.

He wondered who Jack had in Montana to put the drone in the air. Was he working with one of the other men already at the ranch? Somehow, Logan doubted it. Jack liked to keep secrets. Logan leaned in for a closer look. "But what's this smudgy part in the middle?"

"Near as I can figure out, that's the hedge maze. Thing is, I can't get a clear image of it. I tried several times. See?" Jack handed him more photographs, and Logan examined them. From what he'd heard, the maze was one of Two Willows's most distinctive attractions. Planted by the General's wife when she was a girl, it had grown so high you couldn't see into it from the ground—or from the second-story windows of the house. Brian, Connor and Hunter had all reported back that there was something uncanny about the huge standing stone at its center. He couldn't pretend he wasn't as curious about it as Jack seemed to be. Which made it interesting that Jack was right; the maze was blurry in each of the photos.

"How do you explain that?" Logan asked. "And who have you got on the ground at Two Willows? Brian?"

Jack shrugged. "I can't explain it; that's the problem. How the hell are those women scrambling my drone?"

"I don't know." Logan noticed Jack had evaded his question. Just like he thought; it wasn't Brian—or any of the others, he'd bet. He didn't have time to stand here and grill Jack, though. He gave his desk a last once-over, then lifted his bag. "I've got to go. See you on the other side, man."

Jack got up and faced him. Held out a hand.

Logan, surprised again, shook it.

"Good luck. I think you're going to need it," Jack said.

"Thanks a lot," Logan said wryly.

But Jack was right, and therein lay the problem. He needed to get married and settle his future once and for all, but like the General had hinted, Lena was a capable, independent woman—a fighter in her own right. Uninterested in marriage. How the hell could someone like him change her mind?

As Lena surveyed the tables and chairs set up on the back lawn for Jo's wedding reception, she couldn't help thinking she and her sisters should stop renting the damn things and just buy a set of their own. They seemed to host a wedding every other month here at Two Willows. First Cass had married, then Sadie, now

Jo.

The outside weddings would have to stop, though. Colder weather was drawing in. Jo was lucky it looked like the rain would hold off for a day or two. And besides, no one else in this family was getting married.

Certainly not her.

"You look stunning," Brian Lake said, joining her on the back porch and trying to take the stack of tablecloths out of Lena's arms. Cass's husband had been at Two Willows for months now, and Lena had gotten used to him, but she wasn't used to compliments and she shrugged this one off. Jo had insisted they all go to a beauty salon in town that morning and have their hair—and their nails—done for the wedding. In shifts, of course, since they all couldn't leave the ranch at once. At least one Reed had to be on Two Willows land at all times. Her mother had made that promise when the General first left Two Willows to serve his country—not because he asked her to, but because she somehow thought it would guarantee his safety—and now that she was gone, they'd fulfill it for her.

Lena swore Jo had paid the hairdresser off to make her look as girly as possible. Her dark, straight locks had been pulled back and twisted into a complicated updo, and her angular face was framed by tendrils the woman had curled into corkscrews. Lena had nearly gagged when she looked in the mirror afterward. But then things got even worse. Jo had decided they'd all get makeovers, too. Lena had to submit to being plucked, moisturized, buffed and made up like a beauty queen, rather than the rancher she was.

The final indignity was the fake nails and the layers of polish another worker at the salon had shellacked onto her. She couldn't do a lick of work like this, and how was she going to tackle the evening chores when the time came? She'd spent an hour walking around with her fingers fanned out, afraid to touch anything, before exasperation overcame her caution. If only she could rip the fake nails off—

But Lena suspected they'd been glued into place with an industrial-strength substance that required an equally industrial-strength solvent to dissolve.

Worst of all, she couldn't carry her pistol, and these days she preferred to be armed. Her sleek shoulder-holster was normally easy to hide under a loose shirt or light jacket, but this darn dress didn't come with one. Cass, her older sister, told her she didn't need a firearm today, but to Lena's way of thinking that was a reckless assumption. Three times Two Willows had been attacked by drug dealers who wanted to establish a foothold in Montana. Three times they'd fought them off—with weapons of one sort or another.

"I got this," she said to Brian, refusing to give up the tablecloths. This much she could do, at least. She walked down the steps and began to spread them on the tables, grateful it was a day without wind.

"Really, Lena—you're beautiful." Brian followed her and reached for the rest of them. "You'll be fending off suitors left and right at the reception."

"I don't want suitors, and I don't need any help,"

she snapped. Why was it the minute she put on a dress, guys like Brian thought she became incapable of doing anything? She spread another cloth on a long rectangular table.

"That won't stop men from trying," he told her. "They'll be falling all over themselves."

Was he laughing at her? She'd have punched him if she wasn't afraid of breaking one of these damn nails.

She spread the final tablecloth and turned on her heel, her ankle-length, spring green bridesmaid dress swishing around her legs in an annoying way as she walked up the steps to the back porch. Inside, she found Sadie and Connor organizing the tableware. When Sadie approached with a stack of plates, Lena quickly lifted a tray of glasses to move it to the other end of the large plank table. Just as quickly, Connor moved to try to take it from her.

"I got this," she said and set it down in a better position.

"Can't help wanting to ease the way for a lovely lass like you," Connor said brightly. "Never seen you in finer form, Lena."

Lena rolled her eyes. Connor wasn't nearly as Irish as he liked to pretend sometimes, and she wasn't in the mood for his theatrics today. "Everything ready in here?" she asked—as if she was running this show. Which she wasn't; weddings weren't her thing.

"We're ready," Sadie said.

"Come on, lass. Give a man a little twirl," Connor continued with his overblown Irish accent. He reached out, took her hand and spun her around before she could stop him. "Lovely sight. You should dress up more often."

Lena snatched her hand away.

Sadie nudged her husband, but she was grinning. "Stop riling up my sister. He's right, though, Lena. You should let your girly side out once in a while. It's fun, isn't it?" Like Lena, she wore her green bridesmaid gown and was done up to the nines. Only Sadie seemed to enjoy it.

"It's ridiculous." Lena stalked out of the room, her anger building. Being girly wasn't fun. It was dangerous. She'd learned that the hard way. Once she'd let her guard down around a man. Once—

The memories crashed over her, and Lena, in the front hall now, braced herself against the staircase railing, fighting to push them back. She'd never forget the way Scott had drawn his arm back. The way he'd smashed his fist into her face so hard she'd nearly blacked out. She'd always thought herself an equal to any man.

He'd proved her wrong.

Lena pushed off from the railing, straightened and stalked down the central hall to the front door. Yanking it open, she stepped outside to where the ceremony would be held and pushed the memory to the back of her mind, where it belonged. Scott was gone, and she wouldn't replace him with any other man. She'd keep her distance from them from now on.

Out front, Hunter Powell was setting up chairs in

rows. Jo, her youngest sister, was already upstairs getting ready for her big day. Her husband-to-be looked nervous to Lena. She grabbed several chairs and lugged them over to add to the rows, happy to finally have found something to do.

Hunter hurried over to her, his hand outstretched to grab the chairs from her. "Well, look at you," he said in his honey-smooth Southern drawl, pausing to look her up and down. "You're a knockout, Lena. Didn't know you had it in you. Those Chance Creek cowboys aren't going to know what hit them tonight. Let me help you."

"I've got these." Lena was past all patience. She turned her back on the former Navy SEAL sniper and began to unfold the chairs one by one. Hunter grabbed them to line them up, and she bit back a frustrated groan. "I said I didn't need help."

"Darling, you're too beautiful to lug chairs around You'll ruin your dress."

Lena let out a frustrated groan and gave up. She stalked off around the house, heading past the little cottage Jo and Hunter had built together toward the barn, ignoring Hunter when he called after her. They could all make fun of her if they wanted to. She wasn't beautiful. She wasn't feminine. She didn't care at all about dressing up—

And she didn't care about men.

Bunch of idiots, if you asked her. Assholes. Got in your way. Slowed you down. Shot at you once in a while.

Knocked your lights out if you let them.

Lena stumbled on the uneven ground, caught herself and picked up her pace.

Now they were invading her ranch, wooing her sisters—and marrying them.

So far, they hadn't wrestled control of the cattle operation from her. Brian, Connor and Hunter listened to her when she told them how things should be done, but how long would that last? When would they join forces against her? Overrule her?

If she couldn't take on one man, how could she take on three?

She kept walking, her throat aching with the vicious unfairness of life. She should have been six feet tall. She should have had muscles and strength, and the cutthroat personality Scott had. The kind of personality that let you tell a woman you loved her—just before ramming your fist into her face.

Lena balled her hands to stop their trembling, her fake nails digging hard into the flesh of her palms. She didn't want to think about Scott. And she didn't want to think about Brian, Connor and Hunter, either. She had dreamed for years of finally getting to run Two Willows—her way. But that dream was fading fast.

She didn't know where that left her. She'd never given thought to a life that didn't include living on this ranch, tending these cattle—protecting this land. She'd fought the General tooth and nail for years for the control of it.

Now he was winning by sending husbands.

It had to stop.

WHEN LOGAN PULLED into the long lane that led to Two Willows, he found it lined with cars and trucks, and had to park almost out at the street. He grabbed his bag from the passenger seat, and the small box the General had sent along with him, and walked the rest of the way, taking in the lovely old white-clapboard house the General's wife had grown up in and made the family home. It was a large, generous old Victorian that immediately tugged at Logan's imagination. He'd grown up in Idaho in a town with plenty of houses like this.

His childhood home had been of much newer construction, though, built during an era that didn't prize grace and architecture. A four-bedroom, two-bath structure without much to recommend it except its location on his uncle's large spread. His uncle's place had been the original home on the ranch, of course, and it was old and charming, like Two Willows was. Logan had always felt a sense of relief when he'd entered it. His aunt and uncle, while Catholic, weren't as devout as his parents were. They worked hard but didn't take things so seriously. He'd grown up in a loving home, but the difference between his parents' expectations and his own dreams was so large he never felt quite as at ease there.

Neither of his parents worked the ranch; his mother had been a librarian and his father worked at a hardware store. They'd taken the house on his uncle's spread because family was important to the Hughes—and because the price was right. His father pitched in during the busiest seasons, but once Logan had grown able to do a man's work and could take his place, he'd stepped back from even that.

Logan had spent most of his time helping his uncle and the hands. By the time he'd left for the Marines, he'd known just about everything there was to know about working with cattle, which was part of the reason the General had chosen him for this role.

When his phone buzzed in his pocket, Logan stopped, pulled it out and took the call. It was his brother. "Hey, Anthony."

"Hey, yourself. Mom said you hadn't gotten in touch in a while."

"Been busy." Busy hiding the mess he'd gotten himself into. He didn't want to give his parents any ideas that he might come home.

He still couldn't believe how stupid he'd been, rushing into the Sergeant Major's house—busting down his door—like an avenging angel ready to save a damsel in distress.

"Busy, huh? Too busy to call your mother? She worries, you know."

"Stop playing parish priest with me."

His brother chuckled. "Sorry. It's hard to step out of character, you know?"

Logan did know. He'd worked hard to break out of the character his parents had wanted to cloak him with and become a Marine, instead.

"I'll call her—soon as I can."

"Call her today."

"If I have time. I'm… busy."

"Where are you? Can you at least tell me that? Still in Florida?"

Logan always found it hard to lie to Anthony. Ten years older than him, Anthony had always held the upper hand in their relationship and was a man of the cloth now, like their much older brother, James. James was a missionary in Ethiopia. No one expected him to call home all the time.

"No—I'm in… Montana."

"Montana? What kind of mission are the Marines running in Montana?"

"You wouldn't believe it if I told you. And I can't tell you, so don't ask."

"Already did," Anthony pointed out. "You know, if you had to join the military, the least you could've done was be a chaplain. It would have eased Mom's heart to know—"

"That wasn't my path," Logan snapped. They'd gone over this a thousand times. His mother had two priests for sons. Wasn't that enough? Why harp on the one that got away? "You can tell her that next time you two talk."

"I know you don't think you have a calling—"

Seriously? They were going to do this again? Logan shoved his free hand in his pocket. "I *know* I don't have a calling."

He had no desire to be a priest. Didn't think God would have him after so many years in the service, anyway. Surely he'd broken far too many commandments to make that even possible, if he'd ever had an inkling that way.

Which he hadn't. Not ever.

So how to explain his dreams?

He wasn't a priest in them, either, he reminded himself. Normally he wasn't one for dreaming much at all.

Which made them even more—

Weird.

"You ever think about St. Michael?" he asked Anthony as casually as he could.

"St. Michael? What about St. Michael?"

Logan couldn't tell his brother he'd been dreaming about the saint. Anthony would have him home and in a collar before he could finish the sentence.

"St. Michael carries a sword." He touched the medallion again. His middle name was Michael—for the saint. His first name represented a touch of whimsy his mother seemingly hadn't had before or since. "He's supposed to be a protector. Like me," he asserted, unsure why it seemed so important to clarify the connection.

"Not exactly like you. He was a saint. You're a Marine," Anthony said.

"I protect people, just like he's supposed to." That's what the dreams had to mean, right? In them, St. Michael descended from the heavens and handed him that radiant sword he was always depicted with. In the dreams, Logan took the sword, held it firmly and wielded it like he knew what it was for.

He always woke with the sense he was supposed to protect—someone.

Which was why, when he'd heard the Sergeant Major's wife yelling, he'd gone charging in like a white knight.

Unfortunately, she wasn't the damsel he was looking for.

And now he'd skunked his career.

He knew Anthony—and his parents—would interpret the dream very differently. "It's symbolic," his mother would say. "The sword is the word of God. You're meant to protect your parish. Come home and take up your calling."

Logan fought the urge to rip the medallion from his neck and toss it away. "Look, I've got to go."

"Call Mom—"

Logan hung up. He'd call his mother.

Just as soon as he caught himself a wife.

KITCHEN DUTY. LENA hated nothing more than kitchen duty, but it was better than simpering around among the guests in this travesty of a dress. Like Brian had predicted, she'd been fending off male attention ever since the reception had started. Jo's wedding had been beautiful, and now her sister was glowing like she'd reached some stage of nirvana. Lena was happy for her. Really. But all this romantic love stuff was pissing her off.

As were her fake nails. Maybe if she scrubbed some dishes, they'd fall off.

Lena slammed a pile of dishes into the sink and ran water over them. Outside, people danced, music and laughter sliding in the open windows to fill the kitchen.

The night was cooling down, however, and already some men were building a bonfire to keep folks warm. Soon autumn would really make its presence known and they'd be in for another hard Montana winter.

Lena didn't mind. She loved every season at Two Willows. Coming home from the barns on a cold, crystal winter evening, every star a bright pinprick in the sky—

Those were moments to live for.

She could almost enjoy herself if there weren't so many damn men around the place these days. She'd come across Brian, Connor and Hunter having a chat about how to handle security on the ranch once Hunter left with Jo on their honeymoon They hadn't even bothered to add her to their little conference, although she'd always guarded this property with her life. When she'd burst in to add her two cents, they'd all looked guilty, like they'd been caught doing something wrong.

Which they had.

They'd underestimated her again. Just because Scott had gotten the drop on her didn't make her useless. She'd been caught off guard once and only once. It would never happen again.

"We didn't want to bother you—it's your sister's wedding," Hunter had said.

"It's *your* wedding!" she'd cried back at him. He'd exchanged glances with the others, as if he hadn't understood the distinction. Apparently, men were supposed to handle things like security. Women were supposed to slither around looking sexy. She would bullwhip the lot of them if she could get away with it without upsetting her sisters.

Instead, she'd given them a piece of her mind and left them to it. They could make all the plans they wanted; she was the one who knew Two Willows like the back of her hand. She could keep it secure. When her mother died eleven years ago, and the General refused to come home, she'd pledged to keep her sisters safe.

Although lately she'd been failing on every front.

But that was the past, she told herself sternly. She'd learned her lesson.

Someone knocked on the front door, and Lena dried her hands, relieved to get away from the dishes—and her ugly thoughts. She had to get things back in hand. No more self-defeating thoughts. No backing down from the job she'd worked toward her whole life.

This was her ranch. Hers. Not Brian's or Connor's—or Hunter's, for that matter.

Her cattle operation.

She hoped they understood that.

The knock sounded again.

She hoped the General understood that, too. Two Willows wasn't Reed land—it had belonged to the Griffiths—her mother's family.

He didn't get to call the shots here. Much as he thought he did. He'd sent three men, and her sisters had married them. He'd better not think he could—

She had almost reached the door when the knocking became a thunderous pounding.

Irritated, Lena yanked the door open—saw a tall man, with the shoulders of a fullback and biceps of an MMA superstar, his blue eyes flashing with humor, his mouth tugging into a smile as he took her in.

"Hello, baby girl. My name's—"

"Oh, hell no!" Lena slammed the door shut.

And locked it.

Chapter Two

WHEN THE DOOR swung open again a few seconds later, it wasn't Lena who beckoned Logan inside. It was her younger sister, Alice, the otherworldly beauty Jack Sanders was supposed to marry. A white cat twined its way around her feet, gave him a baleful look and stalked away up the hall.

"Excuse my sister's behavior," she said. "It's been a long day, and she's tired."

"More like pissed off," Lena shouted from somewhere behind her. "He's all yours, Alice."

"Come on in." Alice opened the door wider, her expression half chagrined, half amused. "I assume the General sent you?"

Logan nodded. "Guess I don't make the best first impression." It wasn't the first time a woman had slammed the door in his face, though. He suspected he'd survive, but this wasn't a promising start.

"You're not here for me," Alice said after considering him. "But I'm not sure I understand…" She trailed off and glanced in the direction Lena had disappeared.

Logan heard clearly what Alice didn't say: Why

would the General send someone like him for Lena? Was he so unqualified she could see it just by looking at him? He didn't usually lack for female company, but he'd never considered marriage before, either. Maybe that's what she saw.

"She'll come around. After all, how can she pass this up?" he quipped to cover his discomfort and indicated his body as if it were a prize on a television game show.

"Uh… sure." Alice led the way down the hall toward the back of the house, leaving Logan with the sinking feeling he'd blown another first impression.

Batting a thousand.

As usual.

He touched his St. Michael medal. He could use a saint's protection—from himself. One thing for sure, he knew how to stick his foot in his mouth.

Alice stopped, and he nearly walked right into her. She spun to face him.

"Faith… and a sword."

He waited for her to clarify her pronouncement, but she didn't. "What about them?"

"You're going to need a lot of faith to win her—and as strong as my sister is, she's going to need help before all is said and done. I'm not sure where the sword comes in." Alice's shoulders slumped a little, and she shook her head. "Sorry. It felt important to say that, but my radar's off these days. Nothing is clear."

Radar? Did she mean the hunches she was supposed to get? The men who'd arrived in Chance Creek before him had told him all about those. Logan wasn't one to believe in that kind of thing, but then he wasn't one to have dreams about saints, either.

Was Lena the woman he was supposed to protect?

Alice kept going, and he followed her through the kitchen into the backyard, where Hunter and Jo's wedding reception was in full swing. Hearing the live music, seeing the swaying bodies on the makeshift dance floor and the happy conversations taking place all around him, made Logan relax. Nothing was going to happen tonight. All he had to do was get himself settled in as a guest at Two Willows—and give Jo her wedding present from her father.

The bride and bridegroom stood near the dance floor, chatting with friends. As he approached them, Logan had to smile. Hunter was the happiest he'd ever seen the Navy SEAL. Jo was petite and beautiful in her wedding gown, beaming at her husband with so much love it eased Logan's heart even more. Hunter was a good man. He deserved to be loved like that.

Would anyone ever love him that way? He searched for Lena in the crowd but didn't see her.

Probably not.

"Hunter, Jo, this is Logan Hughes. The General sent him," Alice said.

"I've got something for you," Logan said to Jo after he'd shaken hands with Hunter, as if they'd just met, rather than having spent months in each other's company already. He presented Jo with the gift the General had sent with him. "For you. From your father."

"The General?" Jo's face clouded a moment, but

when she undid the wrapping paper, opened the small
box and pulled out the locket he'd sent, she softened.
"It's a lot like the one he gave to my mother," she said,
touching a necklace she wore. "My sisters and I have
been sharing it between us, but each time one of us gets
married he sends us one of our own."

"He loves you very much."

Jo nodded but dipped her head.

Logan knew why. The General hadn't come to her
wedding. He hadn't come to Cass's or Sadie's either,
though.

"When will he come home?" she asked him suddenly.

"I wish I knew. But I don't. He left for the Middle
East this morning. It's going to be a hard trip."

Hunter came to his rescue. "One more dance before
we head out," he told his new wife.

"Or two. Or three," she said, happy again.

When they'd left, Logan scanned the crowd a second time but didn't see Lena until he turned back
toward the house. Through the open windows he saw
her crossing and re-crossing the kitchen. Cleaning up,
he realized.

Avoiding him.

To hell with that, Logan thought. He was here to
catch a bride.

Time to start.

ALICE WAS A traitor. How else to explain why she'd
opened the door and let that... man... walk in. He'd

been sent by the General, anyone could see that, and she already had three interlopers to contend with.

Considering she and Alice were the only two unmarried sisters left, it didn't take a genius to figure out Logan was meant for one of them. Whether the General sent the men for that purpose, or they'd concocted the scheme to win Two Willows for themselves by marrying his daughters, she couldn't be sure. For all their pretense they hadn't known each other before coming here, it was clear to her they had.

She stacked the dishes more vehemently than was prudent, creating a massive pile, and carted them to the sink, just making it before most of them slid from her fingers into the soapy water. Jo jumped back and narrowly avoided the splash. Still holding a lone wooden spoon, she surveyed the puddle of water at her feet. Damn it, couldn't one thing go right?

A slow whistle behind her made Lena spin on her heel.

There he was. Leaning up against the doorjamb.

Watching her.

"Baby girl, I knew from your photographs you were pretty," Logan said. "But they didn't do you justice. You're hot."

Was her mouth hanging open? She was pretty sure her mouth was hanging open.

No one spoke to her that way. No one.

Except Scott.

Lena pushed that thought into the far recesses of her mind.

"How about we start over? I'm Logan Hughes. Your dad sent me here to take care of you," he continued, apparently unaware of her fury. "I know it's been dangerous around Two Willows this summer and fall, but you don't have to be afraid anymore—"

Afraid? Did he think she was *afraid*? Did the General think she was?

Logan broke off and chuckled. "Hell, I can't even finish my own thought. You're too distracting. This is why I could never be a priest." He looked her up and down. "I like what I like: girls who aren't afraid to be girls, you know what I—? Ow! Fuck!"

He tried to grab the wooden spoon, but Lena was too fast for him. She got in a few good whacks to his shoulders, chest and head before he could grab for it again, but it was the crack across his mouth that gave her the most satisfaction. *Girls who aren't afraid to be girls.*

Logan snatched the spoon away. "Shit, woman, have you lost your mind?"

"Have you lost yours? I'm not some girly-girl you can sweet talk into your bed, asshole. Get the hell out of my house. I don't want you, and I never will!"

She stalked out of the room, barely registering the shock, then pain, then determination that flashed in his eyes. She made it up the stairs, into her room—

And slammed the door hard enough to rattle every window in the house.

This was the joker the General had sent to be her husband?

He must despise her more than she'd ever guessed.

LOGAN WAS GRATEFUL for his heavy work coat when he met up with Brian and Connor in the barn the following morning. Hunter and Jo had left the night before on their honeymoon to the east coast, and he meant to pitch in and do his part of the chores before he confronted Lena again. He'd gotten an eyeful of the burned-out stables on his way here and was glad that no one—and no horses—had been injured in the blaze. He'd heard about the way Jo had run into the flames to rescue her animals, and how Hunter had finally gotten her out of there.

Things could have ended much worse than they had.

The main barn was untouched, however, and housed Atlas, Lena's stallion—singed in the blaze, but better now—in a quickly built temporary stall. Connor had told him the other horses had been boarded at other ranches for the time being.

He called a greeting to the other men, wincing a little because his mouth still stung. Lena had gotten a good hard crack at him with that spoon.

He probably deserved it.

A smarter man would have noticed right away last night Lena looked far different than she'd ever looked in her photographs. He had, actually, but hadn't put two and two together to realize how out-of-character it was. He'd meant to compliment her and had stuck his foot in his mouth instead. Typical.

"Hey, Logan. Ready to work?" Brian called back. He was playing with a couple of dogs. Jo's, Logan guessed.

He knew she bred McNabs for their cattle herding tendencies.

"Sure thing."

"Good. There's a lot to do," Connor said. Another dog chased his heels. "This is Max," he said, giving the dog's head a pat. "Those are Champ and Isobel."

"Nice to meet you, Max." Logan bent down and ruffled the dog's ears.

He was happy to see Brian and Connor again. While they hadn't served together actively, they'd all gotten to know each other during their stint at USSOCOM, and soon the three of them easily came up with a plan to divvy up the work. They were about to get to it when Lena strode in, her jaw set, and pushed her way among them.

"I suppose you're gloating, aren't you? You think you've won. Well, you haven't!"

"Lena—"

Lena cut Brian off. Like the rest of them, she wore jeans, boots and a sturdy fall coat to ward off the coolness of the morning. Her hair was pulled back in a tight ponytail. Her fancy nails were gone, and she didn't have a lick of makeup on. She'd come to work, that was clear.

Nothing girly about her.

"I'm not going to let a bunch of strangers run this ranch!" she asserted.

"You aren't making sense," Brian said. Connor winced, and even Logan, new as he was here, could see Brian had taken the wrong tack.

"Not making sense? You think I'm going to sit and watch while the four of you men take over? You think I'll let you steal my land right out from under me? I've seen how this goes before, remember?"

"Lass, you've got it all wrong," Connor tried.

"Don't *lass* me. I'm not some child you can bribe with pretty phrases and lies." She looked at each of them in turn. "I can still drive you off this land; just like I've driven off everyone else who hasn't belonged here. You think I can't?"

Logan held his tongue. No, she couldn't. Not him, at least. But she didn't know that yet, and he wasn't so rash he'd be the one to tell her.

"Get out of my barn!" she burst out. "Now—I don't want to see a single one of you for the rest of the day!"

The men exchanged startled looks, and Lena balled her fists, obviously ready for a fight. Logan grabbed Connor. "Let's go."

"But—"

"You heard the lady. Let's go." He pushed Connor toward the barn door.

Brian followed, frowning, and when they reached the back porch of the house, he demanded, "Why did you let her run us off? She can't run this place alone. We're all supposed to—"

"If I don't marry Lena, none of us gets to stay here," Logan told him. "The more we try to force the issue, the worse it's going to get. You all have lived with her. I haven't. But even I know when a woman is about to snap. First you came, then Connor, then Hunter—and for whatever reason, she allowed that to happen. Now the General has sent her a husband. We can't pretend she doesn't know that. We've got to cut her some slack—let her feel she's got some kind of control over her life."

He knew how bad it felt when someone else tried to take control.

"We need to step back and let Lena take the helm until we know where her weaknesses lay. Then we can step in to help and she'll be grateful—not pissed." As he'd learned so painfully, it didn't make sense to save someone who didn't need saving.

"Since when do you know anything about human nature?" Brian demanded, but Logan could tell he was speaking from surprise, not derision.

Logan knew why. Most of the time he was so quick to joke around no one took him seriously.

But he was serious about marrying Lena and staying the heck away from Idaho. That meant stepping up his game.

"Lena wants control of the ranch. She wants to run the cattle operation the way she thinks it ought to be run. According to everything you guys have told me, it's what she's wanted all her life, but the General has never let her do it. How'd you feel if you were standing in her shoes?"

"So, we just hand it over to her and walk away? Then what? Go get jobs in town?" Connor asked.

"No. We stay right here." He mulled it over. "As

Lena's hired hands," he added, a grin tugging at his mouth. Why not? It was a tidy solution.

Brian whistled. "You know what? That's kind of brilliant."

"I don't know." Connor scratched the back of his neck.

"Think about it," Brian said to him. "How many times have you disagreed with Lena's ideas so far?"

"Not many," Connor admitted.

"Me, neither. She knows what she's doing. Anyone can see that."

"Except the General," Connor pointed out.

"I think he sees it, even if he doesn't want to act on it," Logan said. "But we won't act like hands forever; just until she learns she can trust us. Then we can all work together."

"You think she'll ever trust us?" Connor asked him.

Brian answered him. "I don't think Lena is unreasonable. I think the General's the one who's pushed her too far. Logan's right; we just need to let the pendulum swing back the other way."

Connor took a deep breath. "I guess I can do that. For now."

"I can, too," Logan put in. It had been ages since he'd ranched on anything like a daily basis. Letting Lena call the shots—for now—would give him a chance to catch up on any changes in protocol that might have occurred over the years.

"What about rebuilding the stables?" Connor asked.

"We'll let her take lead on that, too," Brian said.

"Here's the plan: we report for duty each morning, do the jobs she assigns us and keep our mouths shut. You think that's possible, big guy?"

Logan snorted. "It's possible…" He'd do his best because he thought it was the best plan. But Brian was right.

Keeping his mouth shut wasn't going to be easy.

LENA HAD OFTEN done the chores with only Jo's help, so it was no struggle to get the basics done this morning. She'd taken an active interest in every part of the cattle operation from the moment she'd learned to ride a horse—which wasn't too long after she leaned to walk. Back then Amelia had ruled the roost with the aid of a trusted overseer who'd contributed to Lena's education. He was older than her parents, however, and retired only months before Amelia died.

By that time Lena felt she knew enough to run the place herself. She'd never understood the General's need to impose his will on her from a distance. Maybe if he'd come to see the ranch himself, he'd realize how good she was at running the place. Instead, he'd only ever looked at the monetary reports sent by the overseers and never commented that the ranch was far more profitable when she ran it.

He just didn't care. Not about her. Not about Two Willows. And not only did he not care—he continually found ways to undercut her and ruin her plans. This wasn't the first time he'd tried to replace his daughters with sons. She remembered one hot July afternoon back when she was seven, back when she and her sisters treated their father like he was some kind of god who arrived home on leave occasionally to be doted on by all of them. She'd hung on his arm, telling him about her horse, her archery practice, her cattle wrangling skills.

And then her cousins had arrived.

They were distant cousins, barely kin as she understood it. Something about great aunts and uncles that made her parents welcome them even though they were strangers. Earl Reed and his wife, Nancy, were a boisterous pair, and their four sons were half-wild, raised on a ranch down in Colorado. They were just passing through on a vacation to Glacier National Park and only spent two nights at the ranch, but Lena hated every minute of it because their presence turned the General into a traitor.

He no longer seemed to hear a word she and her sisters said. He was too busy playing catch with the boys, riding horses with them—Lena and her sisters' mounts, which meant they had to stay at home. Racing with them, inviting them along to do chores.

When Lena couldn't stand it anymore, she rebelled. At the end of the second dusty, hot afternoon, she saw the General leading Earl and his sons to a watering hole on Two Willows property. *Her* watering hole. Lena slipped after them, found them stripped down, splashing and laughing in the creek, and decided she'd had enough. She would be included if it was the last thing she did.

Lena stripped, too, and ran to cannonball into the

water.

The General's bellow stopped her short.

"Get out of here, girl, and put your clothes on! Get back home to your mama. You trying to disgrace us all?"

She'd never moved more quickly. Never felt such shame. She grabbed her clothes, streaked away like a cougar was chasing her. Hid in the barn until her cousins left the following afternoon, Alice sneaking her food and water. Her mother appeared late that night and gave her a battery-operated lantern and a blanket to make her hideout more comfortable.

"You're getting older, sweetheart," she said. "People are funny about bodies. There isn't anything wrong with them, but people like to pretend there might be."

"He yelled at me."

When Amelia sat down, Lena had curled against her mother, the ache in her heart so sharp she thought it would shred her inside.

"He was trying to protect you. It's hard to understand, but boys and girls are different, and it gets complicated as you get older. All you need to know is your father loves you, and your cousins will leave tomorrow. Everything will go right back to normal; you'll see."

Her mother had been wrong about that. Lena couldn't unlearn what she'd come to understand that day. Like Amelia said, boys and girls were different. Boys could do whatever they wanted. Girls couldn't. Not unless they fought and fought and fought for that right.

It was the only time her father had put his worldview into words so succinctly, but his actions made his feelings loud and clear as the years went by. Men were in charge; women weren't. Men could run ranches; women couldn't. Men could be trusted to watch over themselves; women needed to be supervised.

Now there were four men at Two Willows.

Four men to impose their will on her.

Maybe she should just give up.

Exiting the barn, she came face to face with the charred remains of the stable and stopped in her tracks. She couldn't give up. She had to rebuild it, and that would be much harder to accomplish on her own.

She wasn't on her own, though, she told herself. She still had four sisters, and she could organize the rebuilding of the stables if they would agree to help her.

Of course, she knew what they would say: let the men do it. They didn't realize the General hadn't sent the men to help them; nor had he sent them as ready-made husbands.

He'd sent the men to *replace* them.

One by one he was getting the sons he'd always wanted. Brian had replaced Cass. Connor had replaced Sadie. Hunter had replaced Jo—

And Logan was here to obliterate her in the General's eyes.

Of course, she and her sisters would still exist. Still live at Two Willows.

The General didn't care about that.

Finally, he'd have an army of men living at his wife's ranch. Men loyal to him.

Men he could control.

Her dream of running the cattle—of making this one of the pre-eminent ranches in the land—

Would die.

A breeze whispered over her cheek, cold and sharp, another hint of the hard winter ahead. She'd fought the General for eleven years. She had to keep on fighting.

She couldn't let him win.

She was still standing like that, contemplating the burned-out stables, sorting plans in her head, when a fluttering piece of white cloth caught her attention. Lena straightened.

Someone was coming down the track from the house, waving a white handkerchief at the end of a long stick, a couple of dogs following briskly at his heels.

Logan—with Champ and Isobel.

Lena sighed. Who else?

With her hands braced on her hips, Lena waited for him.

"Make it fast."

"I come in peace," he told her when he approached, Champ and Isobel running circles around him, sniffing and investigating their surroundings. "With a message from Brian and Connor, as well as myself."

"Spit it out. I've got work to do." He was handsome; she'd give him that. An intelligence lurked in his eyes despite his joking manner. Lena wondered what he was like when he stopped messing around, then nearly groaned. She didn't care if Logan was smart or as dumb as a stump. Either way, he was far too dangerous to let past her guard.

"You didn't ask us to come here. Your father sent us without consulting you. We get that—and we wish it was different."

"So?" If he thought he was scoring points, he wasn't. He was right; she didn't want him here.

"So, Brian loves Cass, and Connor loves Sadie—and you know Hunter loves Jo. Anyone could see that last night. They aren't going anywhere. But that doesn't mean we have to be your enemies. None of us want that."

"No, you just want to run the show and boss me around—"

"You're wrong. We want the opposite of that."

"You want me to run the show and boss you around?" she asked sarcastically. Did he think she was stupid? She bent down absently to give Isobel a pat.

"Exactly."

When he didn't elucidate further, Lena let out a huff of exasperation. "I told you not to waste my time." She stood up again, and Isobel wandered off.

"You know Two Willows. You grew up here. This is your mother's ranch. You should be the boss. None of us is clamoring for the job."

"And you'll what—follow orders?" She wasn't buying it.

He flashed a grin that made her swallow. Hell, he

was handsome, wasn't he? "Yes, we will. All of us have made careers out of following orders. You might not believe this, baby girl, but we're just happy to be here. Alive. Working. With a chance to make a home for ourselves here. All of us love ranching. We've got it made at Two Willows. So, boss us the fuck around. We'll do our best."

"What if your best isn't good enough?" This had to be a trick, and Lena hated tricks. Hated the hope that coursed through her veins at his words. Scott had fooled her, too, she reminded herself. Pretended to care for her when he was using her all along.

"Then shit-can us and kick us to the curb," Logan told her. "Come on—we'll be a kick-ass crew of hired hands. The best you ever had."

"Hired hands? What does that mean? You'll want to be paid?"

Logan thought about it. "Guess we will. Fair wages. We've got to be able to take our wives out to dinner now and then, don't you think?"

"You have a wife?" Somehow the thought of it twisted her gut.

"Not yet." And before she could stop him, Logan took two steps forward, bent down and snatched a kiss, jerking back out of the way again before she could slug him. "I'd say that's a start," he added and walked away jauntily, whistling for Isobel and Champ to follow him. The little furry traitors did. "We'll look for a roster of chores in the kitchen at lunchtime," he called over his shoulder.

Lena scrubbed his kiss off her lips with the back of her hand and watched him go, pissed and shocked and… thrown off-kilter.

He was an ass. A cocky bastard. And she hadn't liked his kiss. She didn't know why her heart had leaped when they touched or why her lips still tingled. She was not attracted to the Marine. At all.

But if the men really wanted to be hired hands, she'd boss them around. And Logan? She'd make sure he paid dearly for that kiss. By the time she was done with him, he'd be too tired to try anything like that again.

Chapter Three

THANK GOD HE had fantastic reflexes, honed by his time in the military, Logan thought as he strode toward the house, the dogs racing ahead of him. It had been worth risking an uppercut to his face to get that kiss—and to see Lena's expression afterward. She'd been shocked. Outraged, maybe.

But he didn't think she'd been disgusted.

Her mouth had been soft under his, and his body thrummed with interest when he thought of kissing her again. He needed to be patient, though. Give her time to get used to him. Used to the idea he meant to be her man.

Lena's man.

He liked the sound of it. Liked the solidity it would lend to his life. The period it would put to his parents' dream of him entering the priesthood. And if Alice was right, and Lena was the woman he was meant to save, so much the better. Anything to get St. Michael out of his dreams.

He spent the rest of the morning in the guest room answering emails that had accumulated in the last weeks of his service, checking news sites, and generally wasting time until lunch. When the noon meal rolled around, Logan couldn't help but feel anticipation, mixed with a dash of concern. What if Lena blew them off?

But she didn't. She rose to the challenge they'd given her and posted a roster of duties near the kitchen door—the first thing he saw when he walked in.

The second thing he saw was Lena. Her watchful gaze resting on him.

He checked the roster again.

There were a lot of jobs listed under his name.

But if she thought she could run him off with hard work, she was mistaken. He might be a joker, a class clown when the situation warranted it. He was also a Marine. And Marines weren't afraid of hard work.

In fact, when the meal was over, the busy afternoon came as a welcome relief from all the months he'd spent at a desk at USSOCOM. For the first time in ages, he made use of the muscles he'd spent years building.

"Feels good, doesn't it?" Brian remarked at one point when they passed each other between the barn and the pastures where the cattle grazed.

"Feels fucking amazing," Logan told him.

It was nearly dinnertime, and the sun was low on the horizon when Lena came to check on them, ticked off the jobs on a list she'd written on a piece of note paper and sent them back to the house for dinner.

"What about you?" Logan asked when everyone else turned to go.

"Be there in a minute. I've got a couple of things to

finish." She kept her gaze on the paper in her hand, refusing to meet his.

"We did everything you asked." He wanted to be sure she knew that. He had a feeling Lena would do what she could to send him packing.

"I know that. Go eat." She waved him away.

He wanted another kiss, and he followed her into the barn when she walked past him. When she realized he was still behind her, she faced him and put her hands on her hips. "Scram!"

"I can help, whatever it is," he offered. "Get you in to dinner that much sooner. You must be hungry; I sure am." Lena had worked all afternoon, too.

"I don't need any help. There's just something I want to do."

Why was she acting so squirrelly? Was she hiding something? Logan took a step closer. She was definitely hiding something.

"I'll wait for you. We can walk back together."

"I don't want to walk back together."

"Then we can—"

"I want to be alone. Can't you understand that? Don't you ever just want five minutes to yourself?"

Logan backed off at Lena's outburst. He could understand that. All those years in the military, in close quarters with other Marines—

"Yeah, I do. Sorry—hard not to want to spend as much time as possible with such a pretty lady—" Logan jumped out of the way of Lena's fist, bobbed and weaved and caught a chance to snatch a kiss. He ducked out of the barn before she could retaliate. Damn, he liked kissing Lena. All that outrage made her spicy.

He'd have to do it more often, Logan decided, and headed back up to the house, grinning the whole way.

SHE WAS GOING to kill him if he kissed her again, Lena told herself as she climbed the ladder to the hayloft. She made her way to the space under the window she'd claimed as her own after that disaster with her cousins when she was seven, behind the bales of hay. She opened the old steamer trunk she'd brought from the attic as a child, pulled out a dusty horse blanket to sit on, the battery-operated lantern her mother had given her—its light bright enough to read by but safe around all the hay—and the paperback novel she'd taken out from the library.

Redcoats at Dawn was a fast-paced, thrilling spy story that featured an intrepid young Revolutionary War soldier named Caleb who infiltrated the British Forces time and time again, and brought the intelligence he gathered back to General Washington. Lena had long thought she'd make a brilliant spy—and that she'd been born in the wrong era—

And the wrong gender.

To be a man at the dawn of the nation. To fight to form a new country on the ideals of freedom—

To be respected for your accomplishments—

The closest she could come to any of that was to read a damn book.

She turned the lantern on just bright enough to read

by in the lowering light, curled up, her back against a hay bale, and began where she'd left off. Caleb was shadowing the British Forces again, about to slip in among them to figure out their next move. She knew he was going to be caught this time. She could feel it.

At the same time, the British Forces were closing in on the rebel Americans, and even though she knew how the Revolution played out, the claustrophobic feeling was all too familiar to Lena. Her situation was becoming untenable, too. She didn't know how much longer she'd have a place at Two Willows, despite the men's pretense they were merely hired hands. Bad enough Logan had come here to usurp her.

For him to taunt her with kisses was too much.

She lifted a hand to touch her lips, the words on the page blurring as her thoughts wandered.

She wasn't immune to men. When she'd met Scott, she'd been ready for a fun relationship. She'd loved his recklessness. Loved the way he expected her to keep up with him, no matter what they did. She'd loved riding motorcycles with him, taking life fast and loose. Sex with Scott had been reckless, too. She'd thought she'd met her match. Now she knew how stupid she'd been. All along he'd only wanted her ranch—just like Logan. And when push came to shove—literally—he'd knocked her down without a second thought.

She and her sisters got the last laugh, of course. Scott was in jail. She hoped he rotted there.

Lena sighed. As much as she resented the reason Logan was here, she couldn't place him in the same category as Scott. He wasn't a criminal. She couldn't imagine Logan hitting a woman. Brian, Connor and Hunter wouldn't stick by him if he did. As much as it killed her to admit it, the men the General had sent were upright, decent men.

And the way Logan kissed her—

That was different, too. It was a like a greeting. A way for him to let her know he was here and interested. Scott had always grabbed her and pressed her against him like he was trying to leave a mark. She'd thought he was passionate, but she'd been wrong. All of it had been about control.

Logan, on the other hand... well, she couldn't say what he was after, and she had a sinking feeling he might be the man she'd thought Scott had been—a man who liked to throw himself into fun, active pursuits, a man who'd treat her like an equal.

A man who'd blow her mind between the sheets— and allow her to blow his mind, too.

Unfortunately, he was here at the General's beck and call, a man whose mission was to make sure she relinquished her post as overseer of this ranch. To keep her in her place. She couldn't let him do that no matter who he turned out to be.

She was only allowing the men to work with her so she could be like Caleb in her novel, walking among the enemy, listening to their talk.

Learning their plans to take over.

They'd lose in the end, just like the British troops, she told herself, settling down to read again. And she wouldn't miss Logan when he was gone.

But she wasn't sure she believed that.

"WHAT ARE YOU working on?" Logan asked Alice, keeping one eye on the track leading to the outbuildings. Everyone else sat at the kitchen table, finishing their dinner, but she had pushed away her plate a few moments ago, grabbed a sketchbook, climbed up to a perch on the refrigerator, much to his surprise, and started drawing furiously. Logan hadn't eaten yet. He was still waiting for Lena to join them. Getting worried. Maybe he should go track her down.

"Costume sketches."

"For the movie?" Brian had told him she'd been approached by a producer looking for new talent. She'd been offered a chance to become the lead designer on a historical drama, but first she had to submit a number of samples for inspection. According to Brian, she was working against a deadline, stressing the details.

"Yes. It's really exciting—the movie requires tons of costumes for the ballroom scenes—" Alice stiffened. "Incoming!" She set aside her sketchbook and pencil, pushed herself to the edge of the fridge, slid down to put a foot on the counter and leaped to the floor gracefully. When she rushed to the window, Brian and Connor quickly followed, Cass and Sadie scrambling after them to see, too.

"What is it?" Cass asked.

Alice pointed to the sky. Brian swore under his breath.

Then Logan saw it—a small shape hovering above the maze.

"It's another drone," Sadie exclaimed. "Alice and I saw one early yesterday morning. What's it doing on our property?"

Logan stepped out of the house, the others spilling through the door after him. Alice brushed past him, hurrying toward the maze.

"Get out of here," she shouted at the drone. "Scoot! Go!"

"Whoever's driving that can't hear you," Sadie said. She picked up a rock and chucked it at the thing.

Brian lagged back with Logan. "Is that one of ours?" he asked under his breath.

"Pretty sure it's Jack." Logan filled him in on the conversation he'd had with the soldier back at USSO-COM.

"I'll call him. Tell him to get it out of here before Alice goes ballistic. She's pretty protective of that maze." He hurried back into the house, his phone already in his hand. Moments later, the drone buzzed away.

Alice, breathing hard, turned to fix first Connor, then Logan with an angry gaze. "That's not allowed," she said. "This is a sacred space. Not for photographing."

"It wasn't me," Connor protested.

"Come on. Both of you," she demanded and led the way into the maze. Sadie and Cass hurried after her.

Logan followed willingly, puzzling over Alice's anger. Was she upset at the thought someone might learn the way to its center? He'd been curious about the maze since he'd first heard about it, and about the standing stone. According to the other men, no one knew who'd shaped the stone or put it there.

"It's trippy," Connor had told him. "You'll see."

Logan tried to pay attention to the twists and turns they took through the green corridors, but Alice was pacing fast, and he wasn't sure he'd remember. When they turned a corner and entered the center of the maze, Logan understood exactly why the other men had described the standing stone in awe-filled tones. It stood far taller than he'd expected, solid and imperturbable.

Ancient. Although it couldn't be that old, could it?

"Ask it," Alice said, pointing at Connor. "Ask it if it likes to be spied on."

To Logan's surprise, Connor moved willingly to place his hands on the megalith and asked out loud, "Do you like being spied on?" He turned and winked at Logan. "Watch this."

"Watch what—hey!" Logan ducked as a crow swooped down and buzzed them all, showering the ground with a spray of white liquid excrement. It just missed him. Sadie and Cass ducked, too, although they were laughing.

"I'll take that as a no." Connor wrinkled his nose and kept his eyes on the sky. "Can we go back and finish dinner?"

Alice folded her arms over her chest. "You tell whoever is doing this to back off. You hear me?"

Connor didn't respond, and neither did Logan. Alice pointed at the stone. "You want me to sic it on you again?"

"We'll get the word out," Connor finally said.

Good answer, Logan thought, biting back a grin. It neither confirmed or denied their connection to the drone. "I'm starving," he said aloud. "I'm heading back." The others followed him, Connor quickly taking the lead when Logan turned the wrong way.

As they filed back toward the house, Alice asked, "What kind of a man needs to cheat his way through a hedge maze?"

"Someone really unsure about his place in the world," Sadie answered grimly.

Logan wondered what Jack would think about that assessment of his motives.

Back at the house, Logan waited another ten minutes for Lena, but she didn't show up. In fact, Lena didn't return to the house until late that night after he'd gone up to the guest room to bed. The next morning, when Logan got up, aching all over from the unaccustomed work after months behind a desk, he found Cass standing by the kitchen stove, Connor at the scarred, wooden table eating a hearty breakfast and Brian pulling on a jacket before heading outside.

"Lena's left us our assignments." Brian jutted his chin in the direction of the bulletin board.

"I still think you all should get to choose your chores," Cass said. "Lena shouldn't—"

"She's the overseer," Brian told her. "We're just the

help. We do what we're told." He patted her barely rounded belly. "Take good care of my baby."

"I will. But this thing with Lena is going to blow up at some point, mark my words."

"I know what I'm doing." Brian kissed her on the cheek and headed outside.

Cass handed Logan a plate and began to dish him out some eggs and bacon. "Toast is in the toaster," she told him.

"I appreciate it," Logan told her cheerfully. Breakfast was his favorite meal. He grabbed some toast, buttered it, piled it high with eggs and bacon, made a sandwich and sat across from Connor.

Connor watched him. "Morning, baby girl," he said under his breath.

Logan chuckled. Connor was right; this was just like old times back at USSOCOM, although this was far tastier than the take-out breakfast sandwiches he used to get, and he didn't need to kiss a photograph of Lena anymore. Now he had the real thing. Biting into his food, he decided he could be happy here.

Hell, he already was, despite Lena's prickliness. He loved the outdoor work, the camaraderie with the other men and the company of the women.

"I mean it," Cass said. "At some point, Lena will push you too far and you'll all get into a big fight."

"Have a little faith," Connor told her, looking up from his plate.

She snorted. "Don't think you men can get one over on her. She's smart as heck; she'll figure out your trick in no time."

"We're not trying to get one over on her. We're trying to prove we're not the enemy." Logan took another bite. Heaven.

"That might be harder than you think," Cass told him. She dished out a plate for herself and came to join them.

Alice had said a similar thing, Logan remembered.

"We'll just have to do our best," he said.

Connor finished first, thanked Cass for the meal and slipped out the door. By the time Logan made it down to the barn, the other men had already headed out to clear brush where it was encroaching on the northwest pasture, a job he was slated to join them at, according to Lena's list. But when he saw her mucking out Atlas's stall, the stallion tied to a post across the barn, he went to help. Taking the pitchfork from her hands, he edged past her into the confined space and began to pitch the bedding into a nearby wheelbarrow.

"I've got it." She tried to pull the pitchfork from his arms.

"No, you don't. I've got it now," he pointed out. "I'll have this done in a jiffy."

"I don't need your help!"

"But do you *want* my help?" he asked in a silky voice.

He ducked when she tried to slug him, but she landed her second shot—a glancing blow to his chin. He caught her hand. Held it when she tried to pull away, placing the pitchfork behind him, safely out of her reach.

"I don't think our relationship should be violent," he said in a mock-serious voice.

"We're not having a relationship!" She came at him with a clumsy left hook. Definitely not trained in hand-to-hand combat, Logan thought. He blocked the shot and grabbed her left wrist, as well.

"So, this is the point where you overpower me with your super-strength and show me who's the man?" Lena spat at him. She was breathing hard, a wild look in her eyes.

"I'm definitely the man," he said quietly. "And you're the woman. And that doesn't mean anything about our relative positions in life—but it does make things awfully interesting, don't you think?"

He was trying his best to diffuse the situation. Lena was doing her best to pull away. He could barely keep up with the emotions crossing her face as she struggled. Fury, frustration—and something else.

Something awfully like—

Desperation.

Logan let go and stepped back, gut-punched by the realization. Lena whirled around and stalked out of the barn.

LENA AVOIDED THE house at lunchtime, ducking in early to grab a couple of pieces of fruit and escaping again before Cass caught her. By dinnertime she was starving but no less determined to avoid eating at home. She didn't know what she'd do if she came within ten feet of Logan. He'd grabbed her. Held her in place—with no more effort than it took to pat a dog.

She hated the way her heart had pounded. Hated the scream that had built in her throat until he'd let her go. The world had spun. The walls of Atlas's stall had begun to close in. She'd needed to get away, but she couldn't—

She stumbled on the way up the track toward the house but forced herself to walk on. Logan wouldn't have done anything, and if he had...

Lena swallowed the rage rising up in her throat. What would she have done if he had? Scott had proved she was no match for a full-grown man with the desire to hurt her. Logan was a Marine. More muscular than Scott had been. She patted the pistol in its shoulder holster. Much good it would have done her today—if Logan had been a true attacker. He'd gotten to her before she could even draw it.

Swearing under her breath, Lena charged up the back steps, pushed open the door and hightailed it through the kitchen, up the stairs to her room. She changed, ran a hand through her hair, made a quick trip to the bathroom and made it out the door again with a shouted—"Going to town, be back later"—before anyone could reply.

She felt better as soon as she got behind the wheel of her truck and was driving the winding road to Chance Creek. Out here, alone, she could forget about Logan. She cranked the radio up and sang along to the familiar country tune playing on her usual station. By the time she reached town, she was ravenous, so she popped into the Burger Shack, wolfed down two quarter-pounders with bacon and cheese, chased them with a soda and then made her way to the Dancing Boot to try her hand at a couple of rounds of pool.

As soon as she entered the bar she relaxed. She'd been here a thousand times, knew most of the patrons. No one would bother her here.

Heading over to the pool table, she met up with a couple of men she'd known all her life and beat the pants off them, which put her in a much better mood. A couple of beers didn't hurt, either. More than once, she noticed a trio of men looking her way while she played. Strangers grouped by the bar. Lena wondered who they were. The older one kept his eye on her. The younger two—twins by the looks of it—turned to try to get the bartender's attention.

Lena forgot about them when she bent to take her next shot. She won again and wasn't surprised when her competitors said they planned to call it a night. It was early still, but Lena figured she should, too. Plenty of work waiting for her tomorrow, after all.

Before she could put away her cue stick, however, one of the twins she'd noticed plunked a stack of quarters on the edge of the table.

"Name's Harley," he said. "That's Ray." He nodded at his brother, approaching with three beers in his hands.

Lena looked from one to the other.

"Yeah, we're twins," Ray said in a backcountry

drawl that wasn't local. Southern, most likely. He was blond, like his brother. The same light blue eyes. Same weak chin and stocky frame.

"You boys aren't from around here."

"No, ma'am," Harley said. "We're hoping you're up for a game. Too boring to play each other."

She hesitated.

"Come on, we don't know anyone else," Harley said. "We bought you a beer." He nodded to the extra bottle in Ray's hand. Ray held it out to her.

"What about your friend?" She nodded toward the older man, still nursing a drink at the bar.

"That's our uncle. Forget about him. I want a game."

What the hell, she decided. One more couldn't hurt, and she pitied these young men who looked to be kept on a short leash by their uncle. They were young, twenty-two or twenty-three at least. More boys then men. She could keep them in line.

She took the beer, set it aside, racked up the balls for a new game and got ready to break.

"What brings you to town?" She indicated that Harley could start, but he motioned for her to do so.

"Opportunity," Ray said, drawing out each syllable separately.

His brother nudged him.

"What kind of opportunity?" Lena asked.

"The money-making kind. What else?" Ray said.

"Ignore my brother. He talks too much," Harley said. "We're thinking about settling down in these parts.

Right now we're just checking it out. How about you? What do you do in town?"

"I'm a rancher."

She liked the way that sounded. She was a rancher—and would continue to be unless the General screwed things up for her.

"A rancher, huh? Little thing like you?" Harley said.

Lena ignored his attempt to rile her and make her miss her shot. She broke and landed three balls in pockets.

Harley straightened. Whistled. "Guess you can play."

"Guess so." It felt good to show some prowess around men, even if they were little more than kids. With a few drinks inside her and a few games won already, her earlier fears were gone. To hell with Logan, she decided. She didn't have to be bigger and stronger than him to kick him off her property once and for all.

"Seems to me a woman needs help running a ranch, though. You got a husband?"

"Hell, no." She sank another ball. And then another.

Ray snickered. "You a man-hater?"

Lena missed her shot and felt her temper rise. She straightened up.

"She's not a man-hater." Harley edged her aside and lined up his cue to put a ball in a corner pocket. "She's a woman who knows her own mind."

"That's about the size of it," Lena agreed, but her heart sank as Harley made two more shots in rapid succession. He'd be hard to beat.

"I bet the right man could find a way to partner with you," Harley said.

Lena couldn't say why she thought of Logan. She didn't want to partner with him. She wanted to run her ranch, clean and easy. And Harley was trying to throw her off again. She couldn't let him if she wanted to win this game.

Harley missed his shot, and Lena stepped up to the table.

"What kind of opportunity did you say you were in town for?" she asked. Was it her imagination, or did Harley hesitate?

"We're all about horses, me and Ray," he finally said. "We're looking for breeding stock. A stallion, in particular. Heard there are some good ones for sale in town. But don't go spreading that around. People will jack up the price on us."

Lena relaxed. "Jamie Lassiter's the man to talk to about that."

"Lassiter, huh? We'll follow up on that." But he didn't seem too enthusiastic.

"Don't you have horses? Thought you said you were a rancher," Ray asked.

"I am a rancher. I've got horses. Everyone in Chance Creek has horses just about. That doesn't make us breeders. Like I said, you should talk to Jamie Lassiter about that." She took another shot.

"I'm not interested in his horses. I'm interested in yours. Any of 'em any good?" Ray pressed.

She scanned the table. Let the angles play out in her

head. "Hell, yeah. I've got a stallion that puts the rest to shame in Chance Creek County."

It was a familiar boast—she'd made it plenty of times before—but she caught the look that passed between the brothers and wished she'd kept her mouth shut. What had they been communicating to each other? She looked Ray over again. He was young but maybe not quite as harmless as she'd first thought. She needed to be careful; strangers kept showing up in town and causing them problems.

"Little lady, you sure know your way around a pool table," Harley said. Lena looked him over, too, and relaxed again. She was being paranoid. Harley wasn't a criminal. He was just a kid trying to chat up a woman.

A woman way out of his league.

Lena sank the last ball. "You got that right." Her pride at taking the table diminished quickly when Ray stepped up and took the cue from Harley's hand. Damn it, she was done with these two.

"My turn."

"I don't think so. It's time for me to—"

"Chicken."

Lena swore under her breath. "Rack 'em up, and let's play."

Chapter Four

"I THINK IT'S time for me to head to town," Logan said when the clock struck nine and Lena hadn't returned yet.

"She'll come home eventually," Cass told him. They were seated in the living room, Cass working on the ranch's accounts. "I'm sure she's just having dinner with a friend." She paused for a moment and lay a hand on her belly with a small smile.

Logan dropped the magazine he wasn't reading and stood up. "Could use a change of scenery."

Sadie looked up from where she'd been tapping the keys of her cell phone. "She's at the Dancing Boot. Monopolizing the pool table. According to Caitlyn Warren," she added in answer to Cass's upraised eyebrow.

"I wouldn't mind a game of pool," Logan said.

"Good luck. Lena's pretty damn good," Brian said. He was seated near Cass, reading on a tablet. In fact, everyone was bent over some gadget or other. The scene stood in stark contrast to the hundred-year-old plus architecture of the farmhouse.

Once in town, it didn't take Logan long to find the Dancing Boot, and when he opened the door, music spilled out around him. Patrons lined the long bar and sat at small tables around the edges of a sizable dance floor filled with couples dancing to canned music; there was no band on stage tonight.

He spotted the pool table in back and saw Lena bent over it, taking her shot. Two men stood near her, one holding a pool cue in his hand, the other leaning against a nearby wall.

Twins, if he wasn't mistaken. The one standing behind her was checking out Lena's ass while she took her shot. He didn't like the look of either of them. They didn't look like cowboys, though they were dressed much the same as the other men in the bar. They held themselves differently, Logan thought. They were hard around the edges. Brittle. And both of them kept glancing toward an older man leaning against the bar.

Logan shoved his way through the crowd, grateful most patrons backed out of the way when they saw him coming. He didn't want men ogling Lena.

Didn't like the way she was avoiding him, either.

He fished quarters out of his pocket as he went and slapped them down on the rim of the table when he reached it.

"Next game," he said.

"Clear off. I've got next game," the man leaning against the wall told him.

Lena glanced up. Was that relief he saw in her eyes?

"I already beat you, Harley," she told the leaning

man. "And I'm about to beat Ray, here. This man wants to lose his money, too, he's welcome to try."

Logan followed her lead. If she didn't want these men to know they were together, he could play along. For now.

True to her word, Lena made her shots and took the win. Ray couldn't hide his anger.

Harley was staring at the older man again, who finished his drink, set his glass on the bar and straightened. He nodded, and Harley nudged Ray.

"We'll see you around," he told Lena. "I'd like to get a look at that stallion of yours sometime."

Lena shrugged. "I'm pretty busy." She turned to Logan. "Ready to lose, big guy?"

"Ready to play," he countered. Harley looked like he had more to say, but after meeting Logan's gaze he shrugged and left. Ray's shoulders were stiff as he walked away. The older man ushered them out of the bar. Logan watched them go, curious about the relationship between the three men. He waited until they were gone before turning to Lena. "Friends of yours?"

"Like hell." She put her cue back in the rack.

"What are you doing?"

"Going home."

"What about our game?"

"You weren't serious about that, were you? You know I'd kick your ass."

Logan stepped up to her, happy again to have the advantage of height and bulk. He made a big show of looking down at her. "I'd like to see you try."

With growl, Lena grabbed the cue stick again, and for a second he thought she'd take a swing at him. Instead, she said, "Rack 'em and let's get this over with."

Logan racked the balls. Lena took the break. She pocketed a striped ball first, and another one, then missed a shot she really should have made. Were her hands shaking? She was far angrier than she should be at his joking around, Logan thought.

"Do you know the older guy those idiots were with? The one holding up the bar?"

Lena turned to look right where the man had been sitting. When she noticed he was gone, she shrugged. "I don't know any of them. Never seen them before. Harley said he's their uncle."

"Wonder why they're in town."

"They said something about horse breeding. Wanted to know if I had any horses for sale."

It still didn't add up to Logan's way of thinking, and he resolved to keep an eye on the twins and their uncle. It would be too easy to suspect every man who came sniffing around Lena, but trouble seemed to come at Two Willows pretty regularly. Strangers needed watching. It was just how things had to be.

Thinking about the trouble that plagued Two Willows led Logan to think about the last man Lena had dated. Scott had hit Lena, then had attacked her and her sisters when they blew up the drugs he and his friends had been storing on their ranch.

Logan sank two of the solid balls handily. Did a fancy trick to sink another one, but when he tried to repeat it for a fourth ball, he missed. He'd been remembering the way Lena had fought him in the barn. The desperate look in her eye. He'd been kidding around earlier when he urged her to play this game, but even playful intimidation might reduce his chances with Lena. Maybe he needed to romance her instead.

Lena sank one, then another, then a third. She edged around the table to make an easy shot into a corner pocket.

"Let's make this interesting." Logan blocked her way when she tried to skirt the table to make her next shot. "You sink this ball, we go home."

"And if I don't?"

"You dance with me. Just one song," he added when she visibly bristled.

Lena rolled her eyes. "Come on, cowboy—"

"Don't think you can make the shot?"

"For God's sake." Lena nudged him aside with an air of exasperation. Lined up her shot—

And missed.

LENA STAYED WHERE she was, flabbergasted at what she'd just done. She could have sunk that shot in her sleep.

She'd rushed it—that was the problem. Logan had riled her, and she'd rushed it.

But he'd think she missed it deliberately.

"Come on, baby girl," he said, taking the cue stick from her hand and putting it away. "Let's get to it."

"Stop calling me that." Lena's mind raced as he led her to the dance floor, where a crooning love song she'd always hated played over the loudspeakers. Other couples swayed to the music, some of them impossibly close, starting something they'd finish later at home—in bed.

"Stop calling you baby girl? It's just a pet name. It means I like you."

The idiot was grinning. He loved the fact he was making her mad, didn't he? More than one woman on the dance floor was watching them, envy clear in their expressions. She knew why. Logan smiling was devastating. He set her heart thumping, her pulse thrumming. This close, he smelled good. All woodsy and manly, with an undertone of something that twisted her insides into a knot of wanting—

"Well, I don't like you," she declared.

"I bet you do. Just a little bit. In spite of everything you're telling yourself about me. I'm like a puppy dog with muddy paws. You want to be mad, but I'm too darn cute to swat." Logan took her hand in his, placed his other one on her hip and began to sway.

"Oh, I can swat, believe me." But picturing Logan as a puppy did make her see the ridiculous side of the situation. She was overreacting to his messing around. As usual. Logan wasn't like Ray and Harley. He wasn't a stranger anymore, and he wasn't dangerous. The stupid man was incorrigible. Unstoppable when he wanted something.

Did he want… her?

She stopped moving. Logan shifted his stance, pulled her in closer and kept going, dragging her feet over the floor.

She stumbled and caught up. "In case you haven't noticed; I'm not some rag doll you can drag around," she told him.

"Nope, you're a real, live woman, so start dancing, or I'll pick you up and do it for you."

Jesus. He'd do it, too.

Lena began to move with him.

"That's better. This isn't so bad, is it?"

He tugged her in tighter until all Lena could do was reluctantly rest her head against his shoulder and let him sway with her. His cotton shirt was smooth against her cheek, and she could hear his heart beat, a strong, steady pulse. By all accounts, she should have been panicking. Lashing out with all her strength to get out of his embrace. Why wasn't she?

Lena couldn't answer that. Maybe the drinks were keeping her in a mellow mood. Besides, it was just one dance, she reminded herself. She'd danced with lots of men. It didn't mean anything.

Still, she was aware of his hand resting on her hip, the other at the small of her back. His chin touching the top of her head. When was the last time a man had held her like this?

She shifted again, trying to create more space between them. Logan held her in place.

"For God's sake, relax. It's just a dance, and it will be over soon enough."

Unexpectedly, disappointment flooded her, leaving Lena reeling. She couldn't be disappointed about the dance ending. She didn't want to dance with Logan. This feeling was simply... tiredness. She was worn out. Or something.

She couldn't be... enjoying herself.

Lena closed her eyes.

This was wrong.

This whole night was wrong. She tried to draw back again.

Everything had been wrong since—well, since she'd been born.

Wrong gender. Wrong place. Wrong time. Wrong father—

Nothing was right with her life—and she had little faith it ever would be.

"Hey, we're dancing, not getting ready for war," Logan said. Was that frustration in his voice? He sounded as if he wished she was enjoying herself. And he wasn't letting go.

Lena tried to relax.

"That's better. Who taught you to play pool?"

"Jed Henderson," Lena said, giving in to the situation. "He was the overseer at Two Willows before my mother died. He was a real man." She remembered the way he'd taken her seriously—the only man who ever had, as far as she was concerned. He was courteous to all the women on the ranch, but he'd been almost a grandfather to her. Back then, the General was already gone a lot, making his career with the Army. When he came home, he and Jed got on well together, but it was Jed who'd heaped praise on Lena in a way the General never did.

"He must have been good at it."

"He's good at everything."

"You keep in touch with him?"

Lena turned her head. "No."

Logan didn't push the line of questioning, and she was grateful for that. She was ashamed of the way she'd treated Jed. Furious at his defection, as she'd seen it, before her mother's death, she'd refused to speak to him after he retired. The next overseer, and the next and the next, didn't see any value in a young teenage girl's opinions—not like Jed had.

She'd been shunted aside—displaced.

Just like Logan would try to—

"Quit fighting me." Logan's voice was low against her hair. When his breath whispered against her ear, Lena shivered and held her breath as a strand of desire coiled within her.

Where had that come from?

She was done with men. She didn't want Logan.

It was this stupid dance. Being close to Logan—breathing in his scent—had knocked her off balance. And she was done with it.

Lena brought up her arms and shoved him away—hard.

"Hey!" Logan stepped back. But she suspected he'd released her because he wanted to, not because she'd really broken free.

"I'm leaving." But Lena's gaze caught on the neck-line of Logan's shirt, where a medallion he wore had come into view, reminding her of the lockets the General kept giving to her sisters. Despite herself, she leaned in for a closer look.

"What's that?"

"St. Michael." He must have seen her confusion. "You've probably heard of St. Christopher medallions."

"Patron saint of... something?" she managed, dredging the idea from some recess of her brain. She remembered a movie based in Boston. A parish priest and a bunch of Catholic school boys. "You're... Catholic?"

"Two priests for brothers," he said ruefully. "St. Christopher is the patron saint of travelers. So, people wear his medal for protection."

She filed that information away to think about later. "What about St. Michael?"

"Patron saint of policemen, sailors, paramedics, and military men, among other things." He held it up, and she saw it held an image of the saint holding a large sword in front of him. "He's my patron saint. My middle name is Michael."

"Huh."

"Come on, just a few more seconds." He tugged her against him again and held her lightly. Lena lost the will to fight him off. Too many drinks. Too long a day working. A bad combination. She rested her hands on his shoulders as they swayed together. This wasn't... awful, she had to admit. If only the circumstances were different.

If only Logan wasn't the enemy.

But when Logan rested his chin on top of her head again, Lena growled at him. His answering chuckle shook his body—and hers along with it.

"Why do you keep trying to make me feel small?" she demanded. She'd almost been enjoying herself for a minute.

"It's more like I'm trying to make myself feel big," he told her, surprising her with his candidness. "I want to be able to protect you from the bad guys."

"Protect me?"

"Like St. Michael."

She snorted. "Where's your big-ass sword?"

Logan's chuckle rumbled through his body again. "Oh, we'll get to that sooner or later."

WAS SHE THINKING about his... sword? Logan hoped she was, and for good measure, he tightened his embrace and flexed his biceps. He was a big man. Let her think about that.

Lena pushed right out of his arms as the song ended, though. "Time to go home," she declared, heading for the door.

"How about a walk first—both of us could stand to clear our heads before we drive home. You've had a couple of drinks, right?"

"Not that many." But when they reached the street, she turned to walk without another word. Logan matched her pace gratefully.

"Whole place shuts down after dark, huh?" he asked.

"Just about. Not very exciting, I guess."

"I'm a small-town boy," Logan told her. "I know how to make my own entertainment."

"I'm surprised you're not a priest—with your brothers and all."

"Two's enough for any family." He was quiet a moment. "Not for mine, though. You'd think my folks would want a grandkid or two. Instead, it seems like they'd prefer to end the family line once and for all."

She took this in. "Tell me about your brothers. Are you close?"

His hand brushed hers as they walked, but he held back from taking it. He had to build a foundation with Lena that wasn't purely physical. "Not like you and your sisters. I talk to Anthony a fair bit, but he doesn't understand my choices. I talk to James less often. He's in Ethiopia currently. Pretty busy guy."

"I don't know a lot of Catholics," Lena admitted. "The whole priest thing is… weird."

Logan laughed. "I look forward to telling my brothers that. I think they'd like you."

She gave him a sideways look. "Why?"

"Because you say what's on your mind. You've got a good heart."

"Wouldn't they try to convert me?"

"Maybe." He wasn't sure. Another question for his brothers. He caught her looking again. "What?"

"Trying to picture you as a priest."

"Don't bother. Never going to happen."

"Come on. Father Logan. It suits you. And it would certainly make the world a safer place."

She was teasing him. He liked that. "Tell you what; when they let priests marry, I'll put on a collar."

Lena was quiet for half a block. "Your family must have been proud of you when you became a Marine, though."

Logan pushed back at some uncomfortable memories. That hadn't been an easy time. "Unfortunately, they weren't. I mean, they didn't stop me from signing up, but—like I said, man of God was their first pick."

"I let my parents down, too," Lena said softly. "By being born."

Logan stopped short. "Don't say that, Lena. Don't even think it for a minute. You father loves you—that's obvious—"

She snorted. "The General wanted sons. Plain and simple. You don't have to stick up for him; it's a fact of life my sisters and I accepted years ago."

Logan considered his words carefully, something he didn't often do. "If that's true, and I don't think it is, then the General is the biggest ass who ever lived."

She smiled, and Logan's heart rose. He'd made her smile.

Then her expression shuttered. "Race you back to the Boot!" In a flash she was gone. Logan caught his breath. Hell, she was going to win.

He didn't care, he told himself as he exploded after her. The game was on—

And he'd catch her sooner or later.

"THERE IT IS again!" Alice cried several days later, on a morning that had dawned cold and overcast. She, Sadie and Lena were clustered by the back door, about to split up after eating breakfast together around the kitchen table. The men had already dispersed to do their chores. Lena was waiting to hear from a delivery driver coming to drop off building supplies. Within days of the stable burning down, she had found a set of plans online that almost perfectly replicated the building as it had stood before. She'd placed an order for all the materials they'd need, and it was finally on its way. Connor and Brian hadn't been entirely pleased to find out she'd gone ahead without consulting them, but they'd wisely held their tongues about it.

"Where?" Sadie asked, ducking her head to see out the window.

"Right there. Another drone!" Alice yanked open the door and clattered out onto the back porch, and Lena and Sadie followed. Lena expected her to keep going, but Alice stopped at the edge of the steps. "Yeah, you just try and map my maze," she shouted at it. "See what happens!"

Sadie and Lena exchanged a look. Had their sister lost her mind? She'd been edgy these past few weeks, frustrated at the way her hunches had gone wonky. Lena knew it bothered her to function without that extra information, but her hunches had never been exactly dependable.

"What do you mean—" Sadie began, but Alice held up a hand to shush her.

"Just look."

The drone hovered near the edge of the maze, apparently interested in Sadie's garden, too, but just as Sadie took a step to go after it, it lifted a couple of feet and turned toward the maze, picking up speed.

It was at least ten feet higher than the top of the maze, Lena estimated, but when it reached the airspace above it, it stopped short—bouncing back a few feet. It flew in a little circle as if shaking the jolt off and headed toward the maze again.

It bounced off the invisible perimeter again.

"How are you doing that?" Sadie asked Alice, awe tinging her voice.

"I have no idea," Alice said. "I just keep picturing an invisible wall, and the drone keeps bouncing off it. This is the third time it's happened.

"What if it comes when you're not around?" Lena asked.

"I'm not getting many hunches these days, but whenever this sucker gets near, I feel it," Alice told her.

"You can't know that it's not coming if you're not here to see it," Sadie pointed out.

"And yet I do," Alice said simply.

Sadie glanced at Lena again. Lena shrugged. "Nothing that Alice can do makes any sense. Why should this?"

Lena's phone buzzed in her pocket, and she answered it as she watched the drone bounce off the invisible perimeter again. It was kind of entertaining.

"Can't they get an angle shot if they want to photograph the maze?" Sadie was asking Alice when Lena accepted the call.

"Nope," Alice said confidently.

"Hello?" A masculine voice on the line caught her attention.

"Hello."

"Bud here, from the lumber company. I'm almost at your place. Where do you want this stuff?"

"Take the service road down to the barn," Lena directed him.

"Will do. See you in a minute."

She pocketed the phone. "As much fun as this is, I've got to go. Delivery man is here."

Her sisters barely noticed her leaving. Lena didn't mind. Whoever was flying that drone deserved to get the shit knocked out of it. How rude to try to decipher a maze you hadn't even been invited to walk through. She and her sisters had always helped guests navigate the maze. They had a rule not to ever let someone get lost in it. Still, mapping it from the sky went too far.

As she hurried down the dirt track, she considered the project ahead. She'd worried about the actual construction, but with her crew of "hired hands" she figured they'd get most of it done with a little help from contractors. They needed to get going, however, or they'd miss the chance to build it before the snow came. If they waited too long, they wouldn't be able to bring the rest of their horses back home before winter set in.

"Hi, Bud," she called to the driver when he killed the engine and climbed out.

"Hi, yourself," he called back cheerfully as he rounded the truck and put down the tailgate. "I think I've got everything."

"Terrific. Let's get it unloaded, and we'll go over the paperwork." Lena approached the truck eagerly, leaned in and pulled out a stack of lumber. She was looking forward to rebuilding the stables. It seemed like progress, and these days, she'd take that wherever she could.

"Here, let me help you with that," Logan said, appearing around the side of the barn. Champ and Isobel trotted after him, interested in all the fuss. A moment later, Max appeared, too. The dogs ranged around, sniffing the new truck and getting underfoot.

"I've got it," she told him automatically. Logan was still a thorn in her side. It had been a mistake to let her guard down the other night. Now he wanted to hang out with her all the time, and she had to be downright rude at times to get him to clear off.

He seemed to think that one little dance gave him the right to court her. That's what he was doing, even if he hadn't touched her since. He kept his hands—and his kisses—to himself but often stood so close she held her breath. He was driving her crazy in two ways. One, in that she didn't want a man crowding her space. Two, in that his proximity had somehow resurrected her sex drive.

Not helpful.

Logan reached for the wood again.

Lena evaded him. "I've got it," she reiterated. "Get your own stack."

She was grateful when he finally did. Soon Brian and Connor joined them. As much as she resented the men, she had to admit she liked the way they all pitched in without even being asked. She also appreciated the way the lumber folks had coded the cut wood to match the building plans. They'd have the stables built in no time.

"I think your backhoe is on its way," Bud told her. "I passed it heading out from town. Should pull in any minute."

That was good news, too. "As soon as the foundation gets dug, we'll get this sucker built," Lena told the men.

"Sounds good, chief," Brian said.

Lena nearly stumbled. Chief?

Was he making fun of her?

She kept her head down but watched the men out of the corner of her eye to see if they grinned at each other or were laughing behind her back. She saw nothing of the sort. Brian went straight back to unloading lumber, and all the men listened when she directed where the supplies should go. Once, Connor suggested a change, and she'd considered it and agreed before she even remembered she was supposed to be on the watch for insubordination. His suggestion hadn't felt like a ruse to undermine her, though. It was simply a good idea.

They'd nearly finished unloading the truck when a

big orange backhoe lumbered slowly down the lane. The driver hopped out when he reached them, and she hurried to show him the site for the building. First, he'd have to clear away the detritus from the fire. He'd scheduled a dump truck to take the mess away, and right on time, the huge heavy truck rumbled down the lane.

"I think that's my cue to leave," Bud said. His truck bed was empty. Lena thanked him for his time, and when he pulled out, the dump truck took his place.

"Now, we're talking," Brian said twenty minutes later as the backhoe filled the bed of the dump truck. "That pile of stuff has been bugging me for weeks. Our ranch shouldn't look like a pigsty."

Our ranch. Lena's shoulders set and her jaw tightened. Who was Brian to use that language?

She caught Logan watching her and somehow knew he knew what she was thinking. He didn't shake his head or send any other sign of what he thought she should do, and Lena struggled to regain her composure. She had to remember that to Brian it must seem like his ranch. He'd married Cass, after all. He planned to spend his life here.

Brian turned, looked from one to the other of them. "What?"

Lena couldn't form an answer. She longed to spit out the angry words caught in her throat, but she also knew they weren't fair. Cass loved Brian. And Lena loved Cass. She didn't want to kick her sister's husband off the ranch. Didn't want Sadie or Jo to be unhappy, either. That's what made this so hard.

Some of what she felt must have been written on her face, because Brian's shoulders fell. "This is my home now, Lena. I can't keep my feelings separate from the land I'm ranching. I love Two Willows. Maybe I don't have your history with it, but it means a lot to me. All I want is to be a good steward to this land. Is that so bad?"

Pain pierced through Lena's heart. All she could do was turn and walk away. She couldn't express the varied emotions she felt about the tangled mess they'd gotten themselves into. She was grateful her sisters had found true love. She was furious the General had divided them and was close to conquering the ranch.

And it killed her to know he valued these men far more than he ever had his own daughters.

Logan caught up to her, and she wanted to scream. Couldn't he give her one moment of peace?

"We're trying," he said. "That's what making you chief is all about. We get what you feel—"

"How could you possibly get what I feel?" Lena cried. "You have no idea what it's like to look in your father's eyes and see how much you disgust him!"

"You don't disgust the General—"

Now he was trying to rewrite history. She remembered her father's words clearly from that day when she was seven. *You trying to disgrace us all?*

That's what she'd done—disgrace him. Simply by being born a girl.

"Leave me alone!" Lena scraped a hand across her face, horrified to find tears there. What was wrong with her these days?

When he stepped even closer, she shoved him, hard. "I said leave me alone!"

"Okay." Logan held up his hands in surrender. "But I'm here when you're ready to talk."

She was going to kill him. But then she'd end up in jail with Scott, and she'd have to kill him, too. Better for everyone's sake to just get the hell out of here for a while.

She changed directions and made a beeline to the barn, where she quickly saddled Atlas. The backhoe driver had the plans; he didn't need any of them hanging around while he completed his work.

Only when Atlas was galloping over the rutted track that led to the interior of the ranch did some of the tension drain out of Lena's body. Horses understood. They never let you down.

Not like men.

Chapter Five

"I THINK YOU know why I called this meeting," Brian said later that morning.

Connor shifted uncomfortably. He, Brian and Connor stood clustered around Brian's laptop. Jack's face filled the screen.

"I'll bet it's got something to do with Hughes," Jack said. "What's wrong; Lena doesn't find your scintillating personality attractive?"

"She finds me attractive." He didn't like the man's tone. Like he was going to do any better with Alice.

"But every time you go near her she explodes," Brian pointed out.

"Why should she be different from anyone else?" Jack asked pointedly.

"We danced," Logan said defensively. "Once," he added.

All three of the other men shook their heads.

"It's going to take a lot more than one dance to convince her to marry you," Connor said.

"I'm trying. I can't help the fact that she hates the General and anything to do with him. I should have come here undercover. She would have been all over me."

"I'll bet." Jack snorted.

His attitude was beginning to rile Logan. "It's true. We've got plenty in common—"

"Like what?" Connor asked. Not in a snide way—in a curious tone that let Logan know he was interested in the answer.

"Like…" What did they have in common? "We like horses."

"You and everyone else in a five-hundred-mile radius," Brian said.

"We're independent thinkers. We want to do things our way."

"Nice—I'll put that on your wedding cake," Jack said.

"No, wait. We can work with that," Connor said slowly. "You're right; Lena likes to think for herself and do things for herself, too. She likes to be in charge."

"She's made that clear," Brian said ruefully.

"Maybe… maybe you're going at this all wrong," Connor said. "Hold up and listen," he added when Logan bristled. "You're always trying to help Lena, and she's always getting pissed off. Maybe you're the one who needs to *ask* for help. And then let her take charge and help you."

Hell.

That wasn't the way a man was supposed to do things.

Everything inside Logan rebelled at the thought. "I

just said we're similar. I don't like interference. And I don't like to be bossed around," he said.

"Suck it up, Buttercup," Jack said, laughing on-screen. "Time for the big man to play it small for once."

"It's going to be your turn next," Logan told him, stung.

"I'm already getting the lay of the land," Jack assured him.

It was Logan's turn to laugh. "How's that going for you? Got a visual on the maze yet?" On his way back to the house, he and the other men had watched the drone bounce off the invisible wall that delineated the maze's airspace. Alice had been sitting on the back porch shucking corn in easy view, laughing at its lack of progress.

Jack's face fell. "I don't know how she's scrambling my signal, but I'll get through her defenses any minute now."

"Good luck with that," Brian told him. "But maybe you shouldn't rile your bride-to-be too much before you even meet her."

"Information is the key to any mission," Jack said.

Logan excused himself from the room, leaving the others to their talk about USSOCOM and Jack's future plans. He came downstairs to find Alice in the kitchen tucking containers into a big wicker basket.

"Almost ready," she told him.

"For what?" he asked curiously.

"To give you this." She added a bottle of wine, a corkscrew and two plastic cups, then latched the basket.

"All yours." She handed it to him.

"A picnic?" Logan didn't understand.

"You have something to ask Lena, don't you? I figured it would go over better on a full stomach. That's not too heavy, is it?"

Logan hefted the basket. "I've carried a lot worse, but what am I supposed to ask her?" He remembered Connor's idea. He needed a problem for Lena to solve.

"You'll have to figure that out," Alice said, reaching down to pet Tabitha, her white cat. "Better get going. You've got quite a hike ahead of you, and Lena's on horseback."

She outlined the directions to Lena's favorite getaway point and assured him, "We'll keep an eye on the backhoe, so don't worry about anything here. Take your time."

"Will do." He headed out the back door. Was the picnic one of Alice's famous hunches? He supposed it must have been. No matter why she'd thought of it, it was a good idea. Alice was right; he needed to ask Lena a question. Ask her for help.

But what problem could he ask her to help him solve?

As he walked, the sun came out, and Logan's mood improved. Fall was one of his favorite seasons. He thought up ideas and discarded them one after another. He couldn't ask her help with ranching chores; she'd think he was stupid. He couldn't ask her to help him build the stables; she'd say they were *her* stables and then she'd want to build them all by herself.

He didn't have any problems to solve—

Except the trouble with his family.

Logan shook his head. That problem was impossible to solve, and while he welcomed the idea of getting to know Lena—marrying her—sharing more about his past with her felt uncomfortable.

But the longer he hiked, the more he became sure it was the only problem he had to offer her. Who knew? Maybe she'd have some insight he'd never thought of. Stranger things could happen.

"What are you doing here?"

Logan staggered to a stop, so deep in his thoughts he hadn't seen Lena on horseback round a curve in the trail ahead of him.

"Coming to see if you're hungry." He lifted the basket. He'd run out of time to find a different problem to solve.

Family it was.

She pressed her lips together. Scanned their surroundings as if looking for a good reason to say no. "I guess so," she said finally. She urged Atlas to turn around. "There's a spot just up ahead. Meet you there."

She spurred Atlas on, leaving Logan in a cloud of dust to trudge after her. Up here he had a fine view of the rest of the ranch. It wasn't hard to see why Brian already felt attached to the place. He thought he could dig in here, too.

If Lena let him.

Let her solve the problem, he reminded himself. *Let her take charge*.

This wasn't going to be easy.

"What did you bring?" Lena asked when he finally caught up with her.

"I'm not sure; Alice packed the basket." He set it down, opened it up and pulled out a red-and-white-checkered blanket. He handed it to Lena, who spread it on the ground. "Looks like sandwiches, potato salad, pickles..." He took them out one by one, appreciating Alice's attention to detail. There were plates and silverware, chips and apple pie. And, of course, the bottle of wine.

"I'm hungry," he said, realizing it was true.

"Me, too." They settled in, passing the containers back and forth, Lena holding the cups while Logan poured the wine.

It was almost civilized, Logan thought.

But how long would that last?

LENA WASN'T SURE why she'd agreed to this picnic. Maybe because her ride had settled her down and made her realize she couldn't be upset with Brian for falling in love with Two Willows. He was Cass's husband, and it was right for him to stake his claim here, especially with a baby on the way. That didn't mean she had to accept Logan's presence here, though.

Although right now his presence wasn't that bad. He hadn't called her baby girl again, for one thing. Hadn't said much at all, actually. Their companionable silence made her feel mellow, and the food Alice had packed was hitting the spot.

"Out here, you could almost pretend it was a hundred years ago," Logan said suddenly.

She'd had that same thought many times before. Lena liked to come out here and pretend the world was a much newer place. That the continent hadn't been overridden by cars and airplanes, and that there were vast stretches of land sparsely populated, enough for everyone.

"If you could go back in time, when would you go?" she asked him. It was a question she'd pondered often by herself but had never asked anyone else.

Logan thought about that for a good long while. "It's hard to choose. I'd love to go back and see the Romans. On the one hand they seem so modern, and on the other, so incredibly ancient. But mostly I think I'd like to be here in the United States in the 1600s. I'd like to be one of the first Europeans who set out to explore this continent. Just a musket in my hand and a pack on my back, walking into the forest to see what was there. I guess every man wishes he could be a pioneer at some point. How about you?"

"The Revolutionary War," she said without hesitation. "Fighting for freedom. For shared values. Against tyranny—I can't think of anything better than that."

"I imagine you don't picture yourself sitting in a parlor with the other ladies rolling bandages for the war effort?"

She couldn't help but meet his impish grin with one of her own. "Hell, no." That was the last thing she pictured herself doing. "I would've been a spy. A rebel spy. I would have worked for General Washington."

"Can I ask you something?"

Lena hesitated. People only led with that if their question was personal. "I guess."

"Why don't you sign up? Hell, why not be a spy— today? I'm sure you could do it."

"College. Languages. The military. Years away from my home." She waved a hand to encompass the ranch. "It's a nonstarter. Two Willows is my life. It always has been. I was born to run this ranch. That's all I've ever wanted to do."

"I don't doubt it, but I also think you could be an asset to this country. Did your father ever suggest—?"

"No, he didn't," she said shortly. "And my mother wouldn't have liked it, even if he did."

"She would have stopped you from going?"

"No, but—" How to explain to him. "She had a su- perstition. One she really believed." Lena didn't want to expose her mother's memory to ridicule, but sooner or later someone would fill Logan in on her mother's quirks if they hadn't already. "She made a pact with the land. If she stayed on Two Willows—always—the General would remain safe." She braced herself for Logan's derision.

"So... she never left the ranch?" Logan set his sandwich on his plate. "Not at all?"

"No. Not ever. Now she's gone, it's Cass's job mostly—but we all help. There's always one of us here."

Logan nodded. "Brian said something about that, but I didn't understand it. So, you feel since your mother never left the ranch, you should stay, too?"

"I want to stay," Lena said fiercely. "You're right; I would make a damn good soldier—and a damn good spy. But Two Willows needs me."

Logan nodded. "The Revolutionary War?" he said, bringing them back to their earlier topic, as if sensing their discussion had strayed too far for Lena's comfort. "I wouldn't have wanted to be injured back then. Medical treatments were pretty much like torture."

Lena chuckled, grateful to be back on solid ground. "I wouldn't have gotten injured," she said with conviction. "I would've made sure we won the war a year or two earlier."

Logan laughed out loud. "Cocky, aren't we?"

"I know what I'm capable of."

"I bet you do," Logan said, sobering. He lifted his sandwich and took another bite, and his gaze took on a faraway look. Lena wondered what he thought about when he got like that. The career he'd left behind? His family?

"Do you have a girlfriend?" she challenged him.

Logan swallowed the bite he'd just taken. "Do you think I'd be here if I did?"

"Why are you here?"

He looked away again. "The short answer is because your father sent me."

"What's the long answer?" Lena took a sip of her wine. She wondered if Logan would tell her the truth.

"The long answer is… I think fate wants me here."

She sputtered and swallowed, the liquid going down

the wrong way. Logan reached out, clapped her on the back, and her cup went flying, spilling the wine, which drained into the dusty ground beside the blanket.

"Shoot. Sorry." Logan fetched her plastic cup and returned it to her. Lena looked at the dust covering it. He took it away again and replaced it with his.

"You're kind of a menace, aren't you?" Lena asked.

With that rueful expression on his face, he looked like the puppy he'd had her picturing the other day. "I don't mean to be."

She set his cup down and returned to her own sandwich. "Why do you think fate wants you at Two Willows?" she asked.

"It's a little personal."

"Now you *have* to tell me." Lena winced. That sounded a lot like flirting, and she didn't mean to flirt with Logan.

"You know my parents wanted me to be a priest."

"Heaven help us all."

Logan elbowed her.

"Stop it, or you'll send my sandwich flying next," she warned him.

"My parents wanted me to be a priest," he tried again, heaving a sigh. He was even more handsome when he was losing his cool, Lena had to admit. She tried to focus on his words instead of his face. "I never wanted that," Logan went on. "Never had the patience for that kind of thing. But for a while now…" He took a deep breath, and Lena waited curiously to see what he'd say. "I've been having these dreams."

"I don't want to hear any more," Lena said quickly.

He made a face. "Not that kind of dream, although—" He cut off with a grin she was getting to know far too well. "Are you sure you don't want to know? Some of them are pretty interesting…"

"That's it; I'm leaving." Lena made like she'd stand up.

Logan tugged her back down. "Fine, but you don't know what you're missing."

Lena tried as hard as she could not to guess what she was missing, but she couldn't help wondering what Logan thought about when he pictured them together.

Had he pictured them together?

She had, if she was truthful. And when she imagined his hands on her bare skin, well… things got pretty hot.

"Anyway," Logan went on. "These dreams are different. I have this sense that something's wrong. That someone needs help. A woman."

"Okay." Not too out of the ordinary.

"And here's where it gets weird. In my dreams, St. Michael appears." He lifted the medallion. "And he hands me his sword. I know I have to save… whoever it is I'm supposed to save." He broke off for a moment and shook his head. "That's why when trouble came, I did try to save someone. Not with a sword—"

"Save who?" Lena couldn't help asking.

"The wife of a Sergeant Major." His face had gone ruddy, and Lena watched him, fascinated, as he looked anywhere but at her. "I was walking past their house. They lived on base, like me. I heard shouting through an open window. Stuff crashing around. It sounded like a fight, and there was a woman involved." He finally met her gaze. "What was I supposed to do? Let her get beat up?"

Lena swallowed. "No. Of course not." His earnestness told her the incident still bothered him. "What happened?"

"They *were* fighting," Logan said. "But no one was getting hurt. Turns out the Sergeant's wife was taking her anger out on some of their possessions. All I managed to do was punch the guy, embarrass both of them and get myself reassigned to your father's task force."

"It was still the right thing to do." She had to hand it to the General; he sent men of integrity to Two Willows.

"I'd do it all over again if I heard that kind of fighting," he admitted.

"But you just said fate sent you here, because if you hadn't had the dream, you wouldn't have intervened," she pointed out.

Logan seemed to mull this over. He shook his head. "I would always intervene if I heard a woman being hurt. Guess I don't know what the dream means, after all."

"You should talk to Alice about it; she's all about premonitions."

"Maybe I should do that." He leaned back and rested his weight on his hands. "That still leaves me with the problem of my parents. How do I convince them

I'm not priest material?"

He was asking her for parental advice? That was comical. "You realize I don't even speak to the General, right?"

"You had a good relationship with your mother, didn't you?"

Unexpected tears pricked her eyes. Lena blinked them away quickly. She would never cry in front of Logan. Wasn't one for crying at all. Something had her all out of sorts these days.

But she had been able to show her feelings to her mother, and she realized she missed that. "Mom was amazing," she said simply. "I mean, she ran this whole place while the General was gone. She had help, but she held it together, inside and out. She was the heart of the ranch. The five of us can't match her."

"What was she like?" Logan asked softly.

"She always had time to talk. You'd walk into the kitchen thinking you were hungry, and an hour later all your problems would be solved."

"What advice do you think she'd give me?"

Lena considered him. "I think she'd start by asking what your goals are if becoming a priest isn't one of them."

He toyed with his fork. She noticed he'd barely touched his food—odd behavior from a man who loved to eat as far as she had seen. "I want to settle down." He looked almost as surprised as she was by this pronouncement. He shrugged. "It's time."

"What about being a Marine? You're ready to give

that up?" She couldn't explain why warmth had spread through her at his declaration. She wasn't interested in Logan. Definitely not in settling down with him.

"I guess I am. I loved it." He spread his hands wide. "Loved the action. The sense of purpose. The hard work. The camaraderie. But I think I can have all of that here—"

"Here?" Lena set down her plate. "What do you mean here?"

"Lena, you're not dumb; you know why your father sent me."

Lena blinked. She hadn't expected him to come right out and admit that. "He sent you to marry me?" He was right; she had guessed something like that. But knowing it was one thing. Having Logan say it was another altogether.

"He did." His gaze searched hers. "And I'm more than willing. I've been staring at your face back at USSOCOM for months, Lena. Saying hi to your photograph every morning when I went to work."

"Saying... hi?" She couldn't believe what she was hearing.

"Hello, baby girl," he said. And then he leaned over and kissed her. "Now that I've said what my goals are, what advice would your mother give me?"

Slug him. Slug him, a voice in her mind railed. *Do something to stop this right now!*

But Lena couldn't move, because she heard her mother's voice, too, as clearly as if she were here at the picnic. She knew exactly what advice Amelia would give

Logan. *"Stay the course, son. Don't you give up on my girl. She needs you."*

Lena swallowed hard, scrambled to her knees and began to repack the basket. "She'd say it's time to head back."

Logan sighed. "I'm not going to push you. We need to get to know each other first. I'm just telling you how I feel."

"You know how I feel about men," Lena retorted. "Or haven't I made myself clear?"

"We're not all abusive." He reached out to touch her cheek, as if he knew right where Scott had hit her. Maybe he did. Maybe Brian and the others had discussed her at length. The thought made her burn with anger.

She knocked his hand away. "You're not necessary, either."

"Maybe not. But maybe I could be a good addition to your life."

"You know what my mother would say?" Lena exploded, pushed too far. "She'd say give the women of the world a freaking break and go be a priest!"

LOGAN'S WALK HOME was long and dispiriting. Just when he'd thought he was making progress, he'd screwed it up again. It was his own fault for bringing up marriage after fifteen minutes of a shaky truce between them. He was always stepping in it.

Patience wasn't his strong suit.

He was surprised when he rounded a corner near

the ranch and found Lena standing beside Atlas in the middle of the path.

"Something wrong?" he asked.

"Everything's wrong. But at the end of the day, it's not your fault, is it?" she asked dispiritedly.

He was afraid to take the bait.

"I just figured it out—how the General convinces you guys to come here and marry us."

Uh-oh. Logan thought fast. He knew none of the other men had told the Reeds the General had blackmailed them into taking this mission. He could only imagine their reaction to finding out. Brian, Connor and Hunter had all genuinely fallen in love with the women the General had matched them with. No harm, no foul, Logan thought.

"You said you got transferred for interfering in that fight," she went on. "Transferred to serve under the General, right?"

"On his Joint Task Force for Inter-Branch Communication." It sounded official enough—maybe it would put her off.

"On his Joint Task Force for Lying Idiots, you mean."

"Lena—"

"Don't get your knickers in a bunch. I see how it turned out. Brian came because he had to, but he fell for Cass. He couldn't fake that."

"He fell for her," Logan affirmed.

"Connor fell for Sadie. Hunter fell for Jo."

"That's right. No one crossed a boundary." He

wanted her to remember that.

"How is he getting it right?"

Logan didn't have to ask what she meant. "Jack and I were talking about that before I came—"

Fuck. Had he just said that out loud?

"Jack?" Lena raised an eyebrow.

He *had* said it out loud. He thought about lying. Realized it wouldn't work. "The guy your dad picked out for Alice."

Lena scrubbed a hand over her face. "Jesus. You realize this is insane, right?"

"Believe me, I realize it."

She looked him over. "Did you really come here to marry me?"

Logan nodded. What else could he do?

"And you thought you could actually do that? Marry someone you don't know a thing about? Make a life with her—me?"

He chuckled. "I know a thing or two about you, Lena." When she scowled, he went on. "I know you love this land more than your own life. I know you've wanted to be a rancher since before you could walk. I know a man treated you wrong. I wish I'd been here to stop that. I know that if I could ever prove to you who I really am, the two of us could have a hell of a lot of fun. You're wild in the best of ways. You're funny. You're smart. You're... amazing." As he ticked off her qualities, Logan realized he really did know her.

What's more, he liked her. A lot.

Not as a conquest or a mission or anything like that.

As a woman.

Even without the General's interference, if he'd met her in the course of his travels, he'd have fallen for her. And he'd have done his best to capture her heart. Lena was alive in the best of ways. A true match for a man like him.

"This is a strange situation. Stranger still because the man who's trying to get us together is the one who's keeping us apart. If your father hadn't sent me—if you'd met me at the Dancing Boot one night and we'd played a game of pool, what would you have thought of me?"

An emotion flitted across her features before she schooled them into a frown. "I would have been pissed that you beat me," she said flippantly.

But Logan's heart lifted. He'd seen that emotion and knew what it was, because he felt it, too, all the time around Lena.

Desire.

She liked him despite everything she said. Despite her father. If he was smart, he'd get things back on track and stop talking about marriage for a while.

"I know one thing we have in common," he told her. "Our love of history. You've gotten me in the mood to read up on the Revolutionary War since you've been talking about it."

Lena nodded. She seemed to accept it was time to change the subject, but instead of chatting about history, she turned and mounted Atlas. "Better get home before it gets dark."

He expected her to gallop away again, so he was

gratified when she set Atlas to an easy walk, and he could keep pace. They finished their journey in silence, and when they drew close to the outbuildings, Lena surprised Logan again when she suddenly said, "I have a book you can borrow."

"I'd love to borrow a book."

Lena dismounted and led Atlas toward the barn. He helped her get the horse settled in his stall for the night. It was clear the other men had already accomplished most of the chores.

When they were done, Logan headed for the door, but Lena said, "Hold up a minute." She crossed to a ladder that led up to the hayloft.

"Don't think we'll need hay tonight," Logan said.

She hesitated, one hand on a rung. "I was going to get you that book. But it can wait if you're in a hurry to get to the house."

Logan worked to figure out the situation. Did she mean the book was up there? If so, he wanted to know why.

"No time like the present. I can start it before bed tonight."

She began to climb, but she hesitated when he crossed to join her. He set down the basket, intending to climb up, too.

"You don't have to come up here."

"I'd like to—if you don't mind," he forced himself to say. He was going to kick himself if she refused him. He was far too curious to stop now.

Was that a sigh? He was pretty sure that was a sigh,

but she kept going, and he climbed after her.

At the top of the ladder, the hayloft spread out before them, with bales stacked up just as he would've expected. But as they moved past them, he realized Lena had carved out a little space for herself. Under a window sat an old chest. Nearby, on the walls, hung two replica Revolutionary War swords and a musket, the kind of decorations you might find in any military enthusiast's collection. He had to smile; his uncle had some items just like that hanging in the rec room in his basement. Once, as a kid, after watching a movie in which the hero sliced through a piece of parchment with his sword, Logan had tried to recreate the scene. The paper had survived intact, but his uncle's old turntable had gone flying when the dull replica blade smashed into it. Logan chuckled at the memory.

All in all, the loft was a cozy space. A private one. Lena opened the chest, and he caught a glimpse of a battery-operated lantern, a blanket and several books.

As he took it all in, he realized of course a woman like Lena needed a place of her own. The barn made perfect sense. What surprised him was that she was a secret reader. He wouldn't have thought she'd have to hide that particular hobby in a house like Two Willows. All the Reed women were intelligent; it made sense that they all read as much as they liked. But he was beginning to understand Lena was a private person. Maybe she needed a place to dream unseen.

He thought of what she'd said back on the ridge; that she would go back in time to the Revolutionary

War. Maybe she felt as out of place in this world as he sometimes did.

When she closed the chest, stood up and handed him a book, he took it, perused the title and cover, and turned it over to read the blurb on the back.

"Sounds good. Thank you." Against every instinct that made him want to take advantage of the privacy of the loft to kiss her, and maybe even more, Logan turned and made his way back to the ladder. When they were both on solid ground again, he touched her hand. "You'll never climb that ladder and find me in the loft. Not without an invitation. Got it?"

After a moment she nodded, turned on her heel and led the way back out.

THE KITCHEN WAS crowded three days later when Alice suddenly slammed her mug of coffee on the table. She tossed her sketchbook aside and flung her pencil down. "It's back!"

No one had to ask what she meant. The drone trying to map the maze kept arriving day after day, driving Alice into a fury. Lena wasn't used to seeing her normally calm sister so wound up, and when she joined Alice on the back porch, she meant to be soothing when she said, "Don't even pay it any attention; it never gets past your barricade."

Alice didn't answer. Instead, she grabbed the light work jacket Lena wore, yanked it open and reached for the pistol Lena carried in her shoulder holster.

Lena grabbed her wrist. "Hey—that's not cool."

"Then you do it. Shoot it. Take it out." Alice's eyes were wide, her brows furrowed.

"Okay, I'll handle it." A flying, weaving target wouldn't be that easy to hit, but everyone else was safely in the house, and this was private property. What could it hurt?

She pulled out her pistol and took aim. She didn't rush, knowing the drone would buzz around the periphery of the maze for an hour or more before it flew off.

Her first shot went wide, and the door behind her swung open not a second later.

"What the hell, Lena? What are you shooting at?" Brian shouted.

She ignored him. Took a second shot.

Missed again as the drone dove for the maze.

"Damn it."

"Lena, what's going on?" Cass called from inside.

"Alice wants the drone dead," Lena called back.

"Well, so do I," Cass said. "Go for it."

"You heard my sister," Lena told Brian. She noticed Logan standing in the doorway. He folded his arms and leaned against the frame.

She took aim again, but it was harder now that everyone was watching. She told herself to think of it like target practice. She couldn't let her audience psych her out.

After lining up her shot, she took a breath, aimed and breathed out again while pulling the trigger.

The drone crashed to the earth.

Alice whooped and raced toward it. Scooping it up, she headed for the maze. "Come on!" she yelled back to Lena.

Lena emptied the remaining cartridges from her pistol, pocketed them and reholstered it, then jogged after Alice. Logan followed her, but she didn't care. Taking that drone down made her feel ten feet tall.

She caught up to Alice in the center of the maze. Logan, who'd stuck close behind her, came to a stop when she did. Alice held the drone up to the standing stone.

"Your boundaries are sacred again," she announced to it. "Next time I won't wait so long. This is for you." She dropped the drone on the ground and stomped it to pieces. Turning, she smiled triumphantly. "No one fucks with my maze!"

"That's right." Lena cheered her on. When Alice marched past them, leaving the smashed drone behind her, Logan turned to watch her go.

"Jack's gotta be shitting his pants right about now," he said with a grin.

"Good." Lena grinned back. "What's he like?"

"Honestly? Guy drives me nuts, but I think... I think he might be perfect for your sister. She's perfect for him. He'll turn himself inside out trying to figure out how she does what she does."

"That's how it should be."

"That's how it is for me, too," Logan said as they slowly followed Alice out of the maze. Lena had a feeling he was trying to memorize the way.

"You can't figure out how I do what I do?" she scoffed. "All I do is ranch."

"And consume my every waking thought," he admitted. "And most of my sleeping thoughts, too."

Lena didn't know what to say about that. Truth was, she thought about him far more than she wanted to.

"Ready to build that stable?" he asked.

"Hell, yeah." Relieved at the turn of the conversation, she led the way through the rest of the maze and down the rutted track toward the outbuildings. It was clear the weather wouldn't hold for too long, and they needed the stables up and ready to house the horses over the winter.

Several times during the last few days, she and Logan had gone over the building plans. Normally she would have resented his interference, but this time she had to admit he'd been helpful. Neither she nor Logan had worked with building plans before, and although it wasn't a complicated structure, she wanted to take the time to make sure she understood them.

They met up with the rest of the men at the foundation of the new stable. The next few hours would have been satisfying if Logan wasn't always trying to carry things for her or help hold the boards she was screwing into place. Every time she told him she didn't need help, he replied, "I know," and then helped her anyway. By midway through the afternoon, she was happy with the progress they'd made, but she was also thirsty.

"I need to run up to the house," she told the men. "Need anything?"

"A refill on my water would be great. Want me to come with you?" Logan asked.

"Nope. Be back in a minute." She hurried up the track before he could join her, wanting a little space. She wasn't gone long, so when she was walking back down the track, she was surprised to see a truck she didn't recognize heading out the track that led from the outbuildings to the main road. "Who was that?" she called to Logan as she approached. She passed out water bottles and downed half of her own before setting the canister on a handy pile of wood.

"Those twins who were so enamored of you at the Dancing Boot the other night." Logan drank his entire bottle of water in one long gulp. "Needed that, I guess."

"The twins? You mean Harley and Ray? What did they want?"

"They wanted to see that stallion of yours. Told them you were far too busy for that kind of nonsense. I sent them packing. I don't think they'll bother you again."

Lena couldn't believe what she was hearing. "You sent them packing? Without even asking me?"

"Didn't want to send those two goons up to the house. Besides, the other night you made it clear you didn't want them around."

"That doesn't give you any right to decide who I talk to or don't talk to. You're not my father."

"Believe me; I don't want to be your father." Logan waggled his eyebrows at her.

Lena's anger grew. He couldn't distract her with a

funny face. This was serious. She didn't need some… man… making decisions for her.

"Look, they're troublemakers, anyone can see that. I did what needed to be done. I don't know what the fuss is all about."

Now he was going to pretend *he* was the reasonable one? Lena's throat burned with indignation. "First of all, they're kids. Second of all, the fuss is about you sending away people who came to see me. You don't get to make those decisions. Got it?"

"No, I don't *got it*." Logan straightened up. "Your father sent me here to protect you. If someone sets foot on this property and I don't like them, I'm going to send them away. I'm not going to let them think I have to ask permission before I do so."

"You do have to ask permission! This isn't your home or your land. I'm the one who owns this place. I'm the one who runs it. And who the hell says I need protecting?" Lena hated the way her voice rose at the end of that question. She grabbed the closest thing to hand—a crowbar—unsure what she meant to do with it but needing to feel the heft of it in her hand.

"Lena—" Brian said, straightening from where he was going through a pile of lumber. "Be careful."

"Far as I know it's the General's name on the deed to Two Willows," Logan said, ignoring him.

Lena blinked. The *General's* name? "Like hell! Two Willows is my mother's land. The General forfeited any right to it the day he walked away from her funeral." She lifted the crowbar higher. Logan snatched up a shovel and deflected her blow when she swung the tool at him in a wide arc. He blocked her next blow, too.

"Stop it. Jesus, woman, you're going to get yourself hurt! Come on—we both know the General calls the shots here whether you like it or not!"

Lena swung again as hard as she could. Logan repelled the blow with two hands on the shovel. The crowbar bounced off its handle and smashed back into Lena's forehead. She fell to her knees with a cry. The crowbar hit the dirt in front of her, but Lena was too busy cradling her head in her hands to see it. She heard Logan swearing, felt his hands lift her up. As the world tilted, her vision blurred and everything went dark.

Chapter Six

"MAYBE IT'S A sign you're not where you're supposed to be," Anthony said.

Logan clutched his cell phone tighter, pacing the short expanse of the kitchen, wishing he had more room to burn off the energy that raged through him. Lena was resting in the hospital overnight under observation, but the doctor who'd examined her said he didn't think she'd gotten a concussion. She did have quite a bump on her forehead, though, Brian said.

She'd refused to see him when Logan asked to have a minute alone with her at the hospital. Logan had tried to push the matter, but he was unanimously overruled and sent home.

Now he couldn't relax. He was burning with remorse and frustration. He'd only meant to block Lena's blow, not brain her with the crowbar. The look Cass had given him when he'd run into the house, Lena passed out in his arms, should have struck him dead on the spot. Even Alice, who he swore was on his side where marrying Lena was concerned, had *tsked* at him as she rushed to help.

"What do you want me to do, leave? Just walk out before I even know if she's okay. Go AWOL?"

"I still don't see how a Marine can possibly be on a mission in Montana. No, don't tell me; I know. You can't talk about that. But I want you to think about your future—hard."

Logan wished he'd never placed the call. He didn't know why he'd thought Anthony could advise him when a woman was involved.

Lena was going to be furious when she got home in the morning, and he needed to figure out how to calm her down and get her to listen to him. He hadn't realized he'd said that aloud until Anthony said, "You're the one who needs to calm down and listen to reason. Take a few deep breaths."

"That's not going to help me find an answer."

"Then pray about it."

"That's what you always say."

"Because that's always the answer."

Logan hung up on him. It wasn't the answer this time. He needed to act. Do something—say something. Something to make Lena realize that hurting her was the last thing on his mind. She needed to trust him. When he'd kicked the twins off her property, he'd only been acting in her best interests. She'd have kicked them off the ranch as fast as he had if she'd been there. And despite what she'd said, they weren't kids. They were grown men. Only a couple of years younger than she was. Lena was the one who'd overreacted and lashed out at him with a crowbar. She'd sent *herself* to the hospital, to tell the truth.

Not that he'd ever point that out. He didn't have a death wish.

Alice entered the kitchen and set the kettle on the stove. "I'd offer you some," she told him, "but you need something stronger."

"You're right; I could use a drink," he said.

"I meant you need the maze." She nodded toward the darkness beyond the kitchen windows. "You've got a question that needs answering, right?"

"Yeah, I guess I do." But he doubted a bunch of shrubbery could help him.

"Go ask the stone." Alice pulled out a cup and saucer, then rummaged through a basket of tea bags until she found the one she wanted.

"You do realize that's ridiculous, don't you?"

"More ridiculous than knocking your intended fiancée out cold with a crowbar?"

He didn't bother to correct her. That's how the story would go from now on, he mused, as he shrugged into his coat and made his way out the back door. Lena would come off totally innocent. He'd be the crazed Marine with the shovel.

And what would his brothers think if they knew he was about to consult a mystical standing stone about his problems? He crossed Sadie's garden toward its entrance, figuring the day couldn't get any stranger than it already had been. He'd never in his life imagined he'd physically injure a woman with a garden implement. Now Alice was right; he'd knocked out the only one he'd ever considered marrying.

"Ask it about that sword, too. I can't get it out of my mind, and I need to focus on that drone man," Alice called after him.

There was enough moonlight that as his eyes adjusted he could make his way without tripping over any of Sadie's plants, but when he entered the maze the tall hedges cast deep shadows that made the going difficult. He didn't have the way memorized, either, so it took him some time to reach the center, and he probably would have given up if he didn't think it would be just as difficult to find his way back.

When he finally found the stone, it stood tall and slightly menacing, moonlight making its broad flank glow pale. He approached it and was drawn to touch it, finally placing both hands on it, its rough surface cool below his palms.

Am I supposed to be a priest?

Hell, he hadn't meant to ask that. He was supposed to be finding out how to patch things up with Lena.

Still, the question had come to mind, and he forced himself to sit with it. He knew to the bottom of his heart he wasn't meant for the priesthood. So how come it kept coming up? Had his brothers and parents seen something in him he hadn't? Had he really missed his calling all this time?

Is that why he kept having those dreams?

He was sick of wondering.

"Am I supposed to be a priest?" he asked again out loud.

He stepped back but kept his gaze on the monolith, not knowing what to do next. Overhead, clouds scudded across the sky, the gibbous moon playing hide-and-seek.

It was quiet out here.

Peaceful.

Was this a kind of praying? And who was listening if it was? He could almost believe in a benevolent deity out here in the darkness—

"Oh, hell," a female voice demanded. "What are you doing here?"

LENA YELPED WHEN Logan whipped around and dropped into a defensive stance straight out of hand-to-hand combat practice. He straightened when he spotted her. "Jesus. Lena, what are you doing here? Why aren't you in the hospital?"

He looked like he'd seen a ghost. It would have been funny if her head didn't still ache so hard she thought she might pass out.

"I don't need a hospital. It's just a little bump."

"Looks like a pretty big bump from here."

"You didn't answer my question," she said sharply. "What *are* you doing here?"

"Just… needed some fresh air." He was still looking at her strangely, and it was making Lena uncomfortable. It was as if he'd read some answer in her arrival there, and she didn't have any answers for him.

Although she had a thing or two on her mind. "You were out of line this afternoon," she began.

He stepped closer. "First things first. Lena, I'm sorry. I never meant to hurt you. You know that, right?"

His remorse turned her angry words to ashes in her throat. "I... Yeah, I know." She'd been the one to attack him, and she should have known better than to swing a crowbar at a Marine. What had she thought he'd do? Let her take his head off? "I overreacted, I guess." She seemed to be doing that a lot lately. Especially around Logan.

"Maybe we're both a little hotheaded." He sighed. "But I mean it, baby girl. I don't ever want to be the one causing you pain."

That *baby girl* caught her off balance somehow. Before when he'd said it she'd always felt he'd been teasing her. It had been silly, annoying, a little sexy sometimes.

Now it was soft and... intimate.

Lena wasn't ready for intimate. Not with this headache. Not even without it.

"This is a pretty uncanny spot, isn't it?" he asked, gesturing at the standing stone.

"Yes, it is."

"You don't know who set the stone here?"

"No, we don't. It's as if it's always been here, but of course that can't be true. But even the earliest records we've found of the place talk about the monolith."

"And you like history, so you'd know."

It wasn't a question; it was a statement of fact. Something he knew about her. He was right; the maze and the stone were downright uncanny in this kind of light. The stone almost looked—alive. *Sentient* was perhaps a better word.

Like it knew things.

"Do you come here a lot to ask it questions?" Logan asked.

"No. Not since—not since Mom died. I used to come here all the time. I've asked it a million questions in my life, but not since then."

"Why'd you stop?"

He seemed genuinely curious, and Lena found herself answering, as if the night—and the stone itself—had cast a spell on her. "I asked it a question that day. After Mom died. I slipped out late—it was a night like this. And I asked—" Her voice thickened. "If she'd come back." She'd desperately needed her mother to come back. At fourteen she'd been lost without Amelia's calm and loving presence. She'd had to become so hard—so fast.

Logan waited, as still as the stone, and she went on. "It said *no*—in a way that left no room for interpretation. Of course, I already knew that, but—I've never asked it a question since." She forced herself to take a deep breath. Her mother had been gone for eleven years, and she'd accepted her death and moved forward. She was a strong woman now. She was only emotional tonight because she'd nearly put herself into a coma. "Did you ask it a question just now?" Let Logan sit on the hot seat for a while.

"No," he said quickly. "I'm a Catholic, remember? We don't believe in magic stones."

WAS IT HIS imagination, or did a cold breeze whip up around them after he uttered those patently false words? He couldn't tell Lena what he'd asked, though. She'd think he was out of his mind. He'd spent the last week coming at her from every direction, flirting with her, telling her he meant to marry her—and now he was consulting a standing stone about whether to be ordained?

Ridiculous. Proof of his complete inappropriateness for the job if any more was needed.

When he'd turned and seen Lena, his heart had thumped like a hammer hitting a nail. His whole body had leaped with awareness of her.

With *wanting* her.

Just his bad luck she'd walked in on him after his moment of weakness. If she'd come a second earlier, she would have heard his question.

His question. *Am I supposed to be a priest?*

Was Lena his answer?

He suddenly felt sure she was. He wasn't supposed to be a priest. He was supposed to marry this woman. The General had been right; he had sent Logan to the right place.

"You're… lying. I can tell," she said. "You did ask something. Did you get your answer?"

He took her hand and tugged her closer. "Yes, I got my answer."

He was meant to be here after all. Meant to be with Lena.

Meant to marry her.

Logan bent down and kissed her.

Meant to stake a claim to the future he really wanted.

SHE HAD TO stop letting Logan kiss her, Lena thought, but somehow she couldn't back away. She was growing used to his presence throughout her days. He worked by her side, stepped in to help out before she asked him. He saw the sunrise with her, the sunset, did chores with her, ate with her—

He was becoming a member of the family, like it or not. Getting under her skin.

"What is with you?" she asked, unable to stop herself when he broke off the kiss. She turned to lead the way out of the maze.

"Don't know what you mean."

The Marine seemed downright cheerful now, walking along beside her with a jaunty step.

"Why are you—screwing things up for me?"

Logan stopped, caught her hand and tugged her to a halt, too. "Hey, that's the last thing I want to do, you know that, right? Maybe you're the one who needs to answer a question. Why are you always fighting *me*? Why not let me help you sometimes?"

"You know the answer to that. I don't want to lose control of my ranch."

"We've already become your hired hands. What more can any of us do to set your mind at ease?"

He let go her hand and crossed his arms. His biceps bulged against his shirt. He must be a sight in uniform, she thought. Hell, he was a sight no matter what he wore. Not for the first time, she wished circumstances were different. That she'd never met Scott.

That she'd met Logan instead.

"You can't do anything," she said truthfully. Thanks to Scott, she'd be suspicious of men until her dying day.

He chuckled again. "Just like I thought. So, if I can't set your mind at ease, all I can do is follow my conscience."

"You have one of those?" she asked pertly.

"I do," he assured her. "Works well most of the time."

"When you're not braining helpless women."

"Helpless." He snorted. "Lena Reed, you are a torment to men. But you're right; your technique with a crowbar leaves something to be desired."

She turned around in a huff and strode the rest of the way to the house without looking back.

Chapter Seven

AFTER SUCH A beautiful night, Logan couldn't believe how gray and oppressive the clouds were the following morning. A wet mist threatened to become rain, and for the first time he wondered if they'd be able to get the barn done before the really bad weather arrived. He'd handed Lena over to Cass reluctantly when they'd returned to the house the night before. He'd have rather stayed up and kept an eye on Lena himself, but Cass was awake, having gotten a call from the hospital when they discovered Lena was gone, and she insisted on sitting up the remainder of the night to watch her sister.

Still, this morning Lena refused to consider resting. Instead, she arrived at the building site ready to get to work, the bump still prominent on her forehead, and the men hurried to keep up with her. She didn't even seem to mind when Logan stepped in to offer a suggestion about how to frame in the windows. They all knew they were racing against the clock—with no guarantee of winning.

As usual, Champ, Isobel and Max wandered around

the building site until Lena finally phoned Sadie to come and take them away. Sadie arrived and took charge of them, saying she'd take them on a long hike to tire them out.

"Last night must have set you back a bunch," Connor said to Logan in an undertone later that morning. He nodded at Lena, who was deep in conversation with Brian, both bending over plans that riffled in the wind that had been blowing all morning.

"Yeah. But not as much as you might think." He'd connected with Lena last night in the maze when he'd kissed her. Lena hadn't pushed him away. That had to be progress, but he didn't want to talk about that with Connor. "She can't resist my hot body," he joked instead and flexed his arms.

Connor rolled his eyes. "Are those the same muscles you used to knock her out yesterday?"

"I didn't knock her out!" Logan sighed. He didn't know why he bothered to argue. "Anyway, she's back today, isn't she? Working with me? Brian won Cass while fixing the house, right? Why can't I win Lena while building a stable?"

"Yeah, but Cass was the first. Lena watched me build Sadie a walled garden. Hunter built Jo a house. Maybe you need to up your game. Build something specifically for *her*—not the horses."

Logan kept thinking about Connor's suggestion long after they got back to work. It made sense, but there was one problem: he didn't know what Lena wanted. She wasn't into gardening, and he'd heard her talking to Sadie about how much work Jo would have to do keeping her home tidy without Cass to do it for her.

He didn't think Lena was in any rush to move out of her home. What could he build her that would make a real impression?

He mulled over that question for the rest of the morning, through lunch and into the afternoon, until Lena called out, "Take a twenty-minute break, everyone. Go clear your heads; we all need to stay sharp today."

Logan turned toward the house like everyone else, hoping to grab a snack and a drink before coming back. That mist had hung around all day, and he was damp—and a little cranky. But when he glanced back to check that Lena was following the rest of them, he saw her disappear into the barn—

And knew exactly what to build for her.

An escape. Somewhere dry and warm she could slip away to and read for hours at a time. Somewhere no one else knew about—at least at first.

Not a house—no need to get complicated. Lena wouldn't want that. A simple structure, easy to maintain—and heat. A place to store her books.

With comfortable seating and a few other necessities her hideaway in the barn didn't have.

Could he build it on the ranch without her knowing about it?

And where could he tuck it away, hidden from her sisters, but close enough she could easily reach it?

Logan decided he'd start exploring the ranch and making plans. He'd search online for ideas.

A reading hideaway.

The perfect gift for the woman who was going to be his wife.

Even if she didn't know it yet.

"DAMN IT!" LENA shoved Logan away when he stole a kiss later that afternoon. That was twice in twenty-four hours he'd gotten past her guard.

She was losing her touch.

"Baby girl, you know you love it when I do that," Logan said and went back to work, whistling.

"You know I'm going to kick your ass. Just as soon as I've built this stable." She got back to work, too. She was wet and getting cold as the sun sank low in the sky. Her head didn't hurt as badly as it had earlier, but it still throbbed. The damn mist hadn't let up all day, and she'd made the mistake of choosing twenty minutes of reading over returning to the house to warm up and dry off at break time.

"Might want to wait for that bump to heal up before you give yourself a new one…"

"Watch it!"

She caught his grin and had to bite back a smile of her own. What a jerk. It was like having a brother—

Although it wasn't like that at all. With every kiss Logan got deeper under her skin. She kept catching herself… thinking about him.

Thinking about being with him.

It was ridiculous.

Horrifying.

It had been too long, she supposed, and her body was rebelling against her self-imposed moratorium on carnal pleasure. She hadn't been with a man since before the first attack on Two Willows. She'd thought Scott had soured her on men forever, but it seemed like her body had other ideas in mind.

Being close to Logan seemed to rile her up every which way.

Which wasn't good. She still needed to look out for trouble, even if things had remained calm these last few weeks. Somewhere in Tennessee was a group of troublemakers who'd decided to target her ranch. First, they'd sent Bob Finchley and his buddies to try to woo them and trick them into handing over the property. Then they'd stolen Jo's dogs for a diversion and tried to kidnap Jo. When that didn't work, they'd set the stable on fire to get revenge.

Each time she and her sisters—and Brian, Connor and Hunter—had managed to fight them off. So far, they'd won, but who was to say what would happen next? Cab had traced the men back to Tennessee, but he hadn't uncovered the mastermind behind the attacks, nor a solid reason for them above and beyond the drug connection.

She had to assume they'd try again. She couldn't let Logan distract her.

Lena finally gave up on the afternoon when the light got so low that it would have been dangerous for them to keep working. The wind had picked up, and it was outright raining. They secured all their tools, cleaned and dried them thoroughly before putting them away, and then worked together to do the evening chores.

"I hope this storm passes overnight," Brian said as they walked back to the house, stating what was on all their minds.

"We need to work faster," Lena said.

"I think we're working as fast as we can, lass," Connor said.

"We'll get it done," Logan assured her.

Lena wasn't sure they would, though, and the realization felt far too much like another failure for comfort.

At the house, she waited her turn for the shower and came down to dinner in clean, dry, warm clothes, her hair still damp.

Cass was just putting the finishing touches on a pot roast.

"How's it going out there?" she asked with a commiserating smile.

"Not great," Lena admitted. "I don't know if we can get it done before the snow flies."

Cass nodded. Thought a minute. "You know, we haven't asked for much help from our community over the years. We've always hidden away—done our own thing. Maybe it's time to try something different."

"Like what?"

"Like a barn raising. A stable raising," she corrected herself. "What do you think?"

It went against all Lena's desire for independence, but the alternative was possible failure, and she'd hate to have to explain that to the General after everything else that had happened this year.

She couldn't bear to prove him right about her.

"I think you're on to something," she said reluctant-ly.

"Leave it to me," Cass told her, patting her shoulder. "I'll put the word out, and we'll get the stables done in no time.

Chapter Eight

"**R**EADY FOR THE hordes?" Connor asked a couple of days later as they gathered on the back porch ready to walk down to the building site after a hearty breakfast. They'd done their chores before sunup. Now it was time to focus on the stable.

"Do you really think we'll get hordes?" Logan asked.

Connor shrugged. "Time will tell, I guess."

Cass, true to her word, had put out a call for help, and according to her, a fair number of men and women would show up to lend a hand today. She, Alice and Sadie had gotten up well before dawn to cook all morning in anticipation of extra mouths to feed at lunchtime.

"It's a little hard to plan when we don't know how many people will show up," Lena told them. "I might have been optimistic. If that turns out to be the case, then we'll break some of the tasks down. We won't finish today, but it'll push us forward a lot."

"What if no one shows up?" Logan asked.

"Then we'll get back to work."

"Someone will show up, though, won't they?" Connor pressed. Logan understood why; the man had shown Logan his cell phone earlier this morning. The temperature was set to plunge in just a few days, and snow was in the forecast for early next week. They needed help, or there was no way they'd finish in time.

"I'm sure they will," Lena answered.

"You don't sound sure." Too late, Logan wished he'd thought before he'd spoken.

Lena winced. "It's just—we've always kept to ourselves for the most part. We're not bad neighbors, but we're not the best, either. When we were teens, hiding out when we'd kicked out our overseer again, we didn't exactly go around helping other people, you know? I'm not sure if we've built up enough goodwill to expect people to help us."

"Plenty of people come to your weddings," Brian pointed out.

"That's true."

"But weddings mean free food and drinks," Logan said. "Not working all day in the cold."

"Dude, you're not helping," Brian told him. "Come on, let's get ready."

An hour later, Logan was beginning to despair of anyone showing up, and although Lena hadn't said a word, he knew she was, too. He caught her surreptitious glances toward the house—and toward the poor excuse for a sun that had risen above the horizon. It didn't look like it would rain today, at least. But a thin haze of clouds covered the sky, leaving the sun a dim globe behind them. It wouldn't be that warm, but it wouldn't be that cold, either.

"Look!"

Logan followed Brian's pointed finger and smiled. "There come the first of them," he said heartily as a silver truck rolled down the lane toward them. Hope buoyed his heart when Lena smiled, too.

"That's the Cruzes," she said. "Thank God; that'll be a big help. And the Mathesons," she added a second later when several more trucks came into view. "That's almost enough extra hands right there!"

But the help kept coming. Truck after truck pulled in, unloading men, women—and children. Many of the women and kids peeled off toward the house, carrying covered dishes, while the men—and several women and teenagers—joined the growing group at the building site.

Lena busied herself breaking them up into details of four to eight people, consulting her notes as she went. Once again, Logan thought the military had lost out when she hadn't joined up. She was a whiz at organization and at breaking down a task into its component parts.

As the work started, a cheerful hum of voices changed what had been a frustrating struggle into an enjoyable endeavor. Logan worked along with the rest of the men, meeting his new neighbors, pitching in where he was directed—content to let Lena shine.

And she was shining. The happiest he'd ever seen her—directing everyone, thinking of everything, always two steps ahead anticipating problems and the best ways to solve them.

When he'd first stepped back and let her have her way running the ranch, it had been to score points with her, he admitted to himself now. Today his understanding grew. It wasn't simply kind to let her take the lead at Two Willows; it was right. Lena knew everything about this land. She'd grown up here. It had belonged to her family for generations. That meant something. There'd be plenty of work for all of them, and they were all qualified leaders in their own right, so they'd have to discover how to use their qualifications in ways that didn't upset the apple cart at the ranch.

But that was a problem for another time. For now, he needed to focus on the task at hand.

Except—who was that?

Another truck pulled in, and when the doors of the cab opened and two men climbed out, Logan's chest tightened.

The twins.

Back for another try at Lena, he guessed.

"Take over for me, will you?" he asked Luke Matheson, who grunted and stepped in to help raise a section of wall into place. Logan strode toward the approaching men and confronted them a half-dozen paces from the stables. "Why are you here?"

"We heard about the stable raising. We came to help—just like everyone else," Harley said. "Even brought a casserole." He nodded at the dish in his brother's hands.

"A casserole, huh?" Logan hadn't expected that. He

wanted to kick them off Two Willows land, but he didn't know how to do it without raising a fuss at the same time. He couldn't exactly justify his rancor, either. These two hadn't done anything wrong—yet.

Besides, Lena might come after him with that crow-bar again.

"Better get that up to the house," he told Ray grudg-ingly. "I'll check with Lena about assignments for you. Not sure if there's anything left for you to do."

But of course there was, and fifteen minutes later the two men were working with a framing crew. They both climbed ladders with the ease of men who'd done this kind of work before, handy with the tools, comfort-able at high elevations. Logan had to admit to himself they were an asset to the operation, but he'd be damned if he'd say so out loud.

With two of the walls up, the structure was far from steady, but the twins swarmed over it as if it was constructed of steel—and Lena seemed determined to follow their example. Climbing up to check if everything was level, she perched unsteadily at the top of one of the walls. Logan, catching sight of her, put down his tools to go spot her. All she needed was to hit her head again.

He was halfway there when Harley dropped his drill with a shout of warning to the men underneath, lunged forward to try to catch it, gripping the structure with his legs, but only succeeded in grabbing thin air. The force of his movement made the whole wall sway—

And Logan watched in horror as Lena yelped and

lost her grip.

He didn't know how he made it the rest of the way, but a second later, Lena hit his outstretched arms and they both fell to the ground.

"Lena!" Brian came running. So did Connor. As a crowd surrounded them, Lena got to her feet and pushed Logan away.

"I'm fine. I'm perfectly fine," she said, but Logan knew she was shaken. It wasn't that far a fall, but she still could have been hurt badly enough to put her out of the game for weeks.

And they didn't have weeks.

"You need to take a rest," Logan said. "We all do. Lunchtime, folks!"

"Jesus, Lena. I'm sorry." Harley had finally managed to climb down off the wall and fight his way through the crowd. "That was a rookie mistake. I can't believe I lost my grip on that drill."

"Nearly got her killed," Ray said, shooting his brother a look Logan couldn't decipher.

"I didn't try to," Harley shot back.

"Stick with me," Ray said to Lena. "I'll keep you safe from guys like him."

"Fuck you." Harley shoved him.

"Time to eat," Brian said, stepping between the brothers. Ray turned to follow several of the other men toward the house. Harley hung back a moment, then left as well. Logan wanted to go after them, but he didn't want to leave Lena.

"You okay?" he asked her.

"I'm fine," Lena all but growled. "You heard Brian; let's go eat."

But she didn't turn with the rest of the crowd for the house.

And Logan followed her to the barn a few minutes later.

LENA WAS STILL shaking as she climbed the ladder to the hayloft, and when she reached the top, opened the chest and pulled out the old horse blanket, she lowered herself to the floor gratefully and tried to catch her breath. Heat flamed in her cheeks. She'd fallen in front of everyone. She hated to think about how that had looked. Some leader she was turning out to be when she couldn't even keep herself upright.

It had all happened so fast: first she'd been on top of the wall, and then she'd been in Logan's arms.

And if he hadn't caught her—

She knew beyond a shadow of a doubt she'd be racing in an ambulance to the hospital right now with a broken arm—or leg. Or worse. She covered her face with her hands.

How would she have explained that to the General? That she couldn't even build a wall without falling off? It would have been too much.

"Lena? Do you mind if I come up?" Logan called from the base of the ladder.

She nearly refused him, but a moment later she managed, "Yeah. Okay." It wasn't Logan's fault she was such a klutz.

His head and shoulders appeared first, then the rest of him as he climbed into the hayloft. "Are you all right?" He approached her, and she waved him down.

When he'd taken a seat, she nodded. "I really am fine."

"Still, that had to be scary."

"How come no one asks men if they are scared after an accident?"

"Maybe they should."

Yeah. Right. "Look, I don't want any extra attention, okay?"

"Baby girl," Logan said, moving closer despite her protests. "I'm not giving you extra attention because you're some fragile princess. I'm giving you extra attention because you're hot."

Despite herself, Lena laughed. The man was too ridiculous. "You expect me to believe that? Look at me." She knew she was a mess.

"I am looking at you. Tell you what, how about I prove it?"

Before she could stop him, he leaned close and kissed her, bracing his hands on the hayloft floor. She was getting used to his stolen kisses, much to her chagrin, but this one was different. This time he didn't stop with a quick peck. Instead, he kissed her thoroughly, and without making a conscious decision, Lena kissed him back, suddenly hungry for this kind of touch—hungry to prove to herself she really was all right.

"That's more like it," he said several minutes later

when they parted. "Got some color in your cheeks now."

She could certainly feel the heat rising in them. "You're an ass." Lena scrambled to her feet, steadying herself against a wave of dizziness. "I'm starving," she said to cover up her distress. "We'd better get up to the house before everyone else eats up the food."

"Good idea." Logan stood up, too. When a noise down below caught his attention, he strode to the ladder. Lena followed, shaking her head to clear it. She reached the edge of the loft in time to see the barn door shut. "Hello?" Logan called.

Whoever had been in the barn didn't come back.

"Someone probably came to call us to lunch," Lena said and sighed, "then heard us up here." She followed Logan down the ladder, knowing gossip was bound to follow.

"Let them talk," Logan told her when she made it down the ladder.

"I hate it when people talk about me."

"I know." Logan took her hand, and to her surprise, she let him. Outside, he looked around, and groaned. Lena saw why. Harley was striding quickly toward the house, his shoulders stiff.

"He's pissed," Logan said. "Do you think he dropped that drill on purpose?" he added.

"No." She couldn't say why, but she was convinced he hadn't. When people did things on purpose, even if they were trying to act normal, they exaggerated their movements. She hadn't seen anything like that.

"I think he and Ray are fighting over you."

"Huh. Well, let them fight." She wasn't interested in either of them.

Logan's grip on her hand tightened fractionally. "Just as long as you remember who's here to marry you."

BY THE END of the day, the stable's four walls were in place, as were the struts that would hold up the roof. The twins had left at lunchtime. Everyone else who'd come today had promised to come again on Saturday to get the roof on.

Logan eyed the weather report with concern. Toward the end of the week, the temperatures were supposed to drop.

"The weathermen are always wrong," Lena told him when she saw what he was looking at, but when she left, Brian and Connor came to look, and both of their faces echoed his feelings.

"It's going to be tight," Brian said.

"We'd better be prepared to tarp it up at a moment's notice," Connor put in.

He was right. Logan went to town the following day and made sure they had adequate tarps, but he knew a good storm could tear one off a roof no matter how well you secured it. They could only hope the bad weather would hold off.

Meanwhile, there were plenty of chores to keep them busy as they got the ranch ready for cold weather.

The week passed in a blur, and most nights Logan

fell into a deep sleep the minute his head hit his pillow. He still flirted with Lena every chance he got, stole kisses when he could—

But they were both far too busy for much more than that.

As for the hideaway he wanted to build for Lena, he made no progress at all and was beginning to despair when he ran into Cass in the basement one day. She was putting a load of bedclothes into the washer when he came to fetch his things from the dryer. As he watched, she put a hand at the base of her back and stretched, and he noticed the swell of her stomach—bigger than it had seemed just days ago.

He couldn't help wondering if he would ever have a family. If Lena ever became pregnant, he'd do double-duty to keep her safe. He…

Was letting his imagination carry him away.

"Hi, Cass. Just here to get my things."

"I'll do your laundry for you, you know," she said. "I do everyone else's."

"Don't want to impose."

"It's not an imposition. We divvy up the jobs here so that everything gets done."

"And you don't mind getting stuck with the laundry?"

Cass laughed. "I don't mind it nearly as much as I'd mind mucking out a stable." She made a face. "Luckily, I've got two sisters who feel entirely the same about laundry. It works out."

Logan realized this was his chance to talk to someone about Lena. "Got a minute?"

"Sure."

He told her about the hideaway, mentioning that he'd noticed Lena liked to be alone but not spilling the beans about her penchant for historical novels. "I just haven't had time to find a place or get it built."

Cass thought a moment. "I have an idea—but you don't have to agree to it," she rushed to add.

"Lay it on me."

"The attic. We never used to use it because the roof leaked like a sieve. Now it's completely dry, and it's a big space—"

"There would have to be a lock on the door," Logan said, thinking it over. "It would have to be off-limits to everyone else."

"Of course. And you'd need to insulate it somehow so it isn't hot in summer and cold in winter…"

"I can handle that." He was sure he could. And it would be a lot less work than building something from scratch—plus it took away the need to figure out how to heat a little place out in the woods, and it would be handy to Lena all the time. "You're a genius, Cass."

She smiled. "Thanks."

"I'm going to need your help, though—so she doesn't suspect."

"I'm in," Cass said immediately.

LENA WAS SO busy she barely had time to visit the hayloft in the barn that week, and besides, it was getting too cool to be comfortable out there for very long, even with the horse blanket wrapped around her. This happened every fall, and as the slow, dark months passed she was apt to grow cranky with her sisters—and anyone else who got too close. The walls of her small bedroom closed in on her when she retreated there for too long. Sometimes she took long drives in her truck just to get some time alone, but there wasn't room in her schedule for that now.

Lena became as obsessed with the weather report as everyone else as the week went on. Today's job was sheathing the building in plywood.

Tomorrow they'd put on the roof.

If the snow held off.

Lena found herself pulling out her phone and looking at the weather report every fifteen minutes. Only when Brian barked at her to pay attention as they maneuvered a sheet of plywood up to the top of one of the gable ends did she put it away, pride stinging from the rebuke, and promise herself not to look again until they were done for the day. High, thin clouds obscured the sun but didn't bring any bad weather. Still, it was getting cold—which made working with tools far more difficult.

She came back to the house that night with Logan to find several boxes of pizza stacked on the table.

"A movie night?" Lena asked. "I'm not sure I can stay awake."

"These were delivered. By your fan club," Sadie said with a grin. She was setting a stack of plates on the table.

"My fan club?" Lena looked at the boxes again for an explanation.

"Harley. Not sure where Ray was—I thought those two were joined at the hip. I asked him to join us, but he couldn't stay. Just knew we were probably over-worked this week. Nice of him, wasn't it?"

Lena noticed Logan's frown and had to bite back a smile. "Very nice. I'll have to thank him tomorrow." She nearly laughed at the Marine's baleful expression. "Come on, let's eat. I'm ravenous."

"Way ahead of you." Brian grabbed a plate and helped himself to a slice from the top box. "Pepperoni. Awesome." He took a bite right then and there and groaned. "That hits the spot."

Soon they were all arrayed around the table, eating pizza, not much chatter interrupting their meal until they'd each consumed several slices.

When Connor made a frustrated noise, Lena craned her neck and realized he'd been looking at his phone under the table.

"Snow tomorrow night."

His words sank in, and they all stopped eating.

"Then we'd better be up before sunrise and get that roof on as soon as we can," Logan said.

"It's going to be a struggle," Alice said quietly.

Lena knew that was one of her sister's hunches, and her appetite disappeared. "We'll get it done," she assured everyone else. "We have to."

Chapter Nine

THE FOLLOWING MORNING dawned cold with an iron-gray sky overhead.

"I don't like the look of those clouds," Brian remarked when Logan joined him on the back porch. As they walked down to the building site, their breath shone white in the air. Champ, Isobel and Max had tried to join them, but Brian had ordered all the dogs back to the house, and Cass had taken charge of them.

"We'll get 'er done," Logan said, but he wasn't as sure as his words made out. If they didn't, the horses would have to board elsewhere over the winter. It wouldn't be the end of the world, but he knew Lena would feel like she'd failed. He knew the rebuilt stables stood for more than a roof over their horses' heads. It stood for standing strong against the people who had set themselves against Two Willows.

"I MEAN IT. We'll get 'er done," he said again when Lena frowned.

"I'm with you," Brian said. Soon they were back at work, tackling the usual morning chores and then following Lena's commands to set up their materials for the day.

Once again, trucks rolled in as soon as the sun came up. This time the volunteers wore more layers, and the women carried more dishes up to the house. Heartier fare, Logan expected.

They'd need it.

There was less joking today as everyone broke into teams and got to work, and soon sheets of plywood were being handed up to the roof and screwed into place. The twins were back, he noticed, and he had to work hard not to resent it. While Ray looked out of sorts, grumpy as a wolverine anytime anyone came near, Harley was doing everything he could to stay close to Lena, and she seemed to enjoy his company—laughing even now at something he'd said.

"Lena?" he called.

"Yeah?"

He racked his brain for a response that wouldn't give his real motive away. As usual, he'd acted first without thinking. "Need a hand over here."

When she joined him near a pile of shingles, he knew he should come up with a reason to mask his jealousy. Instead, he found himself saying, "I don't think you should encourage that ass."

"We've been over this before," she reminded him.

"I don't like him."

"Don't like *him*? Or don't like me talking to him?"

"Is there a difference? Look, we know nothing about him—or his brother. And he's the idiot who nearly got you killed."

"He dropped a tool—"

"And nearly ended up tipping you on your head. It's my job to keep you safe—"

"Actually, it isn't," she shot back. "It's your job to get to work and get a roof on my stables. It's going to snow any minute, so stop wasting time."

LENA WASN'T THE only one whose temper grew short as the morning advanced, and she knew a real leader would do something to ease the tension. She wasn't sure what to do, though. Ray was the worst of the lot, snapping at anyone who spoke to him. The contrast between his behavior and Harley's made her wonder if Logan was right and the twins had fought over her. She didn't normally think of herself as the femme fatale type, but it was clear something had happened. The looks Ray kept sending Harley made the hair on the back of her neck stand up. Men got like that when their desires were frustrated. She shivered a little. Once she might have been attracted to a man like Ray with his reckless male energy. Not anymore. She wished he'd go home and take his brother with him.

Worse, the roof was progressing more slowly than she'd hoped, people's dexterity hampered by the cold weather. Although they had many hands, more didn't necessarily mean faster where a roof was concerned. Things needed to be done in a certain order. They couldn't all climb up at the same time.

They were making progress, though, and by noon

they were nearly done. Which was good, since the clouds had lowered ominously.

"Lunch break," she called out, expecting the crowd to make a dash for the house to warm up.

"Lena, no disrespect," Luke Matheson called from the roof. "But I think we'd better keep going." He pointed to the sky, just as a lazy flake of snow drifted down and touched her cheek.

"Okay," she decided quickly. "You're right; let's get it done." She pulled out her phone and called Cass. "Hey, we're pushing through, so no one's coming up for lunch yet. Is there any way you can get some hot coffee out here—and something everyone can eat on the go?"

"I'm on it." Cass hung up.

Ten minutes later, a string of figures came out the back door of the house and trudged down the track toward them. Luckily, the snow had only continued to fall a flake at a time, but Lena knew they were pushing it. Even such a slight amount of precipitation would leave things wet and slippery in no time.

She blessed Cass when the women arrived with thermoses of piping hot coffee and easy-to eat sandwiches. The men were back to work in no time, warmed and ready to go.

Still, the job crawled on. The shingles were hard to work with in the cold, and Lena's fingers moved like metal gears left to rust for far too long when she tried to shift one into place.

"At least it's not a metal roof," Logan mumbled the

next time they came close.

He was right. The metal would be slick and danger-ous by now. They were already pushing it being up here in the snow.

The light waned, even though it was barely past noon.

And the snow began to fall for real.

"Damn it." Lena bent to work harder, nailing a shingle in place and reaching for the next one. All around her the sound of hammers redoubled.

"Let's go, boys. Let's move," Brian called out. "We can finish in a half hour if we put our backs into it."

"Someone get a broom up here. We need to keep the snow off this roof," Logan added.

Lena looked up, wishing she'd thought to suggest that.

Harley scrambled past her. "I'll get it. Where do I look?"

Lena told him, impressed by his willingness to keep helping under these conditions. He'd been cocky the first time she'd met him, but she was quickly learning he wasn't the jerk his brother was.

She straightened and caught Logan's dark frown. When she made a face at him, he leaned closer. "I can't help it," he growled at her. "He's such a kiss-ass when it comes to you."

"Maybe you should try that once in a while."

His dark look changed to something far more dan-gerous. "Any time, baby girl."

"Oh, my god. You are incorrigible. Do you ever

think of anything besides sex?"

"Rarely."

She got back to work with a smile, despite the difficult situation. A moment later, Harley returned, and he made it his job to keep sweeping the snow off the roof in between helping with the shingling. The unshingled area was growing smaller by the minute.

Lena's heart lifted. "I think we're actually going to get this done."

She could have eaten her words when the wind whipped up a moment later, sending billows of snowflakes sideways into their faces.

"Jesus," Logan said. "Okay—everyone not actively shingling, get off this roof. We don't want anyone to fall. Brian? Get those last bundles up here. Let's finish off this job."

One by one the men climbed down, leaving just a handful of figures huddled up on the high roof. Brian humped the remaining bundles of shingles up the ladder. Lena kept hammering. So did Logan, Connor and Harley—and Ray, to her surprise. Now that the chips were down, Lena had to admit she appreciated their presence. Both twins had worked hard all day despite Harley's propensity for chatter and Ray's baleful looks.

Lena, on her knees, had bent to tack down a shingle near the edge of the roof when Connor, working higher up, swore and lurched forward. A hammer zipped past her, and Ray, near the ridge of the roof, cursed. "Damn it, Harley! Look what you did."

Lena lunged for it, too, just as Connor slid down the wet surface and knocked her over. He scrambled on all fours and caught himself from sliding farther. Lena fought to do the same, but her momentum carried her forward and she tumbled, coming face to face with the ground twenty feet below her—

Just as a strong hand clamped around her bicep and kept her from falling off the roof.

For a long moment she hung there, legs and torso splayed on the roof, head and shoulders hanging over, staring at the ground far below, where the hammer lay in the newly fallen snow.

"Someone brace me," Logan finally yelled. "If I move, we're both going to fall."

Lena kept as still as possible, aware the slightest movement could unbalance her—and pull Logan down, too.

Someone moved to grip her feet. She felt another presence behind Logan. A moment later, Logan shifted back and pulled her with him. Slowly, he eased her away from the edge of the roof.

When she could push up into a sitting position, Lena finally let out the breath she'd been holding. Stars danced before her eyes, and she had to bend down and put her head between her legs. The world dipped and spun. She put a hand on the roof to brace herself, unable to get her balance back. Connor was holding on to Logan. Harley had been the one to grip her feet.

She felt Logan's hand on her back.

"It's okay. Just breathe," he told her.

Humiliation washed over her as she realized what had nearly happened. A man wouldn't have been bowled over—he'd have had the strength to stop himself. She had fallen because she was too light to keep her footing.

She was always at a disadvantage. Just because she'd been born a woman.

She worked as hard as anyone else. Tried as hard, but she always came up short.

Lena tried to move. She needed to get back to work. Prove to all of them she was as good as they were. But somehow the more time went by, the worse she felt.

She didn't know how long they stayed that way before she allowed Logan to help her over to the ladder, where he climbed down before her, one hand on her waist as she took it rung by rung. Each step down felt like a defeat. Back on solid ground, she sagged against him, hating her own weakness but unable to fight it.

She'd nearly died.

As a rancher, she'd messed up a few times. Had a couple of close calls to danger. And hell, she'd been in a shoot-out just weeks ago—

But she'd never faced death so baldly. Not like she had on the roof. As soon as she'd started to slide, she'd been helpless to stop herself.

She hated feeling helpless.

"It's okay," Logan said again.

Behind him she heard arguing, and she was dimly aware Harley and Ray had climbed down, too, and now were fighting. Other men circled around them, trying to break them up.

Connor, pale as a ghost, came to stand beside Lena. "I'm sorry, lass. Christ, what a stupid mistake to go after that hammer."

"What made you drop it?" Logan asked him, craning his neck to see the argument playing out behind him.

"It wasn't mine. I saw it go past and lunged for it. Should've called a warning and let it go. Nearly got you both killed."

Logan clapped him on the shoulder. "Honest mistake. It was slippery as fuck up there. Any of us could have lost our footing."

"I don't know about honest," Connor leaned in to say. He sent a look over his shoulder at Harley and Ray, who appeared to have noticed the crowd of onlookers. They weren't arguing anymore, but the animosity between them was clear. "That boy's got butterfingers," Connor went on. "That's twice he's dropped a tool. He's got no place on a construction site."

"Harley dropped it?" Logan asked.

Harley turned at the sound of his name. "It wasn't me," he said. "It was—"

Ray grabbed his arm and hustled him away up the track. "I didn't do nothing," he snarled back at Logan.

"Like hell! Lena? It wasn't me," Harley called back as his brother kept hustling him along.

"You think she gives a damn about you?" Ray said loudly enough for all of them to hear.

Harley ducked his head, shoved his brother away

and kept going.

"Good riddance," Logan said as the brothers stalked off toward their truck, but Lena was horrified. Had Harley dropped the hammer? Or had Ray? Was it an accident, or—?

"Forget about them. You two had better get up to the house and get warm," Connor said.

"We'll be right there," Logan said. When Connor was gone, he added, "He's right. It's cold, and you're in shock. We need to get you back to the house."

"Chores," Lena managed through teeth that had begun to chatter. She'd think about Harley and Ray another time. When she was warm, and her brain was working right.

"Brian's got it covered already." Logan nodded at a cluster of men heading toward the barn. She realized they'd already put the tools away.

"Okay." Her whole body had begun to shake, and a moment later when Logan picked her up, she couldn't even find the strength to protest.

BACK AT THE house, Logan kicked off his boots, pulled Lena's off, too, and carried her straight upstairs to her room. She'd sagged against him as he'd carried her up the hill and didn't seem aware of their location until he began to undress her.

"Hey," she protested when he'd gotten off her coat and gloves and began to work on tugging her thick sweater up and over her head. "Hey!"

She batted his hand away and tried to sit up. "What

are you doing?"

"Putting you to bed—after I get this wet stuff off. You're soaked through. Still in shock."

"I can get myself to bed." Her color was coming back. A knock sounded on the door, and Cass poked her head in.

"I've got hot coffee and some stew. Lena, you okay?"

"I'm fine. Logan's making too much of this." But she gratefully took the mug of coffee Cass handed her, blew on it and took a sip.

"I'll get her into bed," Cass told him. "You can come back as soon as she's tucked in," she added with a knowing grin.

"Fine." Logan left the room, frustrated. It wasn't that he wanted to hit on Lena in her condition. He simply didn't want to let her out of his sight. He'd nearly lost her over a stupid mistake this afternoon, and he couldn't help but feel responsible. There'd only been a few feet left to shingle. He should have sent everyone else inside, including Lena, no matter how she protest-ed.

He had to stifle a grin at the thought of how that would have gone. They'd have gotten into a wrestling match up there and probably both would have fallen off the roof.

He sobered again at the realization they'd come pretty damn close. He'd caught Lena at the last possible moment, and only luck had left him in a position to keep her from sliding over and pulling him with her.

That had been a long, awful minute before Connor had shuffled close behind him and helped pull them both back. He was going to make damn sure neither Harley nor Ray got anywhere hear her again.

Voices floated up from the kitchen, where people had congregated to eat now that the work was done. He'd make sure to thank everyone for their help—later. First he needed to make sure Lena was okay.

When Cass came out of the room, she held up a hand before he could even ask a question. "Lena's fine. She ate some food, drank her coffee. She's already going to sleep." She gave him a good long look. "If you're going in there, you behave."

"I promise."

"Should I believe you?" She tilted her head as if considering the matter and sighed. "You're not going to take no for an answer, are you?"

"I just want to be close. In case she needs anything."

Cass softened. "All right."

When he opened the bedroom door, he found Lena curled on her side beneath a pile of blankets. Her eyes were closed but they fluttered open when he came in. He'd never seen her so unguarded, and a warm, painful sensation filled his chest. He wanted to keep this woman safe—forever. He wanted to find a way to break through the walls she'd built so high when it came to men. St. Michael's sword would come in handy right about now.

"What're you doing here?" Lena mumbled.

Logan began to peel off his own clothes.

"Climbing in there with you. To keep you warm."

"Oh, for fuck's sake," she said half-heartedly but didn't protest as he stripped down to his skivvies, circled the bed and climbed in the other side. Nor did she do more than grumble when he moved close to her and circled her waist with one arm.

This was where Lena belonged—right next to him, where he knew nothing could hurt her.

As long as they stayed in this bed, everything would be okay.

LENA WOKE THE next morning to the sound of snoring and stiffened, instantly on high alert, until she remembered Logan climbing into bed.

She hadn't stopped him.

Why hadn't she stopped him?

Then she remembered everything else: losing her balance, rolling to the edge of the roof.

Looking over at the ground below, held in place by Logan's grip on her arm.

He'd saved her life.

And now the Marine was snoring in her bed.

Could she climb out without waking him? She was—not naked, thank goodness—she realized when she peeked down and saw she wore a cami and panties. But she was as close to it as she could get. She wasn't ready for this kind of encounter with Logan. She shifted away from him—

His arm tightened around her waist, and he hauled her back in against his chest.

"Where do you think you're going?" he rumbled softly in her ear.

"I'm getting up. It's morning. There's work to do." She hadn't even thanked the men and women who'd come to help yesterday, she realized with a flush of shame. She'd have to make a passel of phone calls to make up for it—although she was sure her sisters had filled in for her.

"It's early. Plenty of time for another snooze."

She lifted her head to see the alarm clock. "Time to get up in twenty minutes. That's not long enough for a snooze."

He pushed up on one elbow, his other arm still holding her tight to his body. "Plenty long enough for all kinds of things."

Heat suffused her, and Lena stifled a curse. She hadn't meant to react to him that way. But with his broad, muscular chest pressed against her back, his hand dangerously close to her breasts and her bottom snuggled against his crotch, she supposed it was only natural to feel... something.

Lust. That's what it was called.

Her body simply craved what she'd denied it for far too long. She was in the prime of her youth. In bed with a hot Marine. Of course she was turned on.

That didn't mean she'd do anything about it—

Lena sucked in a breath when Logan's mouth found her neck and he began kissing her softly, moving up to nibble on her earlobe, his breath tickling her ear.

Sharp shocks of need lanced through her, and Lena

braced herself, not wanting to move. His hand moved to her hip, held her in place, and she imagined a closer connection. Him sliding into her.

She must have made a sound.

Logan turned her over, and Lena swallowed as her breasts pushed up against his chest and his fingers tightened over her hip.

"You were amazing yesterday."

Lena was lost. What was he talking about?

"I wasn't sure we'd get the job done, but you kept the men going, kept them organized—"

"I nearly fell off the roof."

"That could have happened to anyone." He kissed her.

She couldn't seem to form an answer. She didn't want to think about the roof. Didn't want to think about anything other than Logan's fingers. His hand still perched on her hip, but he was moving it ever so slowly, his fingers curving over her ass.

Her whole body ached for him to pull her close. She wanted to feel him—all of him—pressed against her.

"You weren't so bad up there yourself, you know?" She cursed the waver in her voice. Did he realize what he was doing to her?

"Really?"

Was he fishing for compliments?

"Really. Thank you. For everything," she said honestly. Like it or not, she owed this man her life, and right now she'd have a hard time denying she liked Logan.

Still, she shouldn't let him know that.

Which made it hard to understand why she found herself edging closer, tilting her head and giving him a kiss.

WHEN LENA'S MOUTH brushed his, Logan's world contracted to the size of the bed. Heat throbbed hard between his legs, and his hand curved around her ass, tucking her tighter against him. He didn't care if she felt his arousal. Hell, he wanted her to. Wanted her to know exactly what he wanted.

"This isn't happening between us."

Logan stiffened at Lena's words. It damn sure felt like it was about to happen, but if she was having second thoughts, he'd stop—even if it killed him.

He was pretty sure it would kill him, though.

"I'm not marrying you."

Logan held his breath. Did that mean she still wanted to—

Oh, God.

Lena's hand slipping down between them to curl around the length of him would have brought him to his knees if he wasn't already lying down.

"Why won't you marry me?"

What a stupid thing to say. First make love. Then ask the hard questions. He let his hand begin to explore her body. As his palm moved over her ass again, he snagged his thumb in the waistline of her panties and tugged them down. He wanted to feel skin. As his fingers slid underneath the cotton, she shifted closer to him.

She wanted this, too.

"For one thing, the General sent you. I won't give him the satisfaction."

He took a chance and slipped a hand between her legs. "How about giving yourself some satisfaction?"

When Lena parted for him, he knew he had her—at least for now.

Who knew what would happen afterward. But if he was only going to get one shot to be with her, he'd make the most of it.

If his body let him.

He was so hard, and her light touch, stroking him up and down through the fabric of his boxer briefs, was driving him wild.

Logan shifted and rolled her over, straddled her quickly and, with a single tug, pulled the thin, surprisingly feminine tank top she wore up and over her head.

She didn't fight him, and when she lay back again, her breasts on display, Logan lost what little restraint he'd managed to hold on to.

He framed her shoulders with his hands, bent down and captured her mouth with his, delighted when she answered with equal passion. Still, her breasts beckoned, and when he'd kissed his fill, he slid down to explore them with his mouth, tracing kisses over her soft skin as his hardness bobbed between them, until her hands found him again and her caresses elicited a groan deep in his throat.

This wouldn't be his most expert lovemaking. He was far too gone already, and as luscious as her breasts were, he needed something more—fast. When Lena tugged his boxer briefs down, he took that as a sign she wanted more, too.

He pushed up, kicked off the briefs, settled himself between her legs and nudged against her. He couldn't help himself. She deserved so much more than this crude, fast fuck, but—

Lena palmed his ass with her hands, dug her fingers in and pulled him close.

Logan didn't need any more invitation than that.

He stroked inside her, rewarded by her tight, wet heat. Lena was sweet—so sweet. Crushing her with his weight, feeling her softness part around him, Logan knew there wasn't anywhere he'd rather be. He wanted Lena to feel the same way, and when he pulled out and stroked in again, she sighed beneath him and arched into his touch.

A thought occurred. "Protection? I don't have a condom. And I'm not going to last—"

"I'm on the Pill."

Still, Logan grit his teeth and held still. "You sure about this?" He had to know. He couldn't make a mistake.

"Don't I look sure?"

Her last sentence contained so much frustration, Logan decided to take it on face value.

She gasped as he plunged into her again, her fingers digging into his hips. "Oh—"

His own unintelligible groan mingled with hers as they began to move together. Lena was so hot, so ready for him, her movements nearly undid him right then. Logan gathered her close, wanting to feel all of her as they made love. He wanted to do this with more finesse—wanted to give her everything, but he was locked into a rhythm with her he didn't think he could change.

He didn't want to.

Moving inside of Lena felt better than anything he'd experienced before. She fit him perfectly, and he loved the feel of her skin under his hands. He wanted to touch her everywhere, but all he could do was brace him and move faster within her—bringing them both to the brink.

"Logan—"

His name on her lips brought him crashing over into an orgasm, and she cried out, too, pulsing against him as ecstasy overtook her. Wave after wave of sensation washed through Logan, until he thought his climax would never end.

Eventually it did, of course. As their breathing slowed and Lena relaxed beneath him, hope and—love—filled Logan's heart.

This was where he was meant to be.

Holding Lena.

Loving her.

Forever.

THEY LAY TOGETHER a long time, Logan above her—

Inside her.

When he finally shifted to one side and slid out of

her, Lena almost groaned. She didn't want to face this part.

Thinking about what she'd done.

She wanted to stay where she'd been only moments before—moving with a man—crying out with him.

Feeling—

Good.

But now she had to face the music, because Logan wasn't just any man. He was the man her father had sent to marry her.

And she couldn't pretend he hadn't just moved her world.

Hell, he was good. Or maybe he didn't have to be good; he was simply himself. He fit inside her. Filled her in the perfect way. Made her—

Want him again.

Lena rolled away from him to stare at the wall.

She'd let the Marine make love to her. Let him stroke inside her until she'd cried out his name and ridden a wave of sensation that left her tingling all over. She'd made herself vulnerable to him.

And he'd made her come with such force she felt brand new inside.

And now she wanted him again. Craved him.

But their twenty minutes was up. It was time to get up. Shower.

Shower…

Lena got out of bed in one graceful maneuver, stood for a moment to let Logan enjoy the view, and when she heard him shifting behind her, she walked away slowly. "Time to clean up." He'd either get the invitation or he wouldn't.

She heard his feet hit the floor, and she snagged her robe off the hook behind her door. They'd have to be quiet. This was an old house; no en suite bathrooms here. Just the shared one down the hall.

At least it had a lock.

Cass would already be down in the kitchen. Alice and Sadie both slept in a little later to let the others clear out before they took their turns. The coast should be clear.

Logan had slipped his briefs back on when she turned back and pressed a finger to her lips. They both made their way down the hall as quietly as they could. Once inside the small bathroom, Lena locked the door and got the shower running.

"If we take too long, someone will pound on the door," she warned him.

"I can be quick."

Judging by the state of him in those briefs, he was right.

Lena smiled. She could be quick, too. When he peeled off her robe—and skimmed off his briefs—they stepped into the shower together.

Making love in the old-fashioned shower would be tricky—possibly dangerous—so Lena soaped up her hands, ran them all over his body and then sank to her knees. He was thick and hard, and when she took him into her mouth, he groaned.

"Lena—"

"Shh," she said, pulling back. "Just go with it." She couldn't help herself; he was so damn sexy, and she wanted to taste every bit of him.

Wet, he pushed in and out of her mouth with ease, and she relished the knowledge of how big he was, remembering how he'd felt pushing inside her. She teased him with her tongue, loving how she could make him lose control, and when he finally did, tangling his hands in her hair, moving in and out of her mouth and pulsing with his release, she gripped his hips and swallowed, reveling in the incredible intimacy of the moment.

"Lena," he said again when he was done and he'd lifted her to her feet. The look in his eyes nearly unnerved her. There was something different about him. About the way he touched her.

She didn't want to think about it.

Knew she'd have to soon.

The water was running cooler, and she shushed him, finished cleaning up, giving her hair the quickest wash in history, and then led him to her room, both of them wrapped in towels. It was late. They should be out in the barn already.

The other men would wonder—

Or maybe they wouldn't.

Lena gave in. The way Logan was looking at her—the way her whole body flamed with need—there was no way they'd go anywhere before Logan made love to her again.

She let her towel drop. Let him turn her toward

him. And when he sat on the edge of the bed, she straddled him without being asked.

He was ready again. Lena had the feeling he would always be ready for her, and strange as it was after all that had happened to her—and as much as she hated the fact her father had sent him to Two Willows—she had the feeling she'd always be ready for him, too.

Knowing how he'd made her feel earlier made it easy to be ready. As she lowered her hips and felt him press against her, opening her up to him, she buzzed with longing. Only being with Logan could sate that feeling. If it meant sharing the deepest parts of her with him—

So be it.

Logan slid his hands up and palmed her breasts. Lena arched back, settling lower still—taking him deep inside.

She clung to him as he teased her, already so close to losing control, she didn't know how she could last much longer. When he put his hands on her hips and began to move her against him, Lena gave up and settled in for whatever ride he wanted to take her on.

She wasn't disappointed. She clutched at him as he thrust inside her. Flung her head back and opened her mouth in a silent cry when he brought her to another orgasm. He grunted against her, crushing her to him as he came, too, then fell back on the bed, her on top of him, utterly spent.

They lay tangled like that until Lena's stomach rumbled.

"Time to get up. For real this time."

"Hold that thought. I'll be back in a minute." He slid out of her again, and a few moments later left the room, boxer briefs back on, his jeans in his hands. A trip to the bathroom again—Lena heard the shower running—then his steps went the other way and down the stairs. Some minutes later, he reappeared, carrying plates piled high with leftovers from the dishes everyone had brought the day before.

Lena scrambled to sit up. "What are you doing?" She never ate breakfast in bed. Certainly not that kind of breakfast.

"I explained to Cass you were sleeping late. She agreed that was prudent."

"You... what?"

"Lena, just for once, take it easy and have a little fun."

She opened her mouth. Closed it again.

What the hell.

She took a plate from him, grabbed a chicken leg and took a bite as her stomach rumbled again. "Mmm, this is heaven." She scrambled back to lean against the headboard and tugged the blankets up around her.

Logan joined her. "Baby girl, you haven't seen anything yet."

Chapter Ten

I T WAS LATE morning by the time they got up, and with the chores already done and the barn roof on, Logan realized this was his chance to get to town to order the supplies he'd need to build Lena's hideaway up in the attic. He told Lena he had some personal business to take care of, waited until she'd headed to the barn to check on Atlas, climbed into his truck and pulled out toward town.

He couldn't wait to see her reaction when he'd built the hideaway, and his mind began to turn with ideas for how to make it special. The trick would be to get the wood cut and prepped elsewhere and everything ready for a quick assembly. Then he'd need to get Lena out of the house so the work could be done upstairs. He'd have to organize things with the precision with which she'd organized the barn raising. He was sure he could do it—he simply needed time.

He'd barely walked in the door at the hardware store, however, when he spotted a familiar face. Ray Ellis. And where Ray was, Harley was sure to be near, he thought grimly. Logan made his way closer and saw he was right. Harley was with his brother and uncle, who was lifting a canister of kerosene into their cart.

"That's why it takes time," the older man was telling the twins. "We have to find out what's important—what's worth money—so we can get it secured. Then we can burn the rest."

Logan didn't hear Harley's answer, but he could tell it was a complaint.

"That's the job, so that's what we're going to do," the twins' uncle stated. "Come on." He pushed the cart down the aisle, and the twins followed him.

Cleaning out a house or an old shed, Logan figured. He'd done that once or twice with his uncle as a kid. Some people were worse than pack rats. He couldn't blame Harley for protesting. Sorting through years of accumulated crap—especially if it had been sitting in a leaky outbuilding—was an awful job. The perfect job for a pair of troublemakers like them, as far as he was concerned.

Logan went to talk to the owner of the store about his project, wondering where the Ellises had settled. He hadn't heard about them buying a house yet, but there were several small communities nearby that used Chance Creek as a hub. They could have bought a place out of town.

Later, having found everything he needed, he walked to Linda's Diner, ordered a coffee and a Danish, and when the waitress brought them, asked, "You know a couple of new guys in town. Twins? Harley and Ray Ellis?"

"Can't say that I do." The woman's name tag read Christie, and she seemed a sociable type.

"Late twenties. Husky guys."

"Sorry," she told him. "I'll keep my eyes open for you. You holler if you need anything else."

"Thanks." That clinched it; they hadn't settled in town. Christie was young. She didn't have a ring on her finger. She'd probably know if two new bachelors had moved in.

Silver Falls, maybe? He'd heard it was easy to hide up there.

WHEN LENA ENTERED the kitchen just before noon, Cass was the only one around, and Lena caught her resting her hand on her abdomen with a soft smile on her face that stopped Lena in her tracks.

Most of the time she didn't think about Cass being pregnant. Her sister had so far sailed through her first few months with the serenity of a swan floating on a lake. No morning sickness, no signs at all that she was growing a new life in her womb, but when pressed, Cass said she felt different—whatever that meant.

"Hey," Lena said awkwardly.

Cass turned around. "Hey, yourself. Glad you got some rest this morning. You've been burning the candle at both ends."

"Still should've been up on time." Lena found it hard to meet her sister's gaze. Did Cass know what she'd been doing? Did they all know?

Probably.

"All the chores got done," Cass assured her. "Logan headed to town. Said he'll be back for lunch."

"I know." Lena wasn't sure what else to say—or to do for that matter. Usually her chores kept her so busy she didn't have this problem.

"Set the table?" Cass asked.

"Sure." Grateful for the task, Lena got busy. She didn't know how Cass stood it here in the house day in, day out.

"Lena."

Lena looked up to find Cass pulling more leftovers from the fridge. From the looks of things, they'd be eating casseroles for days.

"It's okay, you know. To be attracted to Logan."

"I'm not marrying him." Why did it hurt to say that? Lena forced herself to continue laying the plates down one by one, then went to fetch a handful of silverware.

"That would be okay, too."

Lena set down the last plate with a thump. "Like hell it would. I see what's happening here, even if you don't."

"What I see is a bunch of highly trained, grown men—men who've led other troops in situations neither of us can possibly imagine—stepping back to let you call the shots. Who else would do that, Lena? You might never meet someone like Logan again."

"Ask yourself why," Lena demanded. "Why are these highly trained men stepping back to let me call the shots? Huh? Why would they do that?" She didn't give Cass a chance to answer. "Because they want our land.

They want Two Willows. They're just waiting until we're all trapped—"

But she couldn't finish that sentence, because it didn't ring true to her anymore. Brian, Connor and Hunter might have relished the idea of becoming ranchers, but they also loved her sisters. No one could deny that. And Logan... Logan seemed to want her this morning—a lot. He'd seemed to want to marry her, too.

She couldn't deny she'd loved every minute of being with him, which made reality that much harder to bear. She couldn't fall for the man her father sent. That was just too—horrifying.

"Brian married me because he loves me," Cass said bluntly, echoing her thoughts. "Because he can't live without me. That's what it means to stand before the altar and pledge your life to another person. If you don't feel that way about Logan, then yeah—you'd better stay away from him. But if you do feel like that about him, don't let him go. No matter how he got here."

Lena looked down at her hands. "What if I don't *want* to feel that way about someone?"

As Cass's expression softened, Lena realized what she'd revealed. Suddenly it was all too much. She needed to move. Needed to do... something. Lena left the dishes, crossed the kitchen, grabbed her coat and burst out the back door.

"Lena!" Cass called after her. "Lena, where are you going?"

"Out!" She had no idea where. All she knew was she had to leave before she thought too hard about why love scared her so badly.

And how she could possibly protect her heart now that Logan had come to Two Willows.

"HEY, BABY GIRL," Logan said when he finally tracked down Lena in the barn late that afternoon. "How's Atlas doing?"

She didn't answer, and Logan's stride hitched. Shit, was she mad? He tried to get a look at her face.

She looked mad.

"What's wrong?"

"I'm not in love with you," she ground out and kept working on the saddle in front of her, rubbing the leather with saddle polish.

Ouch. A quick thrust of the knife to his heart. "Who said you were?" he managed to ask.

"That's what you thought, going to bed with me."

"Jesus, Lena—I don't expect you to—"

"To fall head over heels for you? Good, because I haven't, and I won't."

She was an expert at twisting the weapon in the wound. He struggled to come up with an answer. Something that wouldn't increase her ire but would let her know he was taking this seriously, even if she didn't want to.

"Maybe it'll take a couple more go-rounds." Shit. That wasn't going to help anything.

Right on cue, Lena tossed aside the saddle polish, picked up a nearby rake and brandished it at him.

"This ended badly for you last time," Logan reminded her, swiftly grabbing a straw broom.

"It's going to end badly for you if you don't watch out."

"Lena, come on. I was teasing. Trying to lighten the mood. You know I care about you." He felt like he was wearing a neon sign when it came to his feelings for her. He wasn't used to this, and she didn't seem to realize that.

"I know you want to fuck me." She brandished the rake again. The metal teeth at the end of it could take out an eye if he wasn't lucky. Logan knew he had to fix this fast.

"Yeah, I want to fuck you. And I admire you. And I know you've worked your butt off your whole life to keep this ranch going. All I want to do is help. What's the issue?"

"The issue is—" Lena swung the rake. "Everyone thinks my marrying you is a done deal. They think it'd be... good for me."

Uh oh. Logan thought fast. "Then they're blind. You're fine just the way you are. I'm the one it'd be good for."

Lena wavered. He'd surprised her.

That was something.

But when she pulled the rake back into a batter's stance, Logan braced himself.

"No matter who it's good for, I can't marry you."

"Because of the General," Logan guessed. "Is that it? You hate him so you have to hate me?"

The rake lowered several inches. "Pretty much."

"You know, I don't have all of the story here. Why do you hate him?" He had to keep her talking until she dropped the rake altogether. Her temper had caused enough trouble between them already.

"Because he hates me," she said simply.

Logan's heart contracted. He recognized that look on her face, because he'd seen it in the mirror plenty of times when he'd known he'd let his parents down.

"He doesn't hate you." At least that much was true. He'd never met a man more desperate to win his daughters back over—even if the General's tactics were misguided.

"He wanted a son."

There it was. Lena couldn't change her gender any more than he could change his desire for women. He couldn't be a priest.

She couldn't be a man.

For which he was eternally grateful.

"What if I said I think you're perfect?" he asked her quietly. He wished she could see into his heart and know how much he meant it. She was feisty and smart and funny and a little wild—everything he liked in a woman. He didn't want her to change at all.

"That just makes it worse." But she lowered the rake. He took it from her and set it aside, turning back in time to see Lena's shoulders slump. She scowled. "God, I'm pathetic."

"You're human," he corrected. He took a chance and gathered her into his arms.

"I don't want to be human anymore," she grumbled,

but she didn't push him away.

"I'm glad you are. It makes being with you fun." He lifted her chin with his finger, amazed she let him get away with it. "You're better than any son could have been. You've kept this place going all these years. You got the stable built and the roof put on before the weather got too bad. We'll finish the interior soon and get those horses moved back in. Atlas will be pleased, won't you, boy?" He turned to the big stallion.

"I guess he will. And I guess I did. Is it ever going to feel like enough?" she asked.

"Yes," he said with a wisdom he wished he really had. "Just as soon as you decide it is."

Pity he couldn't seem to apply that wisdom to his own situation. He'd spent the last few days ignoring phone calls from his brother and parents. He wasn't going to become a priest; that much was clear.

He was simply going to disappoint them.

Again.

LENA COULDN'T UNDERSTAND why the interior work on the stables seemed to take longer than the exterior. The electrician dragged his feet, and it took several days when she'd thought he'd be done in one. Brian and Conner pitched in with the finishing work, and Logan did his share, but she began to feel like he was taking every opportunity to slip off to town on errands of his own.

She had no idea what he was doing. Whenever they were together he focused on her and seemed happy to be there. She didn't think there were any issues between them, except a certain hesitance on her side to be intimate with him again.

With most men, she'd worry he'd be angry she wasn't living up to some unwritten sexual bargain, but Logan didn't seem to be avoiding her out of anger.

He was simply... busy. With what, she wasn't sure. He evaded her questions. Kissed her when she asked too many. Joked around all the time and soon got her laughing, took her on hikes when the chores were done and kissed her again. But he never definitively answered her queries—and she was beginning to think he was reconnoitering in town without her. If he thought another attack on Two Willows was imminent, she wanted to know about it, but when she confronted him, he shook off her worries and said he'd tell her if he thought they were in any danger.

The day Jo and Hunter arrived home was a happy one for them all. Jo was over the moon when she saw how far they'd progressed on the new stables and could hardly be dragged away at dinnertime. Her dogs were so frantically overjoyed to see her they couldn't contain themselves. Once she'd oohed and aahed over the new building and played with Champ, Isobel—and Max— until the dogs were wriggling with happiness, she and Hunter joined the others around the big table, where they swapped stories and looked at the photos the newlyweds had taken from their trip back east.

Marriage suited Jo, Lena realized with a pang. Her sister was positively glowing, and while she was raring to get back to all her animals, she was constantly touching Hunter. Snuggling against him. Tilting her face up to meet his kisses.

Watching the way her sisters acted with their husbands, Lena wondered for the first time if she had this whole marriage thing wrong. None of them seemed hemmed in by their men. Brian and Cass complimented each other in a traditional way. Connor and Sadie seemed to have found salvation in each other. Hunter and Jo were simply purely, madly in love.

Lena couldn't deny the affection evident in each couple's relationship was heartwarming, but there was something else there, too.

Trust, she realized with a squeeze of her heart. Each of her sisters trusted her husband through and through.

Had she ever trusted someone like that? Besides her mother?

She couldn't help think of Logan's surreptitious trips to town. No man had ever earned her trust. Certainly not Logan, as much as she'd enjoyed his company lately.

She turned her attention back to Jo's photographs, swallowing her disappointment at the realization.

"No trouble here?" Hunter sounded like he hardly believed it, and Lena couldn't blame him. There seemed to always be trouble at Two Willows these days.

"No trouble," Logan told him.

"Except a couple of accidents," Cass put in wryly.

"Which were just accidents," Lena countered.

"Maybe we've seen the end of it," Jo said happily,

but Lena caught the look the men exchanged. They didn't think so.

She didn't either.

Was there something they knew that she didn't? She was beginning to think it more than likely, and over the next few days her suspicions grew. One of the men always seemed to be missing at any given time. There was never a full complement of trucks in the parking area near the carriage house, never enough hands working on jobs down at the barn or stables. And sometimes trucks she didn't recognize came and went up at the house, but when she asked who'd been by, Cass and her other sisters just shrugged.

"Someone for Sadie," was the invariable answer, and it was true her sister made herbal cures that people came to buy from several counties around, but it seemed to Lena that something was going on—something she was being kept in the dark about.

Sooner or later she'd figure out what it was.

Chapter Eleven

"S HE'S CATCHING ON," Cass murmured to Logan the following morning. "You'd better wrap up your project quick."

"At least all the parts are done that require outside help." It had been a bear to keep Lena from the house when the electrician, insulation and dry-walling guys had come by. There was no way he could hide from her long enough to get those jobs done, so he'd hired them out, but that required the workmen to slip in and out while Lena was down at the barn. More than once he'd had to send a tradesman packing before their work was done. It would be a miracle if the hideaway ever got finished.

"Thank goodness. She keeps asking about the strange trucks. That girl has eyes like a hawk," Cass complained.

"She wants to keep you all safe," Logan told her. "That's a good quality in a sister."

"I guess, but it's annoying when you're trying to get one over on her."

"All I need is an afternoon to finish up the wood-work and shelves," Logan said, keeping an eye on the door. Lena could appear for breakfast any time now.

"She'll hear you if you're up there banging around. She's so suspicious she'll come looking for you if you leave her down in the barn."

"We'd better send her into town, then. Doesn't she have any friends who'd want to spend the afternoon with her?"

"I've got an idea," Cass said and pulled out her phone. She typed a message into it. Waited a moment and then smiled. "Perfect. The ladies over at Westfield are going to invite her to go look at horses with them. They're expanding their business and need another pair to pull a carriage." She laughed at his surprise. "That's right; you haven't met them. They had guests at their B&B when you arrived for Jo and Hunter's wedding, otherwise they would have come. They run a historically themed bed and breakfast, and they always dress like they're characters from a Jane Austen novel. They're adding another carriage. That means more horses. Of course, they could pick them out fine without Lena's help, but that's all right. I told them to keep her until dinnertime, and they'll probably ask her to stay to eat, so you'll have plenty of time."

"Thank you. You're the best sister-in-law ever."

Cass's eyebrows shot up. "Sister-in-law? Is there something you want to tell me?"

Whoops. He was getting ahead of himself. "Not yet."

"ARE YOU SURE you won't stay to dinner?" Avery

Lightfoot asked when Lena opened the door to her truck late that afternoon.

"I'm sure." Actually, she could have stayed for hours given how much help she had now back at the ranch, but Lena was ready to end the visit to Westfield.

She'd enjoyed her time with the women who ran the Jane Austen B&B and had appreciated the chance to catch up with a few of the men who lived on the property, who ran a sustainable community there. Several of them had grown up in Chance Creek, so their paths had crossed before, and it was interesting to hear about all their travels since then and learn about what they were doing now.

Still, by the end of the afternoon, the fluttering and rustling of the women's 1800s-style gowns had begun to drive her wild, and there were simply too many people at Westfield. For weeks now Lena had dealt with what seemed like just as many people at home.

She needed some time alone.

In the spirit of taking the chance that was handed to her, she said goodbye to the inhabitants of Westfield, drove into town and decided to eat by herself at Fila's— a fusion Afghan/Mexican restaurant that had the best butter chicken nachos.

She'd barely been served her meal when Harley and Ray walked in, accompanied by their uncle. They spotted her just as quickly and swerved toward her, but their uncle stopped them with a word, and she had the feeling he was cautioning them. Still, the minute he waved them on, the twins made a beeline for her table.

Their uncle followed more slowly. Lena's heart sank. She didn't know what to make of what had happened on the stable's roof, and she didn't even want to think about the possibility Ray had done something on purpose to hurt her.

"All alone?" Harley asked.

"Where's that Marine?" Ray added sourly.

"I'm taking a break from the ranch," Lena told them shortly. "Just looking for some peace and quiet." Maybe they'd get the message and bug off.

"Then we shouldn't bother you. Come on, boys," their uncle said. He was a tidy man with watchful eyes and a shock of white hair. Lena saw a lifetime of hard living in his weathered features but spotted the intelligence there, too.

Harley hurried to make the introductions. "Lena Reed, meet Beau Ellis. My uncle."

"Mine, too," Ray added.

Lena stopped herself from rolling her eyes and shook hands politely. "Nice to meet you, Mr. Ellis."

She expected him to ask her to call him Beau, but he didn't. Lena was all too familiar with men like him—men from a generation who figured women belonged to a lower order.

Good thing they were dying out.

Ellis appraised her for a long moment. "The boys say you're good with horses."

Surprised, she looked to Harley and Ray, who were watching their uncle.

"Yeah, that's right." She was good with horses. No

lie there.

"I'm looking for an overseer for our breeding operation."

"An overseer?" Wouldn't the twins fill that function?

"These boys lack your experience," Beau told her. "You interested?"

"In a job?" Lena couldn't keep up. Beau wanted her to oversee the twins?

"That's right. Like I said, I need someone to run the show. Heard you were the best. Thought maybe you should come work for us. The boys seem mighty keen on the idea."

The best? Lena wondered who would have told him that. Ray and Harley? Jamie Lassiter was the breeder in these parts, and he had an eye for it. She was more of a dabbler—not a pro. While he waited, Ellis seemed to be assessing her. His invitation hadn't been warm, despite what he'd said about the twins wanting her to take the job. And the last thing she needed was to spend more time around Ray and Harley.

"Do you even have a spread?"

"Not yet. But we will soon."

"Say yes, Lena," Harley coached her. "It's a good job. Plus, you'd be with us."

He wanted more than a coworker, Lena was sure. Harley watched her like a man who wanted to bed her. Whereas Ray—she was beginning to think he'd do anything to thwart his brother. Unease stirred within her again. She didn't want this job. Not with Beau as her boss—or the twins as coworkers.

"I think your information is off," she said truthfully. "I'm no expert at horse-breeding. And I've got my own ranch to run. I'm not looking for work." That ought to end all this.

"Lena—" Harley tried again.

"You heard the woman. She's not looking for work." Ellis cut him off. "Change your mind, you come find me. But don't wait too long." He set off toward the counter to place his order.

"Think about it," Harley urged her. "It'd be a blast."

Ray hadn't said a thing.

"What do you think?" she challenged him.

"If you're smart, you'll say yes."

Lena blinked. It wasn't exactly a threat, but it sure sounded like one.

"No Marines bossing you around," Ray added, as if to soften his message. But Lena didn't think that was what he meant by his first comment.

"Sorry. I can't leave my home." They had to understand that. Maybe they did; some unspoken conversation passed between them with a raised eyebrow and a shake of a head.

Ray shrugged. Harley frowned, but his brother grabbed his arm. "More than one way to skin a cat," he told Harley. "Let's go eat."

"See you, Lena," Harley said, his shoulders slumping as he moved away.

Lena watched them, relieved they'd moved on, but one thought stayed with her. Ray was right; if she took the job their uncle offered, she'd be the overseer and she wouldn't have to share the position with a passel of men.

But no—she'd never leave Two Willows.

Not for the best job in the world—and certainly not to work for the Ellises.

JUST AS CASS had theorized, Lena didn't come home for dinner, and Logan paced the living room, waiting to show her the hideaway in the attic, until Connor finally roared at him to sit down and watch the *fecking* movie playing on the Reed's outdated television.

It was an action flick that finally drew him in with a twist he hadn't seen coming, and when it was over, he looked out the kitchen window to see that Lena's truck was parked near the carriage house.

He hadn't seen her come inside.

"She's in the maze," Alice said from her perch on top of the refrigerator, where she'd spent the last few hours, her cat in her lap and a sketch pad in her hand. "Go find her there."

Logan didn't need to be told twice. He grabbed his jacket and headed out at a fast clip.

He couldn't wait to show her what he'd made for her. He hoped it would prove to her once and for all that he cared for the same things she did—and that he wasn't there to ruin her life, but to improve it.

His steps slowed when his phone buzzed in his pocket, and he drew it out, swearing when he saw Anthony's name.

"I've only got a minute," he said into the phone when he accepted the call. He figured Lena had gone into the maze for a reason; giving her some time wouldn't hurt.

"A minute's all I need. Call Mom, all right? It's killing her that you never get in touch."

It sucked having a priest for a brother. Just a certain inflection in his voice and guilt poured into Logan's heart. Anthony was right; he hadn't called home in ages. He'd been avoiding the confrontation that always happened when he did.

"All right. All right, I will," he said.

"Logan—" His brother sighed. "Don't take too long."

LENA DIDN'T KNOW what brought her out into the maze at this time of night. It wasn't late, exactly, but it was as dark as midnight. Faint starlight shone on the scrim of snow left from the last storm, but it left impenetrable shadows that might have spooked someone less at home in the maze.

As she stood in front of the stone, it seemed taller than usual. More inscrutable. Alien, almost. But it was still the same monolith she'd stood in front of countless times. Maybe she hadn't asked it questions since her mother died. That didn't mean she didn't come to be in its presence. It was part of this ranch. The heart of it in some ways—as her mother had once been.

She wasn't going to ask it a question tonight, either. She didn't have any questions. She wasn't going to take some stupid job working for a man who expected to be called mister. That wasn't a step up, any way you sliced it. And neither was working in close quarters with Harley and Ray. She had a feeling that would be detrimental to her health.

Still, the idea of starting over—walking away from Two Willows, her history here—the General—and beginning again with a new job and a new home somewhere else—

Had a certain charm to it.

She could remake herself based on her work, rather than her sex or her relationship with her father. Know she'd be judged for what she did—rather than for who she wasn't.

Would that be freeing?

Or would it be lonely?

How would her sisters feel if she left?

They'd be hurt—she knew that. But what if she went to work for a local ranch?

She realized she'd been treating her future like there were only two possible outcomes. Marry the man her father sent and live at Two Willows, or refuse to marry him and stay single at Two Willows. She'd never allowed herself to think there was a third option—leave Two Willows altogether. Back when she was a child this same stone had told her she'd always stay, and she'd believed it.

She wanted to stay. She was clear on that. Was it the right thing to do, though?

Would a smarter woman set off for a destiny all her

own? Maybe so. Maybe she was simply a coward doing what she'd always done. Maybe fate hadn't sent Logan here to marry her at all—maybe fate had sent him to wake her up and break her free of the shackles she'd always worn.

Two Willows was just a ranch. Just a piece of land. She could walk away from it.

A cold breeze whipped around her, tossing tendrils of her hair around her face. Lena stood rooted to the spot, wondering if that were true. What would happen to her heart if she left her home?

Would it break?

She leaned forward and placed a gloved hand on the stone's flank, then peeled off the glove and placed her palm there. She wished she could stand like it did. Solidly in its place. Knowing itself through and through. Everything she thought she'd understood about herself seemed wrong tonight.

She'd thought she was supposed to protect this ranch. To love it. To make her stand here side by side with her sisters.

Now she wasn't sure.

The stone was cold as iron under her touch, but she didn't flinch. Its stillness soothed her.

The stone never lied about itself.

Never lied, period.

A good quality.

Should I leave Two Willows? The question came unbidden before she could stop it.

Lena wrenched her hand away. She hadn't wanted

to ask that—because she didn't want to know the answer.

What if the stone said yes?

Horrified by what she'd done, Lena spun around, meaning to make a run for it.

And found Logan watching her.

Her heart pounded hard. How long had he been standing there? Had he heard her question? Had she spoken it aloud?

Lena realized in a flash the Marine was central to her answer. He was part of staying at the ranch. Part of the path to her future—one way or the other. It was as if the night shifted. As if they were the only two people left alive.

It was time to speak the truth to each other, she knew. Time to stop running and evading questions.

Time to face what was in her heart. She knew she'd never leave this ranch. She'd asked that question once before and the stone had answered, leaving no room for uncertainty. The question wasn't whether she'd stay—it was what would staying look like? Would she spend her life alone—at odds with her sisters and their husbands? Or would she marry Logan and join with them sharing this spread?

Another breath of air caressed her face, this time a gentle touch—still cool, but soothing.

Logan took a step toward her and Lena saw clearly now what she'd tried so hard not to see before.

Logan loved her.

He'd been sent by the General, and he loved her. A

Gordian knot she couldn't untie with logic—

A conundrum she had to solve with her heart.

Love and hate sat in the balance, and Lena realized which she chose would dictate the course of the rest of her life. Would she allow her anger at her father to keep her from the man she—

Lena swallowed hard.

She loved Logan.

Damn it, she loved him. Despite everything.

But she couldn't... she couldn't let a man...

The breeze caressed her cheek. She felt something in the air—a sudden fierce sense of her mother's love wrapping around her. Lena thought how dearly Amelia had loved the General—

But that hadn't saved her in the end, had it?

An old sadness welled up inside her, and Lena realized something else. Her anger at the General wasn't for herself. It never had been. It was for her mother. The General hadn't been there the day she died, and he should have been, because he was supposed to protect them all. That was his job. And maybe—maybe—

If he'd been doing his job, he could have saved her.

Because Lena couldn't. No matter how fierce she'd been when the General wasn't around. Even though she'd stepped into his shoes, tried to care for the ranch, care for her family—be the son he thought he didn't have—

It had never been enough—

And her mother—

Her mother had died.

The sound that tore from her throat was the cry of a wounded animal. She'd tried. God knew she'd tried. But her mother had slipped away from them all, leaving behind so much pain. The only person in the world who'd really seen her through and through—gone forever. Lena missed her so much.

And the General—he'd discarded them and never looked back—

Lena remembered those awful years. Their anguish and determination to drive everyone else away.

Didn't the General realize they'd chased off overseer after overseer to make room for—

Him?

Logan stepped forward to take her into his arms, and she fell against his broad chest with a sob she couldn't hold back.

She hadn't known how much pain she'd been holding in her heart. She'd spent a lifetime feeling like she hadn't measured up, but it was the General who'd let them all down. She'd been here when her mother died. She'd rushed to her mother's side and helped make her last moments the best they could be. She'd cared for the ranch and her sisters during those first terrible days when everything had fallen apart. She'd sat beside Alice through the church service at her mother's funeral, and held Cass's hand on the walk to her grave. She'd taken Sadie's elbow when the casket had been lowered into the ground, caught Jo when it seemed she might faint on the way back home and held strong for all of her sisters' sake until it was time to go.

She'd driven them home, even though she hadn't even had a license back then. She'd ushered them into the house. Did her best to heat up food some kind neighbor had dropped by. Stayed dry-eyed and strong while her sisters' tears flowed.

She'd been there.

The General hadn't.

"He's the one who should feel ashamed!" she cried.

Logan crushed her against his chest. Buried his face against her hair.

"He does, baby girl. Don't you see that?" he murmured in her ear. "He's so ashamed he can't come home. That's why he's sending us."

A new pain sliced through Lena, so sharp her grief was as wild as a raven trying to beat its way out of her chest. She fought to hold it in, but it wouldn't stay caged.

She wasn't sure anymore if she was crying for herself, her mother, her sisters or her father, but when her sobs finally slowed, she found she'd broken through the pain to a clarity on the other side. She'd lost her childhood—and it was gone forever. She'd lost her self-respect for so long she'd thought she'd never had it, but now she realized she was wrong. She had respected herself when she was young—until the day her father's outburst had taught her to be ashamed of herself. And that wasn't even his fault; that was the world they both lived in. The one afraid of what a woman's body could do.

She'd lived too long with that fear and with the feeling she'd never be good enough. Lived too long thinking her mother's death was somehow her fault, too. Now Logan's words made her realize her father was very possibly struggling with the same feeling.

What a world, she thought. What a trap we all struggle in.

She took a deep breath and promised herself she'd break free of that trap. She was done feeling ashamed. She was a woman. A strong woman. A determined one.

Her body allowed her to be who she was. Lena Reed. A woman who tried her best. Who loved her family.

Who loved Logan.

As her tears faded, the quiet night sounds invaded her consciousness again. The rattle of the breeze in the hedge.

Her mother was close. She could feel her. And Amelia approved.

This was Griffith land. Her mother's land. And of course she belonged here—on her mother's ranch.

Her ranch.

She belonged here with her sisters, their husbands.

And Logan.

Whether or not the General had sent him.

"YOU OKAY?" LOGAN asked when Lena's tears ended, reluctantly breaking the spell that had seemed to settle around them. Tonight he could believe the standing stone was magic. There'd been a hush around them, as if the world were waiting for an answer that had finally come.

An answer he had missed.

He didn't know what had just happened, but it was big, his instincts told him. He wondered if Lena would let him in on it.

"I'm okay." Her voice was hoarse, and he tightened his embrace. He never wanted Lena to feel pain, and she carried so much of it around in her heart.

Lena wriggled in his arms, and he let her go with a sigh.

"Did you ask the stone a question?" he asked warily. She nodded.

He stilled. What had she asked? Would she tell him?

Lena lifted her gaze to his, and her eyes reflected the starlight. "Now I'm saying yes. To you."

His breath caught. "To me?"

She chuckled a little. "I guess you haven't even proposed yet, huh?"

He didn't need to hear any more. Logan dropped down to one knee. "Lena Reed, I love you. I'm your man, I swear it. Will you marry me?"

Lena looked up at the sky, glanced at the stone. "I never dreamed it would happen here, but it's right, isn't it?"

"It's right," he said, still unable to catch his breath. Lena was going to say yes to him. She was going to be his wife. His. Forever.

She turned back to him, and he took her hand. Waited.

"Yes," she said. "Logan Hughes, I love you, too.

I'm your woman and I'll marry you."

He surged to his feet, cupped his hands under her chin and kissed her. She was soft and intoxicating. Desire shot through him like a white-hot bolt of need. They'd made love before, but that was then, when they were two people coming together to satisfy their bodies. Now he needed more. Needed Lena, heart and soul.

His hands dropped to the zipper of her jacket, and he tugged it down, wanting to be closer to her. Wanting to join with her and never let go. When he'd managed it, Lena shrugged out of it, never breaking off their kiss, then shucked off her shoulder holster, too. She seemed as ravenous as he was, desperate to be touching him. He lifted her sweater, wanting to touch her skin.

Lena struggled with his jacket, and he broke off his exploration of her curves to shrug it off, tossing it to the ground near hers. He yanked off his shirt, uncaring about the frosty breeze playing over his skin. He wanted Lena pressed against him. Nothing between them.

Lena must have wanted it, too, because when he was done struggling with his clothes, he turned to find her topless, her breasts such a sweet sight in the low light. When he cupped them, she closed her eyes, moaned—and shivered, too.

"We won't last long out here," he told her, wishing they could.

"Then let's get going," she urged him.

"Here?" He gestured to the center of the maze.

"Here," she confirmed and stepped back until she was almost at the stone.

Good idea, Logan thought. The frozen ground wouldn't be comfortable. He set to work undoing his belt, and just as before, Lena moved more swiftly than he did. She kicked off her shoes, wriggled out of her jeans, made sure he was watching as she hooked a thumb under the waistband of her panties, slipped them off and almost delicately stepped out of them.

"Your move," she said. She was smiling.

Logan loved her smile.

In a moment he'd stripped naked, too, standing on their clothes in his sock feet to avoid freezing his toes. Lena had kept her socks on, too, which somehow made her nakedness even more delicious.

"You're beautiful," he said. He moved forward, lifted her up so her legs curled around his waist and leaned her against the stone.

Lena's shriek must have woken up the entire county. "Cold! Cold, cold, cold!" She arched her back away from the stone, and Logan quickly pulled back. They heard the back door swing open.

"Logan?" Brian called. "Everything all right out there?"

"Everything's fine," Logan called back.

They waited, holding their breath until they heard the door shut again, and then Lena collapsed against him in giggles.

He'd never heard her laugh like that.

"Now what?" he growled in mock frustration.

"I don't know," she said, still helpless with laughter.

He reached down with her still wrapped around

him, clumsily snagged his jacket off the ground, maneuvered to place it against the stone and then leaned in again.

"That better?" he asked when they were back in their original position.

"Much." Lena sobered and moved against him experimentally. "Oh, that's good."

"Oh, yeah? How about this?" He lifted her a few inches, got himself in position and pushed inside her slowly.

Lena moaned.

Logan smiled. He liked making her moan. Liked making her feel good. Luckily, this was something he knew how to do. But it was cold, a breeze whispering over his bare back even as Lena kept his front warm. This was no time for slow lovemaking. They needed to keep their core temperatures up.

As he increased his tempo, Lena moved with him, her hips meeting his thrusts, her breath speeding up with his. They fit together so perfectly, and when they were close like this, he fought for control.

She was going to be his wife, Logan told himself. He would spend a lifetime with her. Suddenly, he couldn't hold back. He wanted Lena to come, too, and—

Lena cried out, and the raw pleasure in her voice took him with her into his orgasm. Helpless against the waves of sensation overtaking him, Logan gave in to it, rode out the storm while Lena arched against him, and cried out a final time.

When it was over and he'd caught his breath again,

Logan hugged her to him. "I want it to be like this forever," he told her. "I want to feel like this—I want to be close to you."

She clung to him with equal strength. "I want that, too."

She was shivering, and Logan knew he needed to get her inside. "Come on, get dressed. I've got a surprise for you."

"What is it?" When he pulled out of her and set her down, he looked for a way to clean off and bowed to the inevitable. He scooped up some snow and gave himself a quick wash.

Lena cocked her head. "That's taking the whole he-man thing a little far, isn't it?" But she followed suit, yelped again and shook herself and hurried into her clothes. Logan dressed as quickly as he could, and in under a minute they were loping through the maze and crossing Sadie's frozen garden toward the back door.

Inside, they rushed upstairs, split up to go to their separate rooms and met back up in the bathroom. As much as he'd have liked to fool around more under the shower, Logan wanted to show her his surprise even more.

Fifteen minutes later, finally warm and wrapped in robes and slippers, he led the way down the hall to the door that led to the attic.

"Why are we going here? It'll be freezing. Is there a leak?" Suddenly animated, she grabbed for the handle.

Logan let her go, chuckling as she flung open the door. Flicking on the light switch, she took the stairs two at a time and then halted at the top.

"What... happened?" she called back down in surprise.

"It's for you." Logan came up behind her. "A place of your own—where you can escape to now and then—even when it's cold outside."

"But—why isn't cold in here?"

"Because I insulated it—and there's a radiator." He pointed to the unit. "You can set it to any temperature you want. And here's where you can store your books." He led her to the bookshelves he'd built. "And if you want a view while you read, you can sit here." He pointed to the window seat topped with comfortable cushions. "Or if you want to take it easy, you can always sit on the couch." He patted it with pride. Far nicer than a horse blanket on a bale of hay.

Lena surveyed the room, shaking her head. "How did you do all this without me knowing?"

"Not very easily." Logan made himself sound stern. "Do you know how nosy you are?"

Lena laughed, then sobered. "I'm not nosy—I'm inquisitive when people start sneaking around!"

"Did you figure out what we were up to?" he demanded.

"Not one bit. I thought there was some threat to the ranch you weren't telling me. I was getting pissed," she admitted. "Thought I'd have to swing a crowbar at you again."

"I wouldn't keep anything like that from you." He drew her down to sit next to him on the couch. "Lena, this ranch is your pride and joy. I understand that. I'm not going to get in your way. I wish you could believe that."

She took a deep breath and let it out. "I think I'm starting to." But she hopped back up and strode to the bookshelf. "Wait a minute. These aren't mine. Where'd they come from?" she demanded.

Pride swelled Logan's chest. He'd ordered those books himself, and he was rewarded when Lena pulled first one and then another off the shelf where he'd placed them. She turned them over and read the back covers. "These sound fantastic!"

"Glad you like them. They're all for you. This whole room is. I installed a lock on the door, and you'll be the only one with the key."

She looked up. Put the books back slowly. "You did this all for me?"

"That's right." Logan patted the cushion beside him, and Lena crossed the room and sat down again, but she kept a distance between them.

"Why?" she asked, but she was smiling at him. She knew why; she just wanted him to say it again.

"Because I love you, Lena Reed, and I'd do just about anything to make you happy."

LENA COULDN'T REMEMBER the last time she'd ridden in the passenger seat in any vehicle. She wasn't a passenger seat kind of woman, but she'd decided she'd give it a try today. She still couldn't believe the transformation her life had undergone in the past twelve hours. She and Logan had made love again in the attic, then a third time when they'd finally gone to bed together. She'd woken with the feeling something wonderful was going to happen, had opened her eyes, seen Logan sleeping beside her and decided it already had.

She liked Logan in her bed, liked his strength and solidity. He was like the standing stone, she realized. Something she could depend on. A rock to ground herself on.

Logan drove expertly, and after a few minutes she relaxed and watched the scenery go by.

Marriage.

She hadn't ever expected to face it.

But then she'd never expected a man like Logan to walk into her life.

When they arrived at Thayer's Jewelers, she even allowed Logan to walk around and open the door for her before she got out of the truck. Why not be a lady for a day?

Her mother would be proud. And she'd get the joke, too.

Inside the store, however, some of her confidence drained away. She didn't wear a lot of jewelry; studs in her ears were about the extent of it. Necklaces and bracelets could get caught when she was working— could even put her in danger.

She'd never worn rings.

Logan did most of the talking to Rose Johnson, who owned the store, even though Lena and Rose had known each other for years.

"Take your time," Rose said gently when she'd pulled out several trays of rings and placed them on the counter for Lena and Logan to look through. "But take a look at this one; it's a little like your mother's, isn't it, Lena?"

"How do you know that?" Lena was surprised. Had Rose known her mother?

"I saw it in a photograph at your house. It's on the mantel over the fireplace. Photographers used to take pictures like that all the time when a woman got engaged—posing women with their hand in view so you could see the ring. I notice things like that," she added. "Part of the job, I guess."

"Got it." Lena took the ring Rose indicated and immediately felt an affinity for it. A silver band, a large diamond flanked by two smaller ones. Beautiful, yet hinting at strength.

She recalled her mother's hands, so beautiful. So tender and loving when it came to her daughters. So strong when it came to tending her land.

"You have to try on a bunch of them," Logan said, and she did, but she kept coming back to that first one. She'd never felt her mother's presence so strongly since Amelia passed away.

Lena knew—somehow—she approved of this union.

"I like this one," she said, choosing the first ring.

"I like it, too." But Logan was looking at her, not the ring, and as he bent to kiss her, she had the feeling he wouldn't even notice if she substituted an entirely different one.

Men.

When he slid it on her finger, it fit as if it had been made for her.

Maybe it had.

She took it off again and handed it to Rose to complete the sale. Rose held it a moment, got a distant look for a beat, then her eyes filled with tears. "It's perfect," she said.

Lena's heart squeezed. She lived with a sister who caught glimpses of the future, and she knew Rose had a similar talent, although more limited. How much could she see, though? Would her future with Logan be what she hoped it could be?

Rose seemed to sense her concerns and reached out a hand to touch Lena's wrist. "I mean it, Lena. It's perfect."

Lena swallowed in a raw throat and made a show of looking at the other jewelry while Logan paid for the ring. How could things be going so right when they'd gone wrong for so long? Suddenly she had a premonition of her own—that this was the calm before the storm. She had to stay vigilant, even if she was getting married.

But it was hard when Logan was near.

When Rose handed it back to him, he slipped the ring on Lena's finger again, kissed her full on the mouth and said, "There. Now you can't change your mind."

"I guess not," she said shyly as they left the store.

She felt different with the ring on, and she held up her hand to see how it looked.

"Morning!"

Lena stumbled when she realized it was Harley who'd called out. He was walking with Ray and their uncle, Beau.

"Morning," she said, trying to skirt around them.

"Hey, Lena. You thought any more about the job my uncle offered you?" Harley asked.

She could feel Logan's gaze sharpen on her, and she answered forcefully. "I've thought about it. Decided to give it a pass. I'm sure you'll find someone else."

"You're making a mistake, you know." Harley followed her.

"Why's that?" Logan took a step forward that placed him square between her and the other men. Normally such a move would irritate her thoroughly.

But not today.

She was going soft.

Lena touched the ring again. If Harley was smart, he'd back down, she thought as Logan moved even closer, but Harley had never struck her as the sharpest tool in the shed.

"Because it's a hell of an offer. That's why. She should be proud to work for us," Ray put in.

Lena noticed Beau hadn't joined the conversation. His gaze was resting on her hand.

On her ring.

"I see congratulations are in order." He cut right over Logan's answer to Ray's assertion. He reached right out and lifted her hand for the twins to see. "Looks like someone beat you two to the punch, boys. Didn't I hear you two fighting over this little filly? Guess I got fooled, too. Thought you were interested in running a ranch."

"Thought I told you I already have a ranch to run." Lena snatched her hand back. "Come on, Logan. I'm done with this."

"Well, I'm not done. What the hell are you thinking, Lena?" Harley asked. "You and me were just getting started."

"We weren't starting anything."

His expression darkened, and Lena realized too late she *had* started something. A feud with this family of misfits.

"Like hell we weren't." Harley leaned closer. Gone was the "aw shucks" manner that had made her relax around him. Now she saw something else.

Something dark.

"You wanted what I had to offer. You know you did," he went on. "And I went out on a limb for you."

"Shut your trap, Harley. No one likes a sore loser. Told you she wasn't interested in you," Ray said.

Lena followed her instincts and strode toward Logan's truck. Logan followed only a moment later.

"What did you say to them?" she demanded as they settled into their seats.

"That if they come looking for a fight, we'll be ready for them."

Chapter Twelve

WHEN LOGAN ASKED that their wedding might be sooner rather than later, he expected Lena to protest, but she agreed far more readily than he expected.

"Why buck the pattern?" she said lightly when he asked her about it.

Logan knew what she meant; all her sisters had married less than a month or two after meeting their husbands. Why should she be different? Thank God for tradition.

He couldn't exactly put his finger on it, but something was pushing him to speed up the process. For one thing, it would get Jack here quickly. He hadn't seen Alice display interest in any other man—except the one who had offered her the movie job. He wouldn't call that interest, either, except he'd seen her on her phone texting more and more often these past few weeks. When she signed off, her cheeks were flushed and her eyes sparkled. A quiet question or two revealed it was all job-related. Whether her excitement was for the work—or her contact on the movie—Logan couldn't say, but his gut told him it was a bit of both. Regardless, she was a woman going places, and if this movie guy didn't make a play for her, sooner or later some local cowboy would. The General had made it clear that all five of the men in his task force needed to bring this mission to fruition; all five of them needed to marry—or lose the ranch.

Still, it wasn't the thought of losing the ranch that motivated him. With four of his daughters married, he doubted the General would follow through on his threat. On the other hand, the General wasn't exactly known for being a reasonable man. If he got angry, he might lash out, and Logan didn't want to take any chances.

What really propelled him to move forward, however, was a sense of foreboding. The sense that their enemies were gathering strength, getting ready to hit the ranch again. He'd had the St. Michael dream three nights in a row, waking up in a cold sweat beside Lena each time. It still felt like a miracle to lie down to sleep with her each night; what made his dreams so off the wall when his reality was so great?

He could only blame the Ellises for their resurgence. He didn't like the way Lena had "accidents" when they were around. He hadn't liked the look of old Beau Ellis one bit, either, but when he'd poked around in town, no one could tell him much about any of them, and he didn't have time for a more thorough investigation.

With his wedding date set for three weeks hence, Logan had little bandwidth for much else than his usual chores, and finishing up the stable, although he was involved—somewhat—in planning the ceremony and reception. To be honest, it was Cass, Sadie and Alice who were spearheading the initiative to get this wedding off the ground. Lena had definite opinions, and she made them known, but her sisters continually had to remind her of elements she had forgotten to even consider.

Logan tried to stay out of it, except when directly questioned. He wanted Lena to have the day of her dreams, but it soon became clear Lena hadn't been the type of woman to dream about a wedding. He loved her all the more for that. And he thought the celebration she and her sisters were ironing out sounded like it would be a lot of fun, with a minimum of fuss.

Just the way he liked things.

Now it was time to let his family in on the news. First things first; he'd call Anthony and get the lay of the land.

"It's me," Logan said when Anthony picked up the phone, "and before you ask, I'm going to call Mom right after I hang up with you—and tell her about my fiancée."

"Fiancée? What fiancée? When's the wedding?"

"Three weeks. We're going to have to work hard to pull it off, but I think we can do it. Will you officiate?"

"If you're getting married, I'll definitely be there. How's the lucky woman? I'm assuming it's Lena."

"Of course, it's Lena. And she's still in love with me. God knows why."

"You're right; God does know why," Anthony told him. "Because you're a good man and deserve it."

"I thought you might be sore I didn't join you in the priesthood."

Anthony hesitated. "I've been thinking a lot about that. Thinking about my own pride. Seems I still have more than my fair share of it. I wanted to make you over in my image, but that's not my place."

"No one would blame you; our parents made no bones about who they wanted us to be."

"I've been thinking of that, too. You ever wonder why they named me and James for saints, but not you?"

"Hey, I'm Michael, remember?" He touched the medal at his neck.

"Logan Michael. Far as I know there's no St. Logan."

"So? They covered that with my middle name."

"There's more to it than that. I don't know why I never did the math before. Mom was sixteen when she had James. Dad was eighteen. I have a feeling if we really counted, we might find James was conceived before their wedding night."

Logan thought about that and realized it was probably true. "Well, I'll be damned." He'd always thought of his parents as rule-followers. They'd certainly been that way when he was growing up.

"Watch it, or you will be," Anthony said in mock disapproval. "I think maybe a little guilt came into play when they set their hearts on him being a priest," he went on.

"What about you?"

"Maybe it became a habit with them. Maybe there was something else they felt guilty about. Who knew what they got up to back in those days? They held off having me for another fifteen years, didn't they? That's a good long run. James always said Nana was like a second mother to him. Maybe Mom and Dad kept having fun while they grew up a little, and by the time they were ready to settle down for real, they felt guilty again and decided on the priesthood for me, too. Like I said before, it didn't matter. I'd have gone down that road regardless."

"So, what about me?"

Anthony cleared his throat. "Mom was forty-one by the time she got pregnant with you. I don't know this for sure, but it seems like they might not have expected you, either. I honestly don't know if they expected any of us." He chuckled. "That has to be among the top ten things I don't want to ask my mother. Anyway, you came along. I was already talking about a life of service. Now they had another chance for grandkids."

Logan tried to make sense of what his brother was saying. "I don't get it. If they wanted grandkids, why make all that fuss about me becoming a priest, too?"

"You'll have to ask them about that. Whatever they say, remember—they love you. I'm glad you're following your heart."

"I don't even know if Lena wants to have kids." He supposed they ought to talk about that.

"Want some more advice?" Anthony asked. "Don't

tell Mom that until after the wedding."

"Lena isn't a Catholic." Logan had been worried on that point. "And we're marrying here at Two Willows, not in a church."

Anthony hesitated. "You know what? I've heard the love in your voice since the moment you started talking about her, even if I didn't acknowledge it. I have no objection."

"But you can't officiate."

"Not unless I had more time. We'd have to talk to a bishop—"

"I can't wait for that."

"I know." Anthony chuckled. "Do you have a back-up plan?"

"Reverend Halpern married her sisters and their husbands."

"Get Reverend Halpern, then."

"Will you be my best man?"

"You'd better believe it."

LENA MADE SURE the door to the attic was firmly closed and locked before she sat at the window seat, opened her laptop and made a video call to the General.

She knew her sisters' fiancés had each in turn invited the man to their weddings. Each time he'd refused to come. She wasn't going to wait for Logan to go to bat for her. She'd face down the man herself.

"What is it?" the General barked when his image showed up on her screen. He was bent over a desk in an office that definitely wasn't his own. Lena wondered where he was. Overseas, maybe? He was focused on a batch of paperwork he was scrawling on with a pen. He looked older than the last time they'd talked, which was...

Hell, when was it?

The General looked up, his impatience all too clear. "Well...?" His words trailed off when he spotted her. He leaned closer to the screen. "Lena? What is it... what's wrong?" He half stood.

"We're all fine," she said quickly and held up her hand to show him her ring. "Perfectly fine. I'm calling to let you know about my wedding. It's three weeks from Saturday." She waited a beat. "That's your cue to say you're too busy to come."

The General sat down and began to speak, but no words came out. Finally he managed, "Three weeks?" His gaze travelled somewhere to the left of the screen, and she had no doubt he was looking at a calendar. As if he actually needed to do that. He wouldn't come, no matter when it was. When he turned back, there was something in his eyes that gave Lena pause, though. It wasn't hardness—or anger. It was—

Grief.

And it hit her like punch to her sternum.

Her father was grieving. She'd guessed that, but seeing it made it real.

"I want to," he said so frankly Lena believed him. "More than anything, but this situation is escalating—" He waved a hand to encompass his foreign office.

If you want to, then try, she urged him silently. *Break*

free of the guilt that's holding you back. Start fixing this.

But she'd never spoken to her father that way, and she couldn't seem to find the right words to start now. "You could come if you really wanted to." She'd done so much over the years she hadn't thought herself capable of. Couldn't he stretch—just this once?

"I... can't."

Anger flared within her. Yes, he could. But he wouldn't. He wouldn't try—even for her. He'd never valued her—

"God, I'm so proud of you," he said.

Lena clapped a hand to her mouth to stifle a cry of pain. Used the other to slap at the keyboard until she'd killed the call.

No.

No—

He didn't get to have it both ways—

Not this time.

He either loved her enough to break free of the past, or he didn't.

Lena shoved the laptop off her lap, not caring when it fell and hit the ground. She tucked her knees under her, wrapped an arm around her middle and stuffed her other fist in her mouth. She wouldn't cry. Not again. She was done with tears.

She swept two of the cushions off the seat onto her floor, then pounded a third with her fist. Damn him—how could he still make her feel this way?

She stood up and paced the attic. She'd told herself she wouldn't slide back into past habits again, and here she was letting the General ruin her wedding. He didn't get to do that. Didn't get to let his cowardice spill all over her happiness.

This isn't about you, she told herself. *This is about him. His bad choices. His guilt.*

His sadness.

And this was life. Ugly. Messy. Painful.

And so beautiful and clean and lovely at the same time. It had been so the day she'd said yes to Logan, and it would be again in three weeks when she pledged her heart to the man she loved.

And if the General couldn't be there—

That was his loss.

IT TOOK LOGAN some time to make his next call, but when he finally did, his mother answered on the third ring. "Logan! Good to hear from you."

"Just wanted to talk if you have a minute."

"Of course." She sounded happy, and Logan hoped he wasn't about to ruin her mood.

"I'm not going to become a priest." Best to get it over with. Short and sweet.

His mother's silence spun out until she sighed. "I guess I figured that out when you became a Marine."

"You never stopped bringing it up."

"No. I guess I didn't."

"Why? You've got two priests in the family already. Why couldn't you let me be?" He wondered if she'd finally come clean. He couldn't remember why this had seemed so hard to discuss before. Probably because he'd been younger. Less sure of himself. Needing her approval. They'd all let this spin on way too long.

"I guess because I didn't let your brothers be. I'd gone too far to stop."

"I don't follow you."

"I made them both priests; how could I let you be what you wanted to be?" His mother sighed, and there was a world of remorse in the sound. "We were so young when we had James. So guilty for what we'd done—I'm sure you and your brothers figured out our sin a long time ago."

Logan didn't correct her. It had never occurred to him his parents had ever slipped up until his conversation with Anthony.

"We managed to marry fast and fool most people. James came late, and he was small."

"So you dedicated him to God."

"We definitely steered him that way. He ran with it, though. I guess that made us feel better. I don't think he regrets the life he chose."

"I don't think so, either. And Anthony's told me a dozen times he would have tended toward the priesthood no matter what you did." He was glad they were able to talk about it rationally instead of having a fight. He didn't want his mother to be defensive. He simply wanted to understand. "So you didn't force them. And if they both chose their vocations willingly, why worry about me?"

His mother was silent a long time.

"I've never told anyone this part. It's too painful.

I'm not sure you'll understand."

"Try me," Logan told her.

"We tried for so long to have another baby after Anthony was born. We were ready to be parents by then, and we didn't want him to feel lonely. First months passed, then years, one after another until it was clear we were done. Those were hard times. Your father and I fought a lot. We blamed each other. Then, I suppose, we blamed God. We felt… judged. As if He was showing us He'd wanted us to be parents much younger—when we had James—and since we didn't agree, now He was punishing us. It was harder for me than for your father. You know my mother raised James more than I did. I felt like I hadn't measured up and was being deprived of children when I was ready for them as a consequence. I was so confused."

"But you did have me."

"Ten years later! Long after we'd given up. What were we to make of that?" his mother asked.

"I guess I don't know."

"We were thrilled. We made such plans for you. We would raise you, send you to college, marry you off, and the grandkids would pour in! And then…" She broke off.

"Then you felt bad about not steering James and Anthony that way," he finished for her.

"That's right. It sounds pretty darn silly when you put it like that."

Not exactly. Logan was beginning to understand it was human nature to box up difficult feelings. People treated problems like equations. If I do this, then that must be the result. But life didn't fit into tidy boxes. Neither did feelings.

"I guess we're all a little messed up," he said.

She sighed again. "The Marines have made you a man I'm proud of. I want you to know that."

Logan supposed no one was ever too old to appreciate praise from his mother. "Thanks, Mom."

"And you're not going to be a priest." She chuckled. "Anthony says you're in Montana. What's going on there?"

"I'm getting married. In three weeks. And I hope you'll come."

"Married?" she said faintly. "You're getting married? Earl, come quickly," she called. "Logan's getting married!"

The next few minutes were a jumble of congratulations, questions and exclamations as he told his story twice over, once to his mother and then to his dad. Both of them could barely contain their excitement.

"What about grandkids?" his mother asked.

"We'll see. When we're settled into our new lives."

"But you'll live in Montana? Earl, we need to move to Montana!"

"You're only one state over, Mom. It won't be that far to visit."

"Says the man who never visits his mother," she pointed out.

"I swear that's about to change."

"I'M SURPRISED YOU'RE not going to be the one wearing the uniform," Jo said to Lena and ducked as if she expected Lena to take a swipe at her. All five of the Reed sisters were in Alice's sewing studio on the second story of the carriage house. It had been restored to normal after the damage it had received when they'd been attacked some weeks ago, and it reminded Lena of childhood days when they'd used this space as a rainy-day playroom. Costumes were strewn over the central tables—Alice's creations for the movie job.

"Jo," Cass said reprovingly. "That's not nice."

Jo kept angled away from Lena until Lena shook her head at her. "Relax," she said. She was done with violence. "I thought about wearing a uniform," she joked. "Decided not to break tradition."

She stood as still as possible on a little pedestal while Alice crouched beside her, pinning the hem of their mother's wedding dress. Cass, Sadie and Jo had all worn it for their weddings. Now Alice was tailoring it to fit her—and the theme of her wedding.

She and Logan had decided to go with a Revolutionary War theme. Alice had dug out a fine blue uniform for Logan to wear, and more for the rest of the men. Her sisters would wear their spring green bridesmaid gowns, altered to have a more 1775 flair. It was far too cold for an outdoor wedding at Two Willows, so they'd decided to take most of the furniture out of the first floor of the house, set up tight rows of folding chairs for the ceremony, and move them to accommodate folding tables for the dinner. It would be crowded, but they'd make it work. Lena couldn't wait to see the look on Logan's face when he saw her walk down the aisle. He'd loved her in that stupid bridesmaid gown she'd worn at Jo's wedding the night they'd met. He'd probably have a heart attack when he saw her in off-white lace.

"Stand still," Alice murmured.

"Sorry." It was hard to stand still and harder to bear the itchy fabric. How did other women deal with this stuff?

"I've got a list," Cass announced. "One for every-one, actually. We've all got jobs to do to get ready for the big day." She began to hand them out, giving Lena hers last. "I didn't give you too many errands," Cass told her. "I just want you to be ready on Saturday for a full makeover: hair, nails, makeup—the works."

"Fine." Let her sister have her way. It was okay to dress up once in a while, she decided. In between times, she and Logan would have loads of fun without resort-ing to all that frippery. She realized she was smiling and caught Cass's eye.

"I'm so happy for you," Cass said.

"Thanks." She looked over her list again, not want-ing to make too much of the moment. "Candles?" she asked.

"Tons of them," Cass told her. "And fairy lights. You're in charge of the mood lighting for the wedding."

Mood lighting. She supposed she could handle that.

Four hours later, she'd finished the fitting, changed, headed into town and handled all her purchases with panache, filling the back of her truck with boxes of votives, tapers and fairy lights. She'd help string the lights closer to the wedding. Cass could handle the candles.

But now she was hungry.

Really hungry.

Lena realized she'd skipped lunch. Linda's Diner would do the trick nicely, she decided, and after she closed the tailgate, she decided to walk the two blocks to the restaurant.

A cold wind reminded her it was nearly Thanksgiving. The early snowfall had disappeared, but it looked like more was on the way. Soon enough the year would end and a new one would begin. So many things had changed at Two Willows since last spring.

She was happy to reach the diner, her bittersweet thoughts dispelled by the hustle and bustle of the place.

"Hi, Lena," Christie called. "Cass has a booth in the back if you're here to join her."

"Sure." She edged around the waitress and made her way back to find Cass and Brian tucked into a booth at the far end of the restaurant. "Is there room for me?"

"Of course, help yourself," Cass told her.

Lena did so, ordering a hamburger and fries when Christie reached the table. A few minutes later, Cass's and Brian's meals arrived, and she told them to go ahead, grabbing a fry or two from her sister's plate.

"Got my whole list done," Lena told them.

"It was a pretty small list," Cass pointed out. "I'm only about halfway through with mine."

"I'd say I'm two-thirds done," Jo said, approaching with a large number of shopping bags draped over her arm. They stowed them under the table, and Jo slid in next to Lena. She, too, grabbed some of Cass's fries. "I think you gave me all the hard things."

"Did not," Cass said affably. "I always save the hard things for myself."

"Then you've never tried to pick out flower arrangements less than two weeks ahead of a wedding." Alice arrived looking more flustered than usual. "She wanted to use peach roses. Can you believe that? We've had three weddings with the same color scheme, and she'd going to zigzag now? I'll have a Cobb salad," she told Christie, who'd come to deliver Lena's burger.

Lena took it from her gratefully, her stomach rumbling. She took a bite of the burger and swatted away Jo's hand when she tried to steal some fries. Jo waited until she'd grasped the burger with both hands for a second bite and snatched a few off the plate.

"Oh, those look good," Alice said and took a few, too.

"I'm going to need more ketchup." Lena looked around for a bottle on one of the adjacent tables, then decided she'd ask Christie when the waitress got back.

"Did someone say ketchup?" Sadie asked as she drew near with a pile of boxes in her hand that blocked her face from view. "If there's ketchup, there's French fries, and I'm in dire need of French fries."

She awkwardly shoved her way into the booth, the tower of boxes tilting precipitously. "Let me at 'em," she said, peeking around the pile.

"I don't think I've ever eaten at a restaurant with all of you before," Brian said. "We need a bigger booth."

Lena froze, the burger halfway to her mouth. Her sisters froze, too. She could see Cass's mouth move—counting—*one, two, three, four, five*—

"The General!" Jo cried.

Lena saw the moment Brian understood. He dropped his burger on his plate. "Oh, hell. You're all off the ranch—"

She didn't wait for him to finish his sentence. She scrambled up on the bench seat, vaulted over the back and across the next booth, and ran for the door, throwing twenties at Christie as she passed.

"Where's the fire?" Christie called after her.

"No fire," she called back over her shoulder.

No fire—

But with them all off the ranch—

Who knew what would happen next.

"I CAN'T GET ahold of him," Logan told Lena a half hour later. She'd scared the crap out of him when she'd careened into the driveway, screeched the truck to a stop by the carriage house and run inside like a tiger was chasing her. It had taken five minutes for him to make sense of what she was trying to say and why she thought the General might be in trouble. By then everyone else had arrived home, too.

"One of us has to be on the ranch—always," she'd nearly shouted at him. "To keep the General safe. I spoke to him the other day. I don't understand why you can't reach him."

She'd mentioned the superstition before, and he'd noticed the way the women kept tabs on each other almost unconsciously to make sure someone was always at the ranch.

"According to USSOCOM, he's out of range of communications."

"What is he doing in the Middle East?" Cass demanded. "He's not supposed to be in an active war zone these days."

"Normally he's not, but men like him are called in for on-the-ground inspections from time to time. Your father isn't one to shirk his duty."

"So we don't know if he's okay or not." Alice was pacing the living room in a very un-Alice way. She shut her eyes and concentrated but opened them a moment later. "I can't see a thing."

"Let's all take a breath," Brian said.

"How did you all manage to leave the ranch at the same time?" Logan asked. It had never happened since he'd been here.

"We were all too focused on getting this wedding off the ground—" Cass didn't finish her sentence, and he knew she didn't want to blame anyone.

"What's done is done," Connor soothed. "You're all back here now. Nothing's happened."

"You don't know that!"

All of them stared at this uncharacteristic outburst from Alice. She gave a groan and paced again. "I hate this; why can't I see anything? It's been getting worse and worse lately."

Logan remembered what Lena had told him before—Alice found it difficult to see her own future. Was that future getting too close?

Jack would be here soon.

"If something happened to the General, we would know about it," Brian said reassuringly. "He might not be reachable, but you can bet he's able to get word out if necessary."

Logan didn't think the sisters were entirely appeased, but there wasn't much they could do but wait.

"When will he be back in touch?" Hunter asked him.

"Not for another week at least."

WHEN LENA SLIPPED outside late that night, crossed Sadie's garden and entered the maze, she wasn't surprised to find her sisters there before her. When she joined them in front of the stone, she pulled her thick jacket more tightly around her and shivered in the cold. The temperature had dropped steadily all day, and the pinpricks of the stars glittered above her. The stone loomed solid and unknowable, a dark shadow against the sky.

Cass reached a hand out to touch it, but Sadie snatched it back. "I don't think we should ask."

"I do," Jo said. "We need to know."

"We can't stop what happens whether we know or not," Alice put in. "Believe me, I've tried plenty of times."

Lena hated the bitterness in her voice. She knew Alice suffered when her premonitions revealed something bad. "I don't think we should ask, either," she said quickly. "But I think—I think we need to make another promise to make up for the one we broke."

"Like Mom did when Dad left the first time?" Cass asked.

"Exactly like Mom did. She promised she'd always stay on the ranch when the General was gone, and she did. In exchange, the stone kept him safe."

Sadie made a noise, but Lena kept going. "We're the ones who blew it; that means we need to make a new promise. A different one."

"What kind of promise?" Jo asked.

"That we'll stay for good. That we'll all live our lives here in Chance Creek, at Two Willows. We'll make our stand here. We'll protect this land."

"But—" Alice began.

"I don't mean we never get to go anywhere. Trips, vacations, temporary things—those are fine. I mean we pledge that Two Willows will always be our home base. That's what the land wants, right?" Now that she was marrying Logan, it was an easy promise to make.

Her sisters nodded. Alice last. "Yeah, that's what it wants," she echoed.

"Then let's do it," Lena urged. "Now, before something happens."

Cass put her hand on the stone. Jo did, too. Sadie reached out more slowly, but when she laid her palm on the stone, she nodded. "It's the right thing to do," she said.

Lena put her hand on it, too, nearly flinching from the cold. "Alice?" Her breath came out in a white puff, and she shivered again. She couldn't wait to get back inside.

Alice hesitated. "It's just—my costume job—it could take me away for a while…"

"But not forever," Cass told her. "Come on, it's freezing!"

Still Alice held back. "But what if it turns into something—" She shrieked when something swift and white shot past her, dove to touch the ground and flew off again, a tiny mouse in its claws.

Lena's heart beat hard; she'd never seen an owl take its prey so close before. How could it see such a small creature in the dark like that?

Alice slapped her hand on the stone. "Do it!" she said to Lena. "Make the pledge."

"Alice?"

Alice cut off Cass's question. "Say it," she hissed at Lena.

Lena replaced her hand on the stone. "In exchange for my father's safety, and for the safety of us all, I pledge that I will spend my life at Two Willows, guarding it and caring for it as best as I can."

Cass swiftly repeated her words, then Sadie, then Jo. When Alice's turn came, her voice was shaking, and she ran through the words as quickly as she could.

"I pledge that I will spend my life at Two Willows,

guarding it and caring for it as best as I can." It came out as one long, slurred phrase. "Done," she said and slapped the stone. "It's done. I know you heard us."

"Alice, what's wrong? Did you see something?" Cass pulled her hand back.

"Of course." Alice pointed to where the owl had grasped the mouse. "Didn't you?"

Lena shivered as a chill that shook her frame. "What do you think it meant?"

"Isn't it obvious?" Alice was close to tears.

Lena thought about the way the owl had taken the mouse. Swiftly. Silently. One moment there, the next gone.

She shivered again, thinking about her father.

And hoped against hope he was all right.

LOGAN COULDN'T IGNORE the sense of something looming on the horizon—something coming at them— after the day Lena and her sisters had all left the ranch at once. He couldn't say why their silly superstition bugged him, except that with five skittish, spooked women around the place it was easy to catch their anxiety.

He worried less about the General than about the possibility trouble would crop up right here at Two Willows, though. Three times men sent by someone in Tennessee had come after the Reeds. Three times they'd fought them off. Something told him they hadn't seen the end of those troublemakers.

He found himself up earlier than usual, riding out at sunrise to get the lay of the land when the weather allowed, ranging far and wide on foot when the weather didn't. He looked for signs that someone was testing the perimeters of the ranch. Probing for weaknesses. So far, he hadn't seen any, but that didn't mean he was wrong to be vigilant. When he'd first come to Chance Creek, he'd locked his firearm away in his room. Now he wore it from morning to bedtime most days.

He soon found he wasn't the only one who was thinking along those lines.

"It's about time for more trouble, isn't it?" Connor had put it succinctly.

"It's been quiet for far too long," Hunter put in. "I figure it's due to arrive any day now."

It comforted Logan to know that he wasn't the only one with such thoughts on his mind, but at the same time it disconcerted him to know that all the men on the ranch were uneasy. The one person he didn't mention his concerns to was Lena. She was far too worried about her father. Her relationships with her sisters had grown closer amid their shared fears. He didn't want to disturb that. He knew Lena would scoff at him and want to take her part in the preparations the men were making to keep a better watch on the ranch, but she was going to be married in two weeks' time and had plenty on her plate to accomplish. Surely that gave him the right to intercede for her just this once.

In any event, they hardly had to make plans. It turned out that each of the men had been patrolling on his own. Aside from a conversation or two in which they divvied up the times of day and the directions in which they went, there really weren't any preparations for Lena to take part in.

Which was all his way of justifying himself the day Lena caught him heading out on an early morning ride.

"You're patrolling. Without me," she accused without preamble.

He was caught, and he knew it. She knew it, too.

"It's not just you; it's Brian, Connor and Hunter, too. What's going on?"

He finished buckling the strap of the saddle and straightened. "There's nothing going on—yet. That's why we didn't bring you into this; there's no reason for what we're doing. We're just doing it anyway, because trouble seems to come around here pretty regularly."

Lena scowled. "You're all in on it —together? And none of you told me?"

"It's like I said; there's nothing to tell. But have you noticed whenever one of you decides to get married, shit hits the fan?" He meant it as a joke, but Lena's frown deepened.

"So, it's our fault people keep attacking the ranch? And that gives you the right to take over, without even telling me?"

"That's not what I meant. We both have chores to do. You've got the wedding to plan on top of that. I figured you had enough to do." He reached for her, but she sidestepped him.

"Not one week ago you said you considered me an equal."

"I do. That doesn't mean we have to be joined at

the hip. I've got my work, you've got yours."

"But I'm not trying to hide mine!"

Logan blew out a breath. She was right, but that didn't stop his frustration from mounting. Just once couldn't he be the man? He wanted her safe—not out on patrol. He scraped a hand over his jaw. "Look, Alice must be rubbing off on me. I got this sense trouble was coming. Nothing tangible; just a feeling. I started watching out, taking morning rides, looking for signs of trouble—but I haven't seen a thing. I found out Brian and the other guys were doing it, too. All we did was make sure we weren't covering the same ground at the same time. This is the kind of thing we do; it's our job. Do you really have a problem with that?"

"What I have a problem with is men stepping in and making decisions for me without asking."

Logan shoved his hands in his pockets. "I can't win this argument, can I?" he snapped. "You're about to marry me. You have two weeks until your wedding day. Any other woman would be thinking about dresses and flowers and table settings and—" Logan knew he was digging his own grave but couldn't seem to stop.

"I'm not any other woman. I don't care what I wear or whether there are flowers at our wedding. It's just a stupid tradition—"

"Hey, maybe I care about our wedding. Maybe I want it to be something special." Logan lost his temper. He'd reined in his own instinct to lead for weeks. They all had. Didn't she see that? "And it's not just your responsibility to care for this ranch. It's *our* responsibility. This land doesn't just belong to you anymore!"

Lena's eyes widened before she regained control. "I knew it!" she hissed. "I knew it—you're just like every man I've ever met. All you want to do is take. Take my freedom. Take my home. Steal my land." She clawed the ring he'd bought her just days ago off her finger and chucked it at him. It bounced off his cheek, and he caught it automatically, his heart sinking.

"None of that's true, and you know it." It was her fear talking. And his worry. They should be confronting those fears, not hurling accusations at each other, but he didn't know how to stop the conversation now that it was started.

"All I know is that I was a fool to trust you. A fool to trust any man. And I'm done. There won't be any dresses or place settings or guests. There won't be a wedding. I'm not marrying you. And I want you off my land."

IT WAS COLD in the barn's loft. Bitterly cold. But there was no way Lena was going back to the house, even if dusk had fallen more than an hour ago, and now it was fully dark. She'd spent a long day doing chores alone, snarling at anyone who dared to come too close. It was too dark to work any longer. She envied Jo, with her snug little private dwelling that Hunter had helped her build next to the main house. She needed a hideaway, too, but she'd be damned if she'd hole up in the attic Logan had fitted out for her.

For one week—one week—she'd allowed herself to

get distracted by concerns that were typically feminine. All the questions that needed to be answered for her upcoming nuptials. She'd allowed herself to enjoy it. Had reined in her vigilance, just a little bit, for a few days.

And this is what happened. The General was in danger, and the men had moved seamlessly to take over. Certain they knew better than she did what was good for her. They could have asked. Could have said, "Hey, Lena, would you like us to take this on?" She could have said yes or no. Instead they decided for her.

Men always tried to decide for her.

Was this the kind of life she was going to face? Would she always have to fight for her position here? As much as she hated to admit it, the General did control Two Willows's deed now that Amelia was gone. He could pass it on to whomever he chose. Sell it off if he felt like it. He could sign the deed over to the men and leave her and her sisters out of it. Community property laws would kick in under a dispute, but that didn't help in the day-to-day operations. If she fought with Brian, Connor and Hunter, it would cause a rift in the family anyway.

Lena wished she could turn back time a day and go back to the tight-knit conversations about her wedding she'd been having with her sisters. Even with their worry about the General, she'd enjoyed the closeness she'd felt with them. It had been like being girls again. It had been too long since they'd had the luxury of having fun together that way.

Now it was over. The wedding was off.

She wrapped the horse blanket around herself more tightly and wished she'd stopped to put on more layers before dashing from the house. She'd need to go back and face the rest of them soon anyway, and tell the men to stop interfering.

She'd have to start patrolling herself.

And she didn't feel like patrolling.

She felt—

She felt like a fool.

Lena sighed and buried her face in her hands. The truth was, she'd gone off half-cocked at Logan's interference when he was right; all he was doing was trying to help. Years of frustration in her dealings with the General had taught her to mistrust everyone. Now Logan was paying the price.

This past week had shown her she didn't feel like being in charge of everything anymore. Truth be told, she couldn't be everywhere at once. If trouble was coming—and Logan was right, it probably was—they'd need to work together to hold it off.

It made sense to have men regularly patrolling the ranch. She should have thought of it herself.

Would have, if she hadn't been so wrapped up in worry about the General's safety.

Lena sighed again. It was late, and cold, and if she didn't retreat to the house soon and apologize to Logan, she'd probably freeze to death. Then there'd never be a wedding. And she wanted a wedding. She loved Logan. And she knew he loved her.

Looking around, she had to admit that her old hideaway paled in comparison to the beautiful attic room Logan had built for her. She would've liked to move the old chest, the swords and the musket into the house and display them there. Reminders of her family's past amid the present she'd been building with Logan.

Regret cut deep inside her. Far deeper than she'd like to admit. She truly loved Logan. Would he still want to marry her if she admitted her mistake? Or had she proved to him she wasn't worth the effort?

God, everything was a mess.

A sound brought her to full alert, and Lena suddenly realized she'd left her shoulder holster and pistol in the house in her room when she'd confronted Logan early this morning, then hadn't stopped to put them on during her headlong flight to the barn. She was unarmed. What if it was another attack?

Another noise, closer this time, brought her to her feet. She glanced around, looking for some way to protect herself, and her gaze landed on the ancient weapons hanging on the wall above her. The little fabric sack hanging next to the musket held the preparations for priming and firing the weapon, Lena knew. But no one had done that for years; not since before her mother's death. Black powder rifles were the General's pet hobby, and he used to take his collection out on the Fourth of July so the two of them could take turns cleaning and priming the muskets. Lena always made it a race, and she could load a charge and a musket ball in a twist of paper, ram it down the barrel, aim and shoot almost as fast as he could. But muskets were notoriously unreliable. It was no help to her now. She grabbed one of the swords instead.

Her heart pounding in her chest, she listened again. If it had been one of her sisters, or one of the men, they would've turned on the light by the door. She had chosen to sit up here in the darkness because of her mood, and she didn't want to risk being spotted while she figured out who it was.

All was silent in the barn.

Maybe she was imagining things.

When a dim beam of light shone suddenly in her eyes, Lena called out in surprise and raised the sword high.

"What are you going to do with that stupid toy? Bounce it off my head?" Logan demanded. He climbed the rest of the way into the loft.

Lena lowered the sword in relief. "What the hell are you doing? Why didn't you just turn on the light?"

"I tried. Several times. The bulb must have burned out. And this flashlight is nearly dead, too. We'd better find some new batteries for it."

Lena thought about replacing the bulb high on the barn ceiling and stifled a groan. It was such a pain in the ass to reach. "You're lucky I didn't hurt you." This sword was no toy, no matter what he said.

"You couldn't have touched me," he scoffed. He was angry still, she realized. Pushed past what he could take by their earlier argument. She needed to tell him she'd realized her mistake, but she couldn't let that arrogant statement go by unchallenged.

"Oh, really?"

Logan walked over to the wall display and set down his flashlight, its dull beam immediately half-swallowed up by the layer of hay on the floor. He took down the other sword. Held it up. Tested its weight with a swoosh or two through the air. He was angry, that was clear, and he was looking at the sword like it disgusted him, too. She understood why. Both swords needed polishing. She'd neglected the old weapons shamefully.

"You think you're a match for me?" Logan asked. "Prove it."

"You want to have a sword fight?" In this low light, Logan looked dangerous. All Marine. No softness about him. She realized how much he'd been holding back around her all this time. Reining in his own strength.

"Chicken?" he goaded her.

"Hell, no." This was a bad idea, though. The swords might be ill-cared for, but they were still sharp.

"Then let's make this more interesting." Logan took a couple of practice swings.

Where had she heard that before?

At the Dancing Boot. Their bet over the pool table weeks ago had led to everything else that had happened. That had been the first time they'd danced.

Lena shook her head. "I don't think so."

"So, you're chicken, after all."

Oh, what the hell. "Lay it on me, then. What's this big wager we're going to make?" She was beginning to remember why she'd run out here in the first place.

Logan always thought he had the upper hand.

Logan swung the sword a few more times. "If I win, you marry me. If I lose, I'll leave the ranch."

He must be feeling as reckless as she was right now, if he was willing to wager their future on a fight. Anger flared in her. Men treated everything like a game. Logan's eyes glittered in the moonlight that flowed through the window, brighter than the burning out flashlight.

"Deal," she snapped. To hell with trying to reason with him. He wanted to fight. They'd fight.

"Ready?"

"Whenever you are." This was insane. The General had never allowed her or her sisters to play with the swords. *Weapons are to be respected at all times,* he'd always said. Apparently, Logan hadn't gotten the same message from his parents. Or the military.

Or maybe he just didn't care. Maybe he wanted to win so badly he'd throw caution to the wind.

A moment later, she didn't have time to think about any of that. Logan crashed his sword against hers with a blow so powerful he nearly knocked it out of her hand. Probably his plan—to end this battle before it even began. Lena wasn't having it. Maybe she'd never trained with the sword, but that didn't mean she be an easy adversary.

The clash of their weapons reverberated in the small space, and soon Lena was fighting with everything she had. Logan didn't hold back. He was treating her the way he treated any adversary. Gunning for the win.

Her estimation of him rose in the next few moments, as she realized he wasn't going to give her any quarter. She wouldn't give him any, either. She fought back, parrying each of his thrusts with a blow of her own. Soon she began to wonder how long she could keep this up. The light in the loft was getting dimmer by the minute. The sword was heavy, but its weight didn't seem to bother Logan at all. As a rancher, she worked hard and did a lot of heavy lifting in the course of her days, but she hadn't spent years as a Marine—not like him.

Her glance flicked to his bicep, so big the span of both her hands couldn't encompass it. What had she been thinking taking this bet? She was going to lose—and that meant marrying him.

Which she meant to do anyway, but he didn't know that.

Logan crashed his sword against hers again, with a blow that reverberated up her arm and made her wince. Lena was slow to parry back his next blow, and Logan moved in for the victory. Beneath them she heard Atlas moving in his makeshift stall, the clash of the swords making him nervous. This had to stop soon, or he'd spook. But Lena knew she wouldn't be the one to end this fight. She couldn't accept defeat—even at the hand of her intended.

Logan crashed his sword against hers again, and again, and again, a series of battering blows that left her weaker each moment. She gripped the handle of her sword with both hands, not wanting to lose this contest, but she didn't parry Logan's next blow quite in time, and her wrist bent back with the force of it. She nearly dropped her weapon but held on, swung—and missed. Logan swooped his sword around, caught hers on the back swing, where her grip wasn't nearly as strong, and knocked it out of her hands. It went clattering right over the edge of the hayloft, fell and landed with a thud on the wooden floor far below.

Atlas whinnied nervously, but Lena was only half aware of him. Her chest heaved with her deep breaths, and her gaze was locked on Logan, who'd raised his sword in a victory salute like a fierce warrior of old. He turned the sword down, jabbed it into the floorboards and approached her as the flashlight died, leaving them in darkness. Lena didn't move. Not even when he took her into his arms, pulled her close and claimed a victory kiss.

Frustration warred with desire in her. Frustration at herself. She loved this stupid, reckless man. She loved him as much for the fact that he'd try to win her back with a sword battle as for the fact that he cared so much about her and her ranch he'd head out early each morning in order to patrol it. He was stubborn. All men were stubborn to the point of stupidity. But he was loyal, he worked hard, he loved this land and he loved her. Enough to put on this crazy display. And bet his heart—and his future—on the outcome.

When Logan stiffened, she thought it was because he expected her to be angry at him. But a second later, he covered her mouth with the palm of his hand and whispered in her ear, "Shh."

Lena stiffened, too, wondering what he'd heard. That was Atlas again, shuffling in his stall, unhappy about the strange noises from their swordplay, no doubt.

"It's just—" she began.

He cut her off, his words barely a whisper. "Someone's coming."

Lena stilled, every nerve on edge, and listened harder but stayed perfectly still, trusting the Marine's instincts. Logan dropped his hand and crept toward the edge of the hayloft. The barn door opened. A light flared—a battery-operated lantern like the one Lena read by in the loft.

"Help me over here," a man's voice called softly beneath them.

Harley. She was sure it was him. Now she heard the footsteps Logan must've heard before. There was a rattling. That was the handle of the stall door. Atlas whinnied again, this time a sound of warning.

Harley and Ray had come to steal her horse.

HAD HE ACTUALLY come down to the barn without a real weapon? Logan bit back a curse as he realized he had. He'd showered after his workday was done, wanting to look his best when he asked Lena to reconsider her decision, and hadn't put his holster back on. The two men below them were trying to steal Lena's stallion. Because Lena had chosen him over one of them?

Or because they'd been sent by the same criminal family from Tennessee that kept coming after the Reeds?

The men who'd attacked the ranch before had been after significant amounts of money, though—money they thought they were owed because the Reeds had destroyed an entire shipment of drugs stored on their land. A breeding stallion was worth a lot of money, but nowhere near enough to pay that back.

But Logan had been thinking over the last few days about the raids on the Reed place as he'd spent hours walking and riding its perimeter. What struck him as odd was that in some ways, with each successive attack, their enemies' goals had seemed to get smaller. First they'd tried to mastermind a takeover of the entire ranch. Then they'd gone for a sum of money—far less than the worth of this place. Then they'd burned the stables, an act of revenge rather than one that would line their pockets. Now they were after a single horse?

What was going on here? What was the real goal? What had started out as an operation worthy of a criminal organization was fast becoming the work of someone—

Desperate.

Unless this attempted theft had nothing to do with the other attacks at all.

But Logan didn't have any more time for questions. He could hear Atlas shifting and scrambling in his makeshift stall. The horse was getting riled up, and any country boy worth his salt knew that an angry stallion was a dangerous animal. Did those two yahoos really think Atlas would meekly allow them to lead him out of this barn by the halter?

Speaking of which…

Did those idiots really think they could halter the animal *after* they'd let it out?

"You got your lighter?" Harley asked.

"Of course. You heard what Uncle Beau said; this time the job's gotta be done right. No one gets out alive."

Logan's heart plunged, and behind him he heard Lena's indrawn breath. As Atlas whinnied again, scrambling and shifting in his stall, Logan thought fast. The Tennessee goons had tried arson once before and failed. Were they about to try it again?

No one gets out alive.

That meant it wasn't the barn or the stables they planned to burn this time. If it was, Harley would've said *nothing* is going to get out alive. *No one* meant people. And people meant Cass and her unborn baby. Alice, Jo and Sadie—and Brian, Connor and Hunter.

Logan realized in a flash they couldn't let these men free Atlas, because as soon as they did, they'd go set fire to the houses. And who knew what they had done in preparation for setting them alight? Set up explosives? Soaked the wooden cladding in gasoline? Or—Logan remembered seeing the twins in the hardware store— kerosene?

He turned to tell Lena to stay right here, only to find her directly behind him. She stood still as a stone, listening to every word the men below them said.

"I'm starting to think we should let this animal burn, too," Harley said a moment later.

"Uh, uh. Uncle Beau has got big plans for this horse," Ray said. "It's going to be the start of our empire. We'll breed him until he gives up the ghost and then sell him for dog food." Atlas shuffled in his stall again, letting out a sharp whinny. "Shit, you're right; this animal's a menace. Buddy," he said to Atlas. "You'd better calm down right now, or I'm going to shoot you in the head."

Logan should've seen it coming. He knew Ray's words would infuriate Lena. It still surprised him when she launched herself out of the hayloft with a rebel yell loud enough to wake everyone within a five-mile radius. Logan rushed to the edge, sure he'd see her twisted body on the ground below, but Lena had landed on Harley and Ray, and was locked in a wrestling match with both.

Logan swore, grabbed the nearby sword and swore again at its uselessness. There was nothing for it, though. He rushed to the edge of the hayloft, slid down the ladder, landed hard, regained his balance—and charged.

Harley yelped when Logan struck him with the flat of his sword, and Lena brushed past him, headed for Atlas's stall. When she threw the door open and the horse charged out, Logan thought for one grateful moment it might do the trick. The stallion reared up, and both Harley and Ray scattered from under its hooves, but then Atlas, the ungrateful beast, raced straight for the door and out of sight. That left two men with pistols, Lena unarmed and him with his stupid replica Revolutionary War sword. He was afraid Lena would try tackling the men again and get herself shot, but in the first girlish move he'd ever seen her make, she raced for the ladder instead, clambered up it and into the loft.

Harley lurched after her. "Lena, stop it! I'm not going to hurt your horse, I'm trying to save it. Just like I wanted to save you!"

Logan went after him, but when Ray took a shot at him, he dove for the floor, rolled behind a cord of stacked wood and thought fast. How the hell could he fight these guys? All he could hope was that someone up at the house had heard that gunshot and would come to investigate—armed. He hoped to God Lena stayed hidden up in the loft. She might buy herself enough time until the cavalry came.

"Forget about her. Split up," he heard Ray say. He peeked around to see what was happening and was rewarded with a shot that ricocheted off the top of the stack, the wall of the barn and buried itself in a wooden post. Logan ducked down again. Sooner or later one of them would be able to get an unobstructed shot at him. He needed more cover, and that meant he had to move. He waited until he thought both men were in motion before he lunged into the far corner of the barn where stacked supplies and tools made a barrier of sorts. Another shot rang out, ricocheted off a metal shovel and penetrated the wooden floorboards. The twins had definitely split up and were circling around trying to get an angle on him. Logan realized if he was careful he might be able to give Ray a nasty surprise. Moving ever so slowly, judging each step before he took it, he edged around the back of the stacked supplies, trying hard not to betray his position. The other men didn't seem to realize that he had moved. He saw Ray slipping carefully toward where he'd just been. *Come on*, he thought. *Just another step. That's right. One more—*

Thunk! He brought the hilt of his sword down hard on Ray's head, and Ray keeled over, unfortunately dropping his pistol more than a yard away from where Logan stood. If he tried to get it, he'd expose himself.

But it was his only hope.

"Ray? Ray, where are you?" Harley hissed.

Logan held his breath. Thank God Ray was out cold on the floor. If only he could reach that pistol before Harley came to look for him, he'd get the situation well in hand.

But Harley was smarter than that. When he edged toward Logan's position, he held his pistol out in front of him, his finger on the trigger, and Logan knew the other man would get a shot off if he lunged for Ray's weapon. His sword wouldn't do him any good.

"I've got you," Harley said. "I can see you back there, Hughes. You think you're invisible, but you're not."

Logan didn't move a muscle. He wasn't sure if Harley was bluffing or not, but Harley's Glock was pointed mighty near his heart. This was all going to be over in a few moments, and the most he could hope to do was lunge out of the way. After that, he didn't have a plan.

"Come on out of there, fight like a man, you little shit," Harley said. "If it hadn't been for you, none of this would have happened. Lena would have fallen for me, and I could have saved her. Put your hands up, drop whatever it is you're lugging around. Now."

If Harley couldn't see the sword, then he didn't have as good an angle on him as he was making out. Maybe there was still time—

Harley took two steps forward and pointed the gun right in Logan's face.

Or maybe his time was up.

HOLD THE GUN. Grab the paper twist that holds the black powder. Open it with your teeth, pour it into the barrel of the musket. Keep your shaking hands from letting it spill all over the floor. Drop in the lead ball. Ram it home.

Find the flint. Where was it? Where was the damned flint? The musket wouldn't fire without it. Lena searched the little fabric bag with shaking fingers, located it, dropped it, fell to her knees and scrambled around to find it again. Finally—after what seemed like hours—her fingers located it, wedged in a crack between two floorboards. She pried it out, found its place, primed the weapon and scrambled to the edge of the hayloft, crouched on her knees.

Ray lay in a heap on the ground, and Harley was

crossing the barn, his pistol outstretched, pointing it unflinchingly in one direction. Lena followed the trajectory and swallowed when she took in Logan, sword raised, backed into a corner, covered for now, but not for long.

She had one shot, she realized. One shot with an ancient gun, primed with powder that had been hanging here for more than eleven years. This was insane. If she missed, Logan would die. And she didn't want him to die.

Faint for the first time in her life, Lena swayed on her knees before getting a hold of herself. She lifted the musket and cocked the hammer. What had the General always said? *Take aim, then let God do the rest.*

"Come on out of there, fight like a man, you little shit," Harley suddenly called to Logan. "If it hadn't been for you, none of this would have happened. Lena would have fallen for me, and I could have saved her. Put your hands up, drop whatever it is you're lugging around. Now."

Harley couldn't see the sword Logan held, but that didn't mean he didn't have a shot. Lena could almost see Logan considering the odds. There was no way he could win.

She hoped he knew Harley was wrong. She would never have fallen for a man like him. Especially not while there were men like Logan in the world.

Ray moaned where he lay in a heap. He shifted but didn't get up. Good, he was down for the count.

Harley took two steps forward and pointed the gun

right Logan's face. "You're lucky my brother is alive. Now I'll just shoot you instead of tearing you apart limb from limb."

Time was up. Lena sent up a prayer, took aim, sucked in a breath, pulled the trigger—

Fired.

Her shot ripped through the barn. Harley cried out and lurched forward, staggered a few feet and collapsed, uttering a horrible, gurgling sound that made Lena drop to her knees. Ray let out a wail, pushed up to a sitting position and nearly keeled over again, obviously groggy, but managed to stay upright.

Logan dropped beside Harley, moving quickly to try to stanch the wound, but a moment later, he sat back. Lena waited for what seemed forever, too numb to pray or hope—not knowing what to pray or hope for—but when she saw Logan cross himself, cold pierced her.

"He's gone," Logan said.

Gone.

She'd killed Harley?

Lena swayed, put a hand on to steady herself, the musket falling with a metallic thump onto the hay-strewn floor of the loft.

She'd killed Harley—

"You bitch! He did this for you!" Ray fumbled around and lurched to his feet, his pistol in his hand.

He pointed it at Lena, and her breath escaped her.

Logan spun around and swore, dove for his sword and came up swinging.

Ray took his shot. A bullet zinged by Lena's cheek,

burning her flesh. She fell back and clapped a hand to it with a cry. Below her Logan bellowed. When she pulled her hand away, it was covered in blood. Her stomach turned.

She heard a grunt and a smack of metal against flesh.

"Logan?" In a flash, she scrambled back to the edge of the loft. Had Ray somehow managed to shoot him, too?

"Lena!" Logan staggered and turned to look up at her. "Lena? You're okay?"

"I'm okay." She looked beyond him to Ray.

"Don't look. Lena, don't look!" Logan cried, shifting to block her view.

She leaned forward. Why shouldn't she—?

She remembered the sword in Logan's hand.

Swallowed.

"Jesus, baby girl," Logan said from down below. "Why didn't you tell me the blades on these things were sharp?"

Chapter Thirteen

LOGAN DIDN'T THINK he'd ever forget the moment Lena's musket ball ripped through Harley Ellis's neck.

If she'd fired a second later, he didn't think he'd have been alive to see it.

"You would have made one hell of a Revolutionary War soldier," he told her several hours later, when the sheriff had been and gone, a neighbor had brought Atlas back safe and sound, and Harley's and Ray's bodies had been carted off. Cab had told them he and his deputies would hunt down the twins' uncle before the night was out and hold him for questioning. The twins' driver's licenses had been issued in Tennessee. Cab was already sure he'd find a connection between the Ellises and the drug dealers who'd been harassing them for months.

"I wanted to be a spy, not a soldier, remember?"

"I'm glad you decided to be a soldier tonight."

They were seated in the kitchen, lights blazing, mugs of hot coffee in their hands, sweetened with a lot of sugar for the shock Cass seemed to think they both might succumb to. Neither of them had been injured except for Lena's cheek, but once she'd washed the wound it hadn't turned out to be more than a scrape. Still, Logan knew Lena was badly shaken. The fire department had been here, too, and had spent more than an hour hosing down the outside of the houses to dilute the kerosene the twins had spread around their foundations. They didn't find anything else awry on the property. Brian and the other men had teamed up with the sheriff's department to do a thorough search of all the buildings. They'd investigate again in the morning, but with the men taking turns keeping watch tonight— and Harley and Ray both dead—Logan was positive nothing more would happen.

He didn't blame Lena for being overwhelmed, though.

Hell, he was a little off his game, too.

He'd never killed someone with a sword before.

He couldn't believe those old swords were sharp. He could have sworn they were the same cheap knock-offs his uncle had owned. Logan felt sick every time he thought of his battle with Lena. He could have taken her head off when they were fooling around earlier.

Now he caught her eye. "I suppose a gentleman would let you off the hook, all things considered. You lost the bet we made earlier," he elaborated when she raised an eyebrow. "You're supposed to marry me. But a gentleman wouldn't hold you to that after you saved his life."

"Good thing you're not a gentleman," Lena said.

Logan's heart skipped a beat. Did she mean—? He

found he couldn't ask her. Not yet.

"At least now you know what your dream was about," Lena said, leaving him confused until he remembered St. Michael.

"You're right. I got a sword tonight, didn't I? And I tried like hell to protect you, baby girl. And then you went and saved me instead with that damn musket."

"But you saved me, too, so it worked out in the end, didn't it?"

"I guess," he said ruefully.

"I used to have a dream," she said and reached out to take his hand, "that one day I'd meet a man I didn't have to protect myself from. Someone who saw me. All of me. And loved me anyway."

"That's me," Logan said softly.

"And I'm the woman in your dream," she told him. "The one carrying the musket."

LENA RAN HER thumb over Logan's knuckles. His hand was larger than hers. Stronger. And she didn't mind.

They complemented each other. Just like Brian and Cass, Connor and Sadie, Hunter and Jo. Like her mother and the General. She didn't know how she could have missed it at first, that together they were better than when they were apart.

"I've been letting life pass me by," she told him. "Holding myself back from loving any man because I was so angry at the General—and at myself. I hated myself." It was satisfying to put it into words. "That wasn't any way to live."

"But—"

"You make me like myself," she explained, "because you like me."

He nodded. "I do like you." He covered her hand with his. "You are everything I've ever searched for, Lena Reed. Whip-smart, takes no shit, action-packed, funny as hell. What more could a man want in a woman?"

Lena softened. "What more could a woman want in a man?"

"Muscles?" He struck a pose. Lena reached out and patted his bicep.

"You've got those."

"Wit?" He waggled his eyebrows.

"You've got that, too."

"A hell of a way about him in the sack?"

"We can hear you, you know!" Sadie called from the living room.

Lena laughed out loud. "I'm not sure about that last one. Maybe we need to try it again." She kept her voice low enough only he could hear. She hoped.

"Sounds like a plan." He stood and led her upstairs, but Lena tugged him past their bedrooms and continued to the attic, where they could finally have privacy. For the next several hours, Logan demonstrated all his moves.

She liked those, too, as it turned out.

Later, tangled together on the couch, Lena rested her head on Logan's chest. She was done fighting him— done fighting her fate.

Logan seemed to be thinking along the same lines. He reached down to paw through his clothes and pulled out a little box she recognized. When he opened it up, her heart squeezed.

Her ring. The one she'd thrown in his face.

"I think it's time to try this again," Logan said. "Lena, you know who I am and what I have to give you. And I hope now you trust me a little bit. All I want is your happiness, and I hope you'll always tell me if I fall short and give me the chance to get back on track—before you swing a crowbar at me—or a sword. Lena, will you marry me and make me the happiest man on the planet?"

"Yes," she said, and let him slide it onto her finger. It felt right there. A reminder of his love. A promise of their future.

"Don't take it off this time."

Chapter Fourteen

"LOGAN!"

Two weeks later, at the Chance Creek Regional Airport, Logan's mother burst through the door after disembarking her plane and rushed to throw her arms around him. His father quickly followed.

It was James's turn next, and his oldest brother made a big show of shock at Logan's appearance.

"You're not my little brother, you're a monster. Look at you!"

"Less preaching, more working out—that's what you need," Logan advised him. He was touched that James had come all the way from Africa for the wedding. It had been years since they'd been in the same place.

"I don't get much time for working out," James told him.

Anthony hugged Logan last. "I'm really happy for you. You look great," he said.

"Right back at you."

"Look at my three sons," their mother said. "I'm so proud of all of you. I wish you all lived closer, though."

"Aida, you promised," their father said.

"All right, all right; I'll save it for the reception, when everyone's had a little wine. I *am* proud of you, though," she told Logan as she linked an arm through his. He led her and the rest of the family toward the baggage carousel.

"For what?" he teased her.

"For finding a woman and settling down. Finally."

"You've got the General to thank for that," he said.

"When am I going to meet this General?" Aida asked.

"I wish I knew."

"YOU LOOK STUNNING," Alice said, twirling Lena around to stand her in front of the mirror in her bedroom. Lena took in her own reflection and had to agree. That was one good thing about tomboying around most of the time. When you finally did your hair and nails, the results made everyone flabbergasted.

She flicked her fingers. "Stupid nails again."

"You can survive one day with them." Cass smiled. "Alice is right; you're beautiful, Lena. Logan won't know what hit him."

"Four married, one to go," Jo said, punching Alice's shoulder lightly. "Who will the General send next?"

Alice got a distant look in her eyes. "I don't know—and it's driving me crazy."

Alice had seemed strained these days, and not just because of the deadline for her sample costumes. Lena knew she was mostly worried about the General; they all were. And Lena had questioned more than once if she should be going through with this wedding right now—especially since Beau Ellis had never been found.

Her sisters had assured her it was what the General would want. "He sent Logan, after all," Jo said. "And Beau must be a thousand miles away by now. We won't see him again."

Lena had gone with the flow. Truth was, she didn't want to put off the wedding. She wanted to step into her new life with Logan, even if they hadn't worked out all the details of that yet.

For one thing, she wasn't sure what name to take. She'd always thought of herself as Lena Reed and thought taking a man's name was an old-fashioned custom. On the other hand, as Cass pointed out, Reed was her father's name—another man. Besides, there were the children to think about.

Children.

She'd never thought of children. Wasn't sure she ever wanted to, either. But she found herself thinking it would be okay if she ever decided she wanted to think about it. Logan's mom was gunning for grandkids and made no bones about it. Logan told her he was willing to wait until they had more time to talk it over.

That was all she could ask for.

"Ready?" Cass asked. "It's about time for us to take our places."

"I'm ready," Lena said.

But as they made their out into the hall, they spotted a man Lena recognized just cresting the stairs.

"Jed?" she cried. "Jed Henderson? Is that you?" She hurried to greet the overseer she hadn't seen in years. Too late she remembered how surly she'd been when he left Two Willows. She hoped he could forgive her.

"Sorry for intruding right before your big moment," he said. "I just had to see you before you walked down the aisle. I wanted to make sure... well, to make sure that man waiting for you at the altar was right for you. It's your father's job, I know, but he hasn't been around much, has he?" he pointed out dryly. "I guess I'm a poor substitute, but I've let you down all these years. I couldn't stand it if I held back now and regretted it later."

"You let me down?" Lena was incredulous. "I was the one who was awful to you."

"You were hurt. I should have prepared you better before I retired. It hurt me, too. Leaving you. You... meant a lot to me. Don't have children of my own, you know."

"Thank you." It was all she could think of to say. "I'm so glad you came. It means a lot to me. I've thought about you so much over the years—everything you taught me."

"I'm glad to know I was of service," he said simply. "Now I've taken too much of your time. You need to get going. Don't keep that young man waiting. I've taken a peek, and he looks like a good candidate. You're sure he's the one?"

"I'm sure." She was, and she was grateful to be able to say so. "But, Jed. Don't go yet. I know this is last minute, but…" She took a breath. "I was going to walk myself down the aisle. Like you said, the General isn't here. Would you consider… would you…?" She found she was afraid to put her question into words.

"I'd be mighty proud to walk you down that aisle." Jed's smile spread ear to ear, leaving no doubt of the old man's sincerity, and Lena's heart rose. She'd be proud, too, to walk by this man's side. Jed was proof that men could be heroes. Logan was proof of that, too. Lena came to a decision on a matter that she'd been debating for days.

"We have to hurry," Cass said. "We should have been downstairs already."

"Ready?" Jed asked Lena, crooking his arm and offering it to her.

Lena linked her arm through his. "Ready."

"READY?" ANTHONY ASKED Logan as they took their places along with Brian, Connor and Hunter near the altar that had been constructed at one end of Two Willows' living room. Reverend Halpern was already waiting for them, smiling and calm, ready to perform the ceremony. With the men's Revolutionary War uniforms and the setting of the old house, Logan could believe that he'd traveled back in time.

He was more nervous than he'd imagined he'd be—mostly because he couldn't believe Lena hadn't changed her mind again. More than once he'd thought she would. She was balky as an unbroken horse, that one. But she'd held fast to her promise to him and had worn her engagement ring happily—without throwing it in his face again. She'd been softer lately. More willing to talk to him. More willing to share her duties around the ranch.

She confessed her worry about her father more than once and allowed him to be there for her. It was as if she was testing the waters—seeing what a relationship with a man could look like. And liking the results.

Logan liked them, too.

Spending time with Lena was better than just about anything else—except spending time in bed with her, where they found themselves compatible in all kinds of ways.

He couldn't wait for the winter to pass so they could ride together. Camp, maybe. Explore Montana together. Meanwhile, he'd enjoy their warm nest on the top floor—when she invited him.

His family had taken to her on the spot when they met her, Anthony and James instantly at ease enough with her to joke around—usually at Logan's expense.

Only the General's absence was a blot on their happiness. He hoped the man was okay. Hoped to hear from him soon so they could all rest easy. He knew all the Reed women were expecting the worst after breaking tradition and leaving the ranch at the same time.

"Here they come," Anthony said, and Logan turned his eyes to the stairs, down which Jo was already stepping slowly in her bridesmaid gown. Sadie came after her, followed by Alice and then Cass.

Then Lena came into view, on the arm of a man he

didn't recognize. It had to be Jed Henderson. He'd made sure Cass sent him an invitation to the wedding. Lena needed men she trusted in her life.

But Logan only had eyes for Lena. Her wedding gown had been transformed into an old-fashioned dress.

And she was… stunning.

Lena… but even more Lena, if that was possible. Logan didn't know how to put it into words.

She walked proudly down the aisle between the rows of chairs. When she reached the altar, Jed gave Logan a little salute, kissed Lena's cheek and stepped back.

Logan took her hand, not able to take his gaze from her face when she tilted her chin up, caught him looking and smiled. "Hey, baby girl."

Brian groaned, then chuckled. "It's never going to stop, is it?"

"Nope," Logan said happily. He looked Lena up and down appreciatively.

"What?" she whispered. "Why are you looking at me that way?"

"Because you take my breath away, Lena Reed."

Her eyes shone, and he saw so much love reflected there, he knew they'd be happy, come what may.

"Dearly beloved," Halpern began.

Logan squeezed Lena's hand. She squeezed his back.

"We are gathered here today…"

LENA FELT HER mother's presence as she stood in front

of the altar and listened to Reverend Halpern repeat the words she'd heard so many times. She wished she knew where the General was and how he was faring, but uncertainty was part of life and she'd come to realize there was nothing she could do now but wait. She'd made her pledge to the stone, and she'd stick to it. Maybe she and her sisters should have done that long ago, rather than letting their mother's promise speak for them.

She was glad for Logan's strong presence beside her, and if she was honest she was glad for this silly dress. Just for once she wanted to feel soft in contrast to Logan's strength. She wanted to bend to fit him, to be supple in his hands.

Then she'd go back to being a ball-buster.

A ball-buster who shared his last name.

Lena and Logan Hughes.

She bit back a grin and glanced up to see an answering one on Logan's face. Did he feel like she did? Like they were getting away with something?

Surely someone would stop them.

Logan spoke his vows in a clear, steady voice, and she hoped she sounded as sure of herself, because she was. When he slipped her wedding ring on her finger, her heart swelled with so much love she thought it would burst.

And when Reverend Halpern announced they were husband and wife—and told Logan he could kiss the bride—she went up on tiptoe, nearly breathless with anticipation.

This was the man she loved—and she planned to spend a lifetime with him. A lifetime that was starting today.

Logan leaned down, kissed her thoroughly and whispered, "My mom says it's time to get started on those babies."

"She did not!" But at the moment it sounded like a very good idea. Working on them—if not having them quite yet. "Behave yourself."

"Never." He kissed her again, lifted her up off the ground and swirled her around. "Not as long as I'm with you."

She decided she could live with that.

Epilogue

ALICE DIDN'T THINK she'd ever seen Lena so happy. Not since their mother had died, anyway. She'd been radiant at the altar, and her smile had been unceasing ever since Logan kissed her and led her back up the aisle. Now they were dancing, their love for each other more than evident.

Alice wished she was dancing, too, but she'd been out of sorts all day, and she supposed she must have shown it, because she hadn't gotten many offers—

And if she was honest, she'd turned down most of them.

She couldn't understand what was happening to her. Her hunches were all messed up. She still got flashes of things that would happen to her sisters—she'd known Jo would spill her wine and had been on hand with seltzer water and paper towels just a moment later—but the hunches that concerned her were intermittent—

As if they were being blocked.

She supposed that accounted for her grumpiness. It certainly wasn't the fact that all four of her sisters were married.

And she didn't even have a boyfriend.

She wouldn't get one, either, hiding away in the kitchen like this. But Reed women didn't meet their husbands-to-be on the dance floor. They met them at the front door, after the General sent them, and she didn't want to think about the General tonight.

It was her fault he'd gone missing. She'd been the last to leave the ranch the day they'd all met up at Linda's Diner and realized what they'd done. She'd spotted another drone in the distance that morning, and had been so furious at the idea that her maze was being spied on, she hadn't thought twice about whether or not one of her sisters were home when she left the ranch later to do her errands.

Now no one knew what had happened to the General, which meant no husband showing up on the steps today for her.

Which was fine: she didn't want one. Certainly not one he'd pick.

Bad enough fate sent her hunches and visions all the time, making her life seem preordained rather than under her control. She didn't need another choice made for her.

But she didn't want the General to be in danger, either.

She lugged the dishes toward the sink and was halfway across the kitchen when her sight overtook her, sending her reeling toward the counter to set them down with a crash.

He was here. The man the General had sent for her.

The doorbell rang.

Alice shook her head. It couldn't be. Not when—

The doorbell rang again, and she realized it was only a matter of time before someone else heard it and went to see who was there.

It couldn't be a husband, she reminded herself. The General was missing. He couldn't send anyone to Two Willows right now. But a shiver traced down her spine. Someone was here with an important message. She knew that in every fiber of her being.

Alice took a deep breath and counted to five, then strode to the front door, her spring green bridesmaid gown swirling around her ankles. The happy hub-bub of the party in the living room swirled around her, but didn't calm her nerves.

She opened the door to find a handsome man with sandy brown hair and blue eyes on the other side. He stood at ease like a soldier, hands clasped behind his back, legs spread in a strong, ready stance. There was a rugged duffel bag on the porch to one side of him.

The man stuck his hand out. "I'm Jack. Jack Sanders. The General sent me. You're Alice."

She nodded. Found her voice. "I knew it would be you."

"I knew you'd say that," he answered.

"You're the one who sent the drone." Alice's throat was dry. This *was* the man the General had sent. The man he meant for her to marry. But where was—?

"You're the one who shot it down."

"Not me; Lena." One point for her.

Jack's eyes narrowed. "Do you know what I'm going to say next?"

She shook her head. Try as she might, she couldn't catch hold of it, but a sudden foreboding filled her. Whatever it was wouldn't be good. Alice shivered and crossed her arms over her chest.

Jack stepped closer, suddenly filling the doorway. His gaze held hers, and she read concern—and a searching hope she couldn't fathom. He cleared his throat.

"I'm afraid I've got some bad news."

Ice water swept through her veins. Of course. She'd known that ever since the owl swooped out of the sky and grabbed that mouse. Alice nodded and waited, unable to breathe, until he said the words already echoing in her mind.

"The General's been hurt. He's coming home."

Be the first to know about Cora Seton's new releases!
Sign up for her newsletter here!
www.coraseton.com/sign-up-for-my-newsletter

Other books in the Brides of Chance Creek Series:

Issued to the Bride One Navy SEAL
Issued to the Bride One Airman
Issued to the Bride One Sniper
Issued to the Bride One Soldier

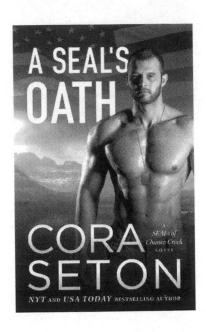

Read on for an excerpt of Volume 1 of **The SEALs of Chance Creek** series – *A SEAL's Oath*.

NAVY SEAL BOONE Rudman should have been concentrating on the pile of paperwork in front of him. Instead he was brooding over a woman he hadn't seen in thirteen years. If he'd been alone, he would have pulled up Riley Eaton's photograph on his laptop, but three other men ringed the table in the small office he occupied at the Naval Amphibious Base at Little Creek, Virginia, so instead he mentally ran over the information he'd found out about her on the Internet. Riley lived in Boston, where she'd gone to school. She'd graduated with a fine arts degree, something which confused

Boone; she'd never talked about wanting to study art when they were young. She worked at a vitamin manufacturer, which made no sense at all. And why was she living in a city, when Riley had only ever come alive when she'd visited Chance Creek, Montana, every summer as a child?

Too many questions. Questions he should know the answer to, since Riley had once been such an integral part of his life. If only he hadn't been such a fool, Boone knew she still would be. Still a friend at least, or maybe much, much more. Pride had kept him from finding out.

He was done with pride.

He reached for his laptop, ready to pull up her photograph, whether he was alone or not, but stopped when it chimed to announce a video call. For one crazy second, Boone wondered if his thoughts had conjured Riley up, but he quickly shook away that ridiculous notion.

Probably his parents wondering once again why he wasn't coming home when he left the Navy. He'd explained time and again the plans he'd made, but they couldn't comprehend why he wouldn't take the job his father had found him at a local ranch.

"Working with horses," his dad had said the last time they talked. "What more do you want?"

It was tempting. Boone had always loved horses. But he had something else in mind. Something his parents found difficult to comprehend. The laptop chimed again.

"You going to get that?" Jericho Cook said, looking up from his work. Blond, blue-eyed, and six-foot-one inches of muscle, he looked out of place hunched over his paperwork. He and the other two men sitting at the table were three of Boone's most trusted buddies and members of his strike team. Like him, they were far more at home jumping out of airplanes, infiltrating terrorist organizations and negotiating their way through disaster areas than sitting on their asses filling out forms. But paperwork caught up to everyone at some point.

He wouldn't have to do it much longer, though. Boone was due to separate from the Navy in less than a month. The others were due to leave soon after. They'd joined up together—egging each other on when they turned eighteen over their parents' objections. They'd survived the brutal process of becoming Navy SEALs together, too, adamant that they'd never leave each other behind. They'd served together whenever they could. Now, thirteen years later, they'd transition back to civilian life together as well.

The computer chimed a third time and his mind finally registered the name on the screen. Boone slapped a hand on the table to get the others' attention.

"It's him!"

"Him, who?" Jericho asked.

"Martin Fulsom, from the Fulsom Foundation. He's calling me!"

"Are you sure?" Clay Pickett shifted his chair over to where he could see. He was an inch or two shorter than Jericho, with dark hair and a wiry build that concealed a perpetual source of energy. Even now Clay's foot was tapping as he worked.

Boone understood his confusion. Why would Martin Fulsom, who must have a legion of secretaries and assistants at his command, call him personally?

"It says Martin Fulsom."

"Holy shit. Answer it," Jericho said. He shifted his chair over, too. Walker Norton, the final member of their little group, stood up silently and moved behind the others. Walker had dark hair and dark eyes that hinted at his Native American ancestry. Unlike the others, he'd taken the time to get his schooling and become an officer. As Lieutenant, he was the highest ranked. He was also the tallest of the group, with a heavy muscular frame that could move faster than most gave him credit for. He was quiet, though. So quiet that those who didn't know him tended to write him off. They did so at their own peril.

Boone stifled an oath at the tremor that ran through him as he reached out to accept the call, but it wasn't every day you got to meet your hero face to face. Martin Fulsom wasn't a Navy SEAL. He wasn't in the military at all. He'd once been an oil man, and had amassed a fortune in the industry before he'd learned about global warming and had a change of heart. For the last decade he'd spearheaded a movement to prevent carbon dioxide particulates from exceeding the disastrous level of 450 ppm. He'd backed his foundation with his entire fortune, invested it in green technology and used his earnings to fund projects around the world aimed at helping him reach his goal. Fulsom was a force of nature, with an oversized personality to match his incredible wealth. Boone liked his can-do attitude and his refusal to mince words when the situation called for plain speaking.

Boone clicked *Accept* and his screen resolved into an image of a man seated at a large wooden desk. He was gray-haired but virile, with large hands and an impressively large watch. Beside him stood a middle aged woman in a severely tailored black suit, who handed him pieces of paper one at a time, waited for him to sign them and took them back, placing them in various folders she cradled in her arm.

"Boone!" The man's hearty voice was almost too much for the laptop's speakers. "Good to finally meet you. This is an impressive proposal you have here."

Boone swallowed. It was true. Martin Fulsom—one of the greatest innovators of their time—had actually called *him*. "It's good to meet you, too, Mr. Fulsom," he managed to say.

"Call me Martin," Fulsom boomed. "Everybody does. Like I said, it's a hell of a proposal. To build a fully operational sustainable community in less than six months? That take guts. Can you deliver?"

"Yes, sir." Boone was confident he could. He'd studied this stuff for years. Dreamed about it, debated it, played with the numbers and particulars until he could speak with confidence about every aspect of the community he wanted to build. He and his friends had gained a greater working knowledge of the fallout from climate change than any of them had gone looking for when they joined the Navy SEALs. They'd realized most of the conflicts that spawned the missions they took on were caused in one way or the other by struggles over resources, usually exacerbated by climate conditions. When rains didn't come and crops failed, unrest was sure to follow. Next came partisan politics, rebellions, coups and more. It didn't take a genius to see that climate change and scarcity of resources would be two prongs spearheading trouble around the world for decades to come.

"And you'll start with four families, building up to ten within that time frame?"

Boone blinked. Families? "Actually, sir…" He'd said nothing about families. Four *men*, building up to ten. That's what he had written in his proposal.

"This is brilliant. Too brilliant." Fulsom's direct gaze caught his own. "You see, we were going to launch a community of our own, but when I saw your proposal, I said, 'This man has already done the hard work; why reinvent the wheel? I can't think of anyone better to lead such a project than someone like Boone Rudman.'"

Boone stifled a grin. This was going better than he could have dreamed. "Thank you, sir."

Fulsom leaned forward. "The thing is, Boone, you have to do it right."

"Of course, sir, but about—"

"It has to be airtight. You have to prove you're sustainable. You have to prove your food systems are self-perpetuating, that you have a strategy to deal with waste, that you have contingency plans. What you've written here?" He held up Boone's proposal package. "It's genius. Genius. But the real question is—who's going to give a shit about it?"

"Well, hell—" Fulsom's abrupt change of tone startled Boone into defensiveness. He knew about the man's legendary high-octane personality, but he hadn't been prepared for this kind of bait and switch. "You yourself just said—"

Fulsom waved the application at him. "I love this stuff. It makes me hard. But the American public? That's a totally different matter. They don't find this shit sexy. It's not enough to jerk me off, Boone. We're trying to turn on the whole world."

"O-okay." Shit. Fulsom was going to turn him down after all. Boone gripped the arms of his chair, waiting for the axe to fall.

"So the question is, how do we make the world care about your community? And not just care about it—be so damn obsessed with it they can't think about anything else?" He didn't wait for an answer. "I'll tell you how. We're going to give you your own reality television show. Think of it. The whole world watching you go from ground zero to full-on sustainable community. Rooting for you. Cheering when you triumph. Crying when you fail. A worldwide audience fully engaged with you and your followers."

"That's an interesting idea," Boone said slowly. It was an insane idea. There was no way anyone would spend their time watching him dig garden beds and install photovoltaic panels. He couldn't think of anything less exciting to watch on television. And he didn't have followers. He had three like-minded friends who'd signed on to work with him. Friends who even now were bristling at this characterization of their roles. "Like I said, Mr. Fulsom, each of the *equal* participants in the community have pledged to document our progress. We'll take lots of photos and post them with our entries on a daily blog."

"Blogs are for losers." Fulsom leaned forward. "Come on, Boone. Don't you want to change the world?"

"Yes, I do." Anger curled within him. He was serious about these issues. Deadly serious. Why was Fulsom making a mockery of him? You couldn't win any kind of war with reality television, and Boone approached his sustainable community as if he was waging a war—a war on waste, a war on the future pain and suffering of the entire planet.

"I get it. You think I'm nuts," Fulsom said. "You think I've finally blown my lid. Well, I haven't. I'm a free-thinker, Boone, not a crazy man. I know how to get the message across to the masses. Always have. And I've always been criticized for it, too. Who cares? You know what I care about? This world. The people on it. The plants and animals and atmosphere. The whole grand, beautiful spectacle that we're currently dragging down into the muck of overconsumption. That's what I care about. What about you?"

"I care about it, too, but I don't want—"

"You don't want to be made a fool of. Fair enough. You're afraid of exposing yourself to scrutiny. You're afraid you'll fuck up on television. Well guess what? You're right; you will fuck up. But the audience is going to love you so much by that time, that if you cry, they'll cry with you. And when you triumph—and you *will* triumph—they'll feel as ecstatic as if they'd done it all themselves. Along the way they'll learn more about solar power, wind power, sustainable agriculture and all the rest of it than we could ever force-feed them through documentaries or classes. You watch, Boone. We're going to do something magical."

Boone stared at him. Fulsom was persuasive, he'd give him that. "About the families, sir."

"Families are non-negotiable." Fulsom set the application down and gazed at Boone, then each of his friends in turn. "You men are pioneers, but pioneers are a yawn-fest until they bring their wives to the frontier. Throw in women, and goddamn, that's interesting! Women talk. They complain. They'll take your plans for sustainability and kick them to the curb unless you make them easy to use and satisfying. What's more, women are a hell of lot more interesting than men. Sex, Boone. Sex sells cars and we're going to use it to sell sustainability, too. Are you with me?"

"I…" Boone didn't know what to say. Use sex to sell sustainability? "I don't think—"

"Of course you're with me. A handsome Navy SEAL like you has to have a girl. You do, don't you? Have a girl?"

"A girl?" Had he been reduced to parroting everything Fulsom said? Boone tried to pull himself together. He definitely did not have a *girl*. He dated when he had time, but he kept things light. He'd never felt it was fair to enter a more serious relationship as long as he was throwing himself into danger on a daily basis. He'd always figured he'd settle down when he left the service and he was looking forward to finally having the time to meet a potential mate. God knew his parents were all too ready for grandkids. They talked about it all the time.

"A woman, a fiancée. Maybe you already have a wife?" Fulsom looked hopeful and his secretary nodded at Boone, as if telling him to say yes.

"Well...."

He was about to say no, but the secretary shook her head rapidly and made a slicing motion across her neck. Since she hadn't engaged in the conversation at all previously, Boone decided he'd better take her signals seriously. He'd gotten some of his best intel in the field just this way. A subtle nod from a veiled woman, or a pointed finger just protruding from a burka had saved his neck more than once. Women were crafty when it counted.

"I'm almost married," he blurted. His grip on the arms of his chair tightened. None of this was going like he'd planned. Jericho and Clay turned to stare at him like he'd lost his mind. Behind him Walker chuckled. "I mean—"

"Excellent! Can't wait to meet your better half.

What about the rest of you?" Fulsom waved them off before anyone else could speak. "Never mind. Julie here will get all that information from you later. As long as you've got a girl, Boone, everything's going to be all right. The fearless leader has to have a woman by his side. It gives him that sense of humanity our viewers crave." Julie nodded like she'd heard this many times before.

Boone's heart sunk even further. Fearless leader? Fulsom didn't understand his relationship with the others at all. Walker was his superior officer, for God's sake. Still, Fulsom was waiting for his answer, with a shrewd look in his eyes that told Boone he wasn't fooled at all by his hasty words. Their funding would slip away unless he convinced Fulsom that he was dedicated to the project—as Fulsom wanted it to be done.

"I understand completely," Boone said, although he didn't understand at all. His project was about sustainability. It wasn't some human-interest story. "I'm with you one hundred percent."

"Then I've got a shitload of cash to send your way. Don't let me down."

"I won't." He felt rather than heard the others shifting, biting back their protests.

Fulsom leaned so close his head nearly filled the screen. "We'll start filming June first and I look forward to meeting your fiancée when I arrive. Understand? Not a girlfriend, not a weekend fling—a fiancée. I want weddings, Boone." He looked over the four of them again. "Four weddings. Yours will kick off the series. I can see it now; an empty stretch of land. Two modern pioneers in love. A country parson performing the ceremony. The bride holding a bouquet of wildflowers the groom picked just minutes before. Their first night together in a lonely tent. Magic, Boone. That's prime time magic. *Surviving on the Land* meets *The First Six Months*."

Boone nodded, swallowing hard. He'd seen those television shows. The first tracked modern-day mountain men as they pitted themselves against crazy weather conditions in extreme locations. The second followed two newlyweds for six months, and documented their every move, embrace, and lovers' quarrel as they settled into married life. He didn't relish the idea of starring in any show remotely like those.

Besides, June first was barely two months away. He'd only get out of the Navy at the end of April. They hadn't even found a property to build on yet.

"There'll be four of you men to start," Fulsom went on. "That means we need four women for episode one; your fiancée and three other hopeful single ladies. Let the viewers do the math, am I right? They'll start pairing you off even before we do. We'll add other community members as we go. Six more men and six more women ought to do it, don't you think?"

"Yes, sir." This was getting worse by the minute.

"Now, I've given you a hell of a shock today. I get that. So let me throw you a bone. I've just closed on the perfect piece of property for your community. Fifteen hundred acres of usable land with creeks, forest, pasture and several buildings. I'm going to give it to you free and clear to use for the duration of the series. If—and only if—you meet your goals, I'll sign it over to you lock, stock and barrel at the end of the last show."

Boone sat up. That was a hell of a bone. "Where is it?"

"Little town called Chance Creek, Montana. I believe you've heard of it?" Fulsom laughed at his reaction. Even Walker was startled. Chance Creek? They'd grown up there. Their families still lived there.

They were going home.

Chills marched up and down his spine and Boone wondered if his friends felt the same way. He'd hardly even let himself dream about that possibility. None of them came from wealthy families and none of them would inherit land. He'd figured they'd go where it was cheapest, and ranches around Chance Creek didn't come cheap. Not these days. Like everywhere else, the town had seen a slump during the last recession, but now prices were up again and he'd heard from his folks that developers were circling, talking about expanding the town. Boone couldn't picture that.

"Let me see here. I believe it's called… Westfield," Fulsom said. Julie nodded, confirming his words. "Hasn't been inhabited for over a decade. A local caretaker has been keeping an eye on it, but there hasn't been cattle on it for at least that long. The heir to the property lives in Europe now. Must have finally decided he wasn't ever going to take up ranching. When he put it on the market, I snapped it up real quick."

Westfield.

Boone sat back even as his friends shifted behind him again. Westfield was a hell of a property—owned by the Eaton family for as long as anyone could remember. He couldn't believe it wasn't a working ranch anymore. But if the old folks were gone, he guessed that made sense. They must have passed away not long after he had left Chance Creek. They wouldn't have broken up the property, so Russ Eaton would have inherited and Russ wasn't much for ranching. Neither was his younger brother, Michael. As far as Boone knew, Russ hadn't married, which left Michael's daughter the only possible candidate to run the place.

Riley Eaton.

Was it a coincidence that had brought her to mind just moments before Fulsom's call, or something more?

Coincidence, Boone decided, even as the more impulsive side of him declared it Fate.

A grin tugged at his mouth as he remembered Riley as she used to be, the tomboy who tagged along after him every summer when they were kids. Riley lived for vacations on her grandparents' ranch. Her mother would send her off each year dressed up for the journey, and the minute Riley reached Chance Creek she'd wad up those fancy clothes and spend the rest of the summer in jeans, boots and an old Stetson passed down from her grandma. Boone and his friends hired on at Westfield most summers to earn some spending money. Riley stuck to them like glue, learning as much as she could about riding and ranching from them. When she was little, she used to cry when August ended and she had to go back home. As she grew older, she hid her feelings better, but Boone knew she'd always adored the ranch. It wasn't surprising, given her home life. Even when he was young, he'd heard the gossip and knew things were rough back in Chicago.

As much as he and the others had complained about being saddled with a follower like Riley, she'd earned their grudging respect as the years went on. Riley never complained, never wavered in her loyalty to them, and as many times as they left her behind, she was always ready to try again to convince them to let her join them in their exploits.

"It's a crime," he'd once heard his mother say to a friend on the phone. "Neither mother nor father has any time for her at all. No wonder she'll put up with anything those boys dish out. I worry for her."

Boone understood now what his mother was afraid of, but at the time he'd shrugged it off and over the years Riley had become a good friend. Sometimes when they were alone fishing, or riding, or just hanging out on her grandparents' porch, Boone would find himself telling her things he'd never told anyone else. As far as he knew, she'd never betrayed a confidence.

Riley was the one who dubbed Boone, Clay, Jericho and Walker the Four Horsemen of the Apocalypse, a nickname that had stuck all these years. When they'd become obsessed with the idea of being Navy SEALs, Riley had even tried to keep up with the same training regimen they'd adopted.

Boone wished he could say they'd always treated Riley as well as she treated them, but that wasn't the truth of it. One of his most shameful memories centered around the slim girl with the long brown braids. Things had become complicated once he and his friends began to date. They had far less time for Riley, who was two years younger and still a kid in their eyes, and she'd withdrawn when she realized their girlfriends didn't want her around. She still hung out when they worked at Westfield, though, and was old enough to be a real help with the work. Some of Boone's best memories were of early mornings mucking out stables with Riley. They didn't talk much, just worked side by side until the job was done. From time to time they walked out to a spot on the ranch where the land fell away and they could see the mountains in the distance. Boone had never quantified how he felt during those times. Now he realized what a fool he'd been.

He hadn't given a thought to how his girlfriends affected her or what it would be like for Riley when they left for the Navy. He'd been too young. Too utterly self-absorbed.

That same year he'd had his first serious relationship, with a girl named Melissa Resnick. Curvy, flirty and oh-so-feminine, she'd slipped into his heart by slipping into his bed on Valentine's Day. By the time Riley came to town again that last summer, he and Melissa were seldom apart. Of all the girls the Horsemen had dated, Melissa was the least tolerant of Riley's presence, and one day when they'd all gone to a local swimming hole, she'd huffed in exasperation when the younger girl came along.

"It's like you've got a sidekick," she told Boone in everyone's hearing. "Good ol' Tagalong Riley."

Clay, Jericho, and Walker, who'd always treated Riley like a little sister, thought it was funny. They had their own girlfriends to impress, and the name had stuck. Boone knew he should put a stop to it, but the lure of Melissa's body was still too strong and he knew if he took Riley's side he'd lose his access to it.

Riley had held her head up high that day and she'd stayed at the swimming hole, a move that Boone knew must have cost her, but each repetition of the nickname that summer seemed to heap pain onto her shoulders, until she caved in on herself and walked with her head down.

The worst was the night before he and the Horsemen left to join the Navy. He hadn't seen Riley for several days, whereas he couldn't seem to shake Melissa for a minute. He should have felt flattered, but instead it had irritated him. More and more often, he had found himself wishing for Riley's calm company, but she'd stopped coming to help him.

Because everyone else seemed to expect it, he'd attended the hoe-down in town sponsored by the rodeo that last night. Melissa clung to him like a burr. Riley was nowhere to be found. Boone accepted every drink he was offered and was well on his way to being three sheets to the wind when Melissa excused herself to the ladies' room at about ten. Boone remained with the other Horsemen and their dates, and he could only stare when Riley appeared in front of him. For once she'd left her Stetson at home, her hair was loose from its braids, and she wore makeup and a mini skirt that left miles of leg between its hem and her dress cowboy boots.

Every nerve in his body had come to full alert and Boone had understood in that moment what he'd failed to realize all that summer. Riley had grown up. At sixteen, she was a woman. A beautiful woman who understood him far better than Melissa could hope to. He'd had a fleeting sense of lost time and missed opportunities before Clay had whistled. "Hell, Tagalong, you've gone and gotten yourself a pair of breasts."

"You better watch out dressed up like that; some guy will think you want more than you bargained for," Jericho said.

Walker's normally grave expression had grown even more grim.

Riley had ignored them all. She'd squared her shoulders, looked Boone in the eye and said, "Will you dance with me?"

Shame flooded Boone every time he thought back to that moment.

Riley had paid him a thousand kindnesses over the years, listened to some of his most intimate thoughts and fears, never judged him, made fun of him or cut him down the way his other friends sometimes did. She'd always been there for him, and all she'd asked for was one dance.

He should have said yes.

It wasn't the shake of Walker's head, or Clay and Jericho's laughter that stopped him. It was Melissa, who had returned in time to hear Riley's question, and answered for him.

"No one wants to dance with a Tagalong. Go on home."

Riley had waited one more moment—then fled.

Boone rarely thought about Melissa after he'd left Chance Creek and when he did it was to wonder what he'd ever found compelling in her. He thought about Riley far too often. He tried to remember the good times—teaching her to ride, shoot, trap and fish. The conversations and lazy days in the sun when they were kids. The intimacy that had grown up between them without him ever realizing it.

Instead, he thought of that moment—that awful, shameful moment when she'd begged him with her eyes to say yes, to throw her pride that single bone.

And he'd kept silent.

"Have you heard of the place?" Fulsom broke into his thoughts and Boone blinked. He'd been so far away it took a moment to come back. Finally, he nodded.

"I have." He cleared his throat to get the huskiness out of it. "Mighty fine ranch." He couldn't fathom why it hadn't passed down to Riley. Losing it must have broken her heart.

Again.

"So my people tell me. Heck of a fight to get it, too. Had a competitor, a rabid developer named Montague."

Fulsom shook his head. "But that gave me a perfect setup."

"What do you mean?" Boone's thoughts were still with the girl he'd once known. The woman who'd haunted him all these years. He forced himself to pay attention to Fulsom instead.

Fulsom clicked his keyboard and an image sprung up onscreen. "Take a look."

Letting his memories go, Boone tried to make sense of what he was seeing. Some kind of map—an architect's rendering of a planned development.

"What is that?" Clay demanded.

"Wait—that's Westfield." Jericho leaned over Boone's shoulder to get a better look.

"Almost right." Fulsom nodded. "Those are the plans for Westfield Commons, a community of seventy luxury homes."

Blood ran cold in Boone's veins as Walker elbowed his way between them and peered at the screen. "Luxury homes? On Westfield? You can't do that!"

"I don't want to. But Montague does. He's frothing at the mouth to bulldoze that ranch and sell it piece by piece. The big, bad developer versus the environmentalists. This show is going to write itself." He fixed his gaze on Boone. "And if you fail, the last episode will show his bulldozers closing in."

"But it's our land; you just said so," Boone protested.

"As long as you meet your goals by December first. Ten committed couples—every couple married by the time the show ends. Ten homes whose energy requirements are one-tenth the normal usage for an American home. Six months' worth of food produced on site stockpiled to last the inhabitants through the winter. And three children."

"Children? Where do we get those?" Boone couldn't keep up. He hadn't promised anything like that. All he'd said in his proposal was that they'd build a community.

"The old-fashioned way. You make them. No cheating; children conceived before the show starts don't count."

"Jesus." Fulsom had lost his mind. He was taking the stakes and raising them to outrageous heights… which was exactly the way to create a prime-time hit, Boone realized.

"It takes nine months to have a child," Jericho pointed out dryly.

"I didn't say they needed to be born. Pregnant bellies are better than squalling babies. Like I said, sex sells, boys. Let's give our viewers proof you and your wives are getting it on."

Boone had had enough. "That's ridiculous, Fulsom. You're—"

"You know what's ridiculous?" Fulsom leaned forward again, suddenly grim. "Famine. Poverty. Violence. War. And yet it never stops, does it? You said you wanted to do something about it. Here's your chance. You're leaving the Navy, for God's sake. Don't tell me you didn't plan to meet a woman, settle down and raise some kids. So I've put a rush on the matter. Sue me."

He had a point. But still—

"I could sell the land to Montague today," Fulsom said. "Pocket the money and get back to sorting out hydrogen fuel cells." He waited a beat. When Boone shook his head, Fulsom smiled in triumph. "Gotta go, boys. Julie, here, will get you all sorted out. Good luck to you on this fabulous venture. Remember—we're going to change the world together."

"Wait—"

Fulsom stood up and walked off screen.

Boone stared as Julie sat down in his place. By the time she had walked them through the particulars of the funding process, and when and how to take possession of the land, Boone's temples were throbbing. He cut the call after Julie promised to send a packet of information, reluctantly pushed his chair back from the table and faced the three men who were to be his partners in this venture.

"Married?" Clay demanded. "No one said anything about getting married!"

"I know."

"And kids? Three out of ten of us men will have to get their wives pregnant. That means all of us will have to be trying just to beat the odds," Jericho said.

"I know."

Walker just looked at him and shook his head.

"I get it! None of us planned for anything like this." Boone stood up. "But none of us thought we had a shot of moving back to Chance Creek, either—or getting our message out to the whole country." When no one answered, he went on. "Are you saying you're out?"

"Hell, I don't know," Jericho said, pacing around the room. "I could stomach anything except that marriage part. I've never seen myself as a family man."

"I don't mind getting hitched," Clay said. "And I want kids. But I want to choose where and when to do it. And Fulsom's setting us up to fail in front of a national audience. If that Montague guy gets the ranch and builds a subdivision on it, everyone in town is going to hate us—and our families."

"So what do we do?" Boone challenged him.

"Not much choice," Walker said. "If we don't sign on, Fulsom will sell to Montague anyway."

"Exactly. The only shot we have of saving that ranch is to agree to his demands," Boone said. He shoved his hands in his pockets, unsure what to do. He couldn't see himself married in two months, let alone trying to have a child with a woman he hadn't even met yet, but giving up—Boone hated to think about it. After all, it wouldn't be the first time they'd done unexpected things to accomplish a mission.

Jericho paced back. "But his demands are—"

"Insane. I know that." Boone knew he was losing them. "He's right, though; a sustainable community made only of men doesn't mean shit. A community that's actually going to sustain itself—to carry on into the future, generation after generation—has to include women and eventually kids. Otherwise we're just playing."

"Fulsom's the one who's playing. Playing with our

lives. He can't demand we marry someone for the sake of his ratings," Jericho said.

"Actually, he can," Clay said. "He's the one with the cash."

"We'll find cash somewhere else—"

"It's more than cash," Boone reminded Jericho. "It's publicity. If we build a community and no one knows about it, what good is it? We went to Fulsom because we wanted him to do just what he's done—find a way to make everyone talk about sustainability."

"By marrying us off one by one?" Jericho stared at each of them in turn. "Are you serious? We just spent the last thirteen years of our lives fighting for our country—"

"And now we're going to fight for it in a whole new way. By getting married. On television. And knocking up our wives—while the whole damn world watches," Boone said.

No one spoke for a minute.

"I sure as hell hope they won't film that part, Chief," Clay said with a quick grin, using the moniker Boone had gained in the SEALs as second in command of his platoon.

"They wouldn't want to film your hairy ass, anyway," Jericho said.

Clay shoved him. Jericho elbowed him away.

"Enough." Walker's single word settled all of them down. They were used to listening to their lieutenant. Walker turned to Boone. "You think this will actually do any good?"

Boone shrugged. "Remember Yemen. Remember what's coming. We swore we'd do what it takes to make a difference." It was a low blow bringing up that disaster, but it was what had gotten them started down this path and he wanted to remind them of it.

"I remember Yemen every day," Jericho said, all trace of clowning around gone.

"So do I." Clay sighed. "Hell, I'm ready for a family anyway. I'm in. I don't know how I'll find a wife, though. Ain't had any luck so far."

"I'll find you one," Boone told him.

"Thanks, Chief." Clay gave him an ironic salute.

Jericho walked away. Came back again. "Damn it. I'm in, too. Under protest, though. Something this serious shouldn't be a game. You find me a wife, too, Chief, but I'll divorce her when the six months are up if I don't like her."

"Wait until Fulsom's given us the deed to the ranch, then do what you like," Boone said. "But if I'm picking your bride, give her a chance."

"Sure, Chief."

Boone didn't trust that answer, but Jericho had agreed to Fulsom's terms and that's all that mattered for now. He looked to Walker. It was crucial that the man get on board. Walker stared back at him, his gaze unfathomable. Boone knew there was trouble in his past. Lots of trouble. The man avoided women whenever he could.

Finally Walker gave him a curt nod. "Find me one, too. Don't screw it up."

Boone let out the breath he was holding. Despite the events of the past hour, a surge of anticipation warmed him from within.

They were going to do it.

And he was going to get hitched.

Was Riley the marrying kind?

RILEY EATON TOOK a sip of her green tea and summoned a smile for the friends who'd gathered on the tiny balcony of her apartment in Boston. Her thoughts were far away, though, tangled in a memory of a hot Montana afternoon when she was only ten. She'd crouched on the bank of Pittance Creek watching Boone Rudman wade through the knee-deep waters, fishing for minnows with a net. Riley had followed Boone everywhere back then, but she knew to stay out of the water and not scare his bait away.

"Mom said marriage is a trap set by men for unsuspecting women," she'd told him, quoting what she'd heard her mother say to a friend over the phone.

"You'd better watch out then," he'd said, poised to scoop up a handful of little fish.

"I won't get caught. Someone's got to want to catch you before that happens."

Boone had straightened, his net trailing in the water. She'd never forgotten the way he'd looked at her—all earnest concern.

"Maybe I'll catch you."

"Why?" She'd been genuinely curious. Getting overlooked was something she'd already grown used to.

"For my wife. If I ever want one. You'll never see me coming." He'd lifted his chin as if she'd argue the point. But Riley had thought it over and knew he was right.

She'd nodded. "You are pretty sneaky."

Riley had never forgotten that conversation, but Boone had and like everyone else he'd overlooked her when the time counted.

Story of her life.

Riley shook off the maudlin thoughts. She couldn't be a good hostess if she was wrapped up in her troubles. Time enough for them when her friends had gone.

She took another sip of her tea and hoped they wouldn't notice the tremor in her hands. She couldn't believe seven years had passed since she'd graduated from Boston College with the women who relaxed on the cheap folding chairs around her. Back then she'd thought she'd always have these women by her side, but now these yearly reunions were the only time she saw them. They were all firmly ensconced in careers that consumed their time and energy. It was hard enough to stay afloat these days, let alone get ahead in the world—or have time to take a break.

Gone were the carefree years when they thought nothing of losing whole weekends to trying out a new art medium, or picking up a new instrument. Once she'd been fearless, throwing paint on the canvas, guided only by her moods. She'd experimented day after day, laughed at the disasters and gloried in the triumphs that took shape under her brushes from time to time. Now she rarely even sketched, and what she produced seemed inane. If she wanted to express the truth of her situation through her art, she'd paint pigeons and gum stuck to the sidewalk. But she wasn't honest anymore.

For much of the past five years she'd been married to her job as a commercial artist at a vitamin distributor, joined to it twenty-four seven through her cell phone and Internet connection. Those years studying art seemed like a dream now; the one time in her life she'd felt like she'd truly belonged somewhere. She had no idea how she'd thought she'd earn a living with a fine arts degree, though. She supposed she'd hadn't thought much about the future back then. Now she felt trapped by it.

Especially after the week she'd had.

She set her cup down and twisted her hands together, trying to stop the shaking. It had started on Wednesday when she'd been called into her boss's office and handed a pink slip and a box in which to pack up her things.

"Downsizing. It's nothing personal," he'd told her.

She didn't know how she'd kept her feet as she'd made her way out of the building. She wasn't the only one riding the elevator down to street level with her belongings in her hands, but that was cold comfort. It had been hard enough to find this job. She had no idea where to start looking for another.

She'd held in her shock and panic that night and all the next day until Nadia from the adoption agency knocked on her door for their scheduled home visit at precisely two pm. She'd managed to answer Nadia's questions calmly and carefully, until the woman put down her pen.

"Tell me about your job, Riley. How will you as a single mother balance work and home life with a child?"

Riley had opened her mouth to speak, but no answer had come out. She'd reached for her cup of tea, but only managed to spill it on the cream colored skirt she'd chosen carefully for the occasion. As Nadia rushed to help her mop up, the truth had spilled from Riley's lips.

"I've just been downsized. I'm sorry; I'll get a new job right away. This doesn't have to change anything, does it?"

Nadia had been sympathetic but firm. "This is why we hesitate to place children with single parents, Riley. Children require stability. We can continue the interview and I'll weigh all the information in our judgement, but until you can prove you have a stable job, I'm afraid you won't qualify for a child."

"That will take years," Riley had almost cried, but she'd bitten back the words. What good would it do to say them aloud? As a girl, she'd dreamed she'd have children with Boone someday. When she'd grown up, she'd thought she'd find someone else. Hadn't she waited long enough to start her family?

"Riley? Are you all right?" Savannah Edwards asked, bringing her back to the present.

"Of course." She had to be. There was no other option but to soldier on. She needed to get a new job. A better job. She needed to excel at it and put the time in to make herself indispensable. Then, in a few years, she could try again to adopt.

"Are you sure?" A tall blonde with hazel eyes, Savannah had been Riley's best friend back in school, and Riley had always had a hard time fooling her. Savannah had been a music major and Riley could have listened to her play forever. She was the first person Riley had met since her grandparents passed away who seemed to care about her wholeheartedly. Riley's parents had been too busy arguing with each other all through her childhood to have much time left over to think about her. They split up within weeks after she left for college. Each remarried before the year was out and both started new families soon after. Riley felt like the odd man out when she visited them on holidays. More than eighteen years older than her half-siblings, she didn't seem to belong anywhere now.

"I'm great now that you three are here." She wouldn't confess the setback that had just befallen her. It was still too raw to process and she didn't want to bring the others down when they'd only just arrived. She wasn't the only one who had it tough. Savannah should have been a concert pianist, but when she broke her wrist in a car accident several years after graduation, she had to give up her aspirations. Instead, she had gone to work as an assistant at a prominent tech company in Silicon Valley and was still there.

"What's on tap for the weekend?" Nora Ridgeway asked as she scooped her long, wavy, light brown hair into a messy updo and secured it with a clip. She'd flown in from Baltimore where she taught English in an inner-city high school. Riley had been shocked to see the dark smudges under her eyes. Nora looked thin. Too thin. Riley wondered what secrets she was hiding behind her upbeat tone.

"I hope it's a whole lot of nothing," Avery Lightfoot said, her auburn curls glinting in the sun. Avery lived in Nashville and worked in the marketing department of one of the largest food distribution companies in North America. She'd studied acting in school, but she'd never been discovered the way she'd once hoped to be. For a brief time she'd created an original video series that she'd posted online, but the advertising revenue she'd generated hadn't added up to much and soon her money had run out. Now she created short videos to market low-carb products to yoga moms. Riley's heart ached for her friend. She sounded as tired as Nora looked.

In fact, everyone looked like they needed a pick-me-up after dealing with flights and taxis, and Riley headed inside to get refreshments. She wished she'd been able to drive to the airport and pick them up. Who could afford a car, though? Even when she'd had a job, Riley found it hard to keep up with her rent, medical insurance and monthly bills, and budget enough for the childcare she'd need when she adopted. Thank God it had been her turn to host their gathering this year. She couldn't have gotten on a plane after the news she'd just received.

When she thought back to her college days she realized her belief in a golden future had really been a pipe dream. Some of her classmates were doing fine. But most of them were struggling to keep their heads above water, just like her. A few had given up and moved back in with their parents.

When she got back to the balcony with a tray of snacks, she saw Savannah pluck a dog-eared copy of *Pride and Prejudice* out of a small basket that sat next to the door. Riley had been reading it in the mornings before work this week as she drank her coffee—until she'd been let go. A little escapism helped start her day off on the right foot.

"Am I the only one who'd trade my life for one of Austen's characters' in a heartbeat?" Savannah asked, flipping through the pages.

"You want to live in Regency England? And be some man's property?" Nora asked sharply.

"Of course not. I don't want the class conflict or the snobbery or the outdated rules. But I want the beauty of their lives. I want the music and the literature. I want afternoon visits and balls that last all night. Why don't we do those things anymore?"

"Who has time for that?" Riley certainly hadn't when she was working. Now she'd have to spend every waking moment finding a new job.

"I haven't played the piano in ages," Savannah went on. "I mean, it's not like I'm all that good anymore—"

"Are you kidding? You've always been fantastic," Nora said.

"What about romance? I'd kill for a real romance. One that means something," Avery said.

"What about Dan?" Savannah asked.

"I broke up with him three weeks ago. He told me he wasn't ready for a serious relationship. The man's thirty-one. If he's not ready now, when will he be?"

"That's tough." Riley understood what Avery meant. She hadn't had a date in a year; not since Marc Hepstein had told her he didn't consider her marriage material. She should have dumped him long before.

It wasn't like she hadn't been warned. His older sister had taken her aside once and spelled it out for her:

"Every boy needs to sow his wild oats. You're his shiksa fling. You'll see; you won't get a wedding ring from him. Marc will marry a nice Jewish girl in the end."

Riley wished she'd paid attention to the warning, but of course she hadn't. She had a history of dangling after men who were unavailable.

Shiksa fling.

Just a step up from Tagalong Riley.

Riley pushed down the old insecurities that threatened to take hold of her and tried not to give in to her pain over her lost chance to adopt. When Marc had broken up with her, it had been a wake-up call. She'd realized if she waited for a man to love her, she might never experience the joy of raising a child. She'd also realized she hadn't loved Marc enough to spend a life with him. She'd been settling, and she was better than that.

She'd started the adoption process.

Now she'd have to start all over again.

"It wasn't as hard to leave him as you might think." Avery took a sip of her tea. "It's not just Dan. I feel like breaking up with my life. I had a heart once. I know I did. I used to feel—alive."

"Me, too," Nora said softly.

"I thought I'd be married by now," Savannah said, "but I haven't had a boyfriend in months. And I hate my job. I mean, I really hate it!" Riley couldn't remember ever seeing calm, poised Savannah like this.

"So do I," Avery said, her words gushing forth as if a dam had broken. "Especially since I have two of them now. I got back in debt when my car broke down and I needed to buy a new one. Now I can't seem to get ahead."

"I don't have any job at all," Riley confessed. "I've been downsized." She closed her eyes. She hadn't meant to say that.

"Oh my goodness, Riley," Avery said. "What are you going to do?"

"I don't know. Paint?" She laughed dully. She couldn't tell them the worst of it. She was afraid if she talked about her failed attempt to adopt she'd lose control of her emotions altogether. "Can you imagine a life in which we could actually pursue our dreams?"

"No," Avery said flatly. "After what happened last time, I'm so afraid if I try to act again, I'll just make a fool of myself."

Savannah nodded vigorously, tears glinting in her eyes. "I'm afraid to play," she confessed. "I sit down at my piano and then I get up again without touching the keys. What if my talent was all a dream? What if I was fooling myself and I was never anything special at all? My wrist healed years ago, but I can't make myself go for it like I once did. I'm too scared."

"What about you, Nora? Do you ever write these days?" Riley asked gently when Nora remained quiet. When they were younger, Nora talked all the time about wanting to write a novel, but she hadn't mentioned it in ages. Riley had assumed it was because she loved teaching, but she looked as burnt out as the rest of them. Riley knew she worked in an area of Baltimore that resembled a war zone.

Her friend didn't answer, but a tear traced down her cheek.

"Nora, what is it?" Savannah dropped the book and came to crouch by her chair.

"It's one of my students." Nora kept her voice steady even as another tear followed the tracks of the first. "At least I think it is."

"What do you mean?" Riley realized they'd all pulled closer to each other, leaning forward in mutual support and feeling. Dread crept into her throat at Nora's words. She'd known instinctively something was wrong in her friend's life for quite some time, but despite her questions, Nora's e-mails and texts never revealed a thing.

"I've been getting threats. On my phone," Nora said, plucking at a piece of lint on her skirt.

"Someone's texting threats?" Savannah sounded aghast.

"And calling. He has my home number, too."

"What did he say?" Avery asked.

"Did he threaten to hurt you?" Riley demanded. After a moment, Nora nodded.

"To kill you?" Avery whispered.

Nora nodded again. "And more."

Savannah's expression hardened. "More?"

Nora looked up. "He threatened to rape me. He said I'd like it. He got... really graphic."

The four of them stared at each other in shocked silence.

"You can't go back," Savannah said. "Nora, you can't go back there. I don't care how important your work is, that's too much."

"What did the police say?" Riley's hands were shaking again. Rage and shock battled inside of her, but anger won out. Who would dare threaten her friend?

"What did the school's administration say?" Avery demanded.

"That threats happen all the time. That I should change my phone numbers. That the people who make the threats usually don't act on them."

"Usually?" Riley was horrified.

"What are you going to do?" Savannah said.

"What am I supposed to do? I can't quit." Nora seemed to sink into herself. "I changed my number, but it's happening again. I've got nothing saved. I managed to pay off my student loans, but then my mom got sick... I'm broke."

No one answered. They knew Nora's family hadn't

had much money, and she'd taken on debt to get her degree. Riley figured she'd probably used every penny she might have saved to pay it off again. Then her mother had contracted cancer and had gone through several expensive procedures before she passed away.

"Is this really what it's come to?" Avery asked finally. "Our work consumes us, or it overwhelms us, or it threatens us with bodily harm and we just keep going?"

"And what happened to love? True love?" Savannah's voice was raw. "Look at us! We're intelligent, caring, attractive women. And we're all single! None of us even dating. What about kids? I thought I'd be a mother."

"So did I," Riley whispered.

"Who can afford children?" Nora said fiercely. "I thought teaching would be enough. I thought my students would care—" She broke off and Riley's heart squeezed at Nora's misery.

"I've got some savings, but I'll eat through them fast if I don't get another job," Riley said slowly. "I want to leave Boston so badly. I want fresh air and a big, blue sky. But there aren't any jobs in the country." Memories of just such a sky flooded her mind. What she'd give for a vacation at her uncle's ranch in Chance Creek, Montana. In fact, she'd love to go there and never come back. It had been so long since she'd managed to stop by and spend a weekend at Westfield, it made her ache to think of the carefree weeks she spent there every summer as a child. The smell of hay and horses and sunshine on old buildings, the way her grandparents used to let her loose on the ranch to run and play and ride as hard as she wanted to. Their unconditional love. There were few rules at Westfield and those existed purely for the sake of practicality and safety. *Don't spook the horses. Clean and put away tools after you use them. Be home at mealtimes and help with the dishes.*

Away from her parents' arguing, Riley had blossomed, and the skills she'd learned from the other kids in town—especially the Four Horsemen of the Apocalypse—had taught her pride and self-confidence. They were rough and tumble boys and they rarely slowed down to her speed, but as long as she kept up to them, they included her in their fun.

Clay Pickett, Jericho Cook, Walker Norton—they'd treated her like a sister. For an only child, it was a dream come true. But it was Boone who'd become a true friend, and her first crush.

And then had broken her heart.

"I keep wondering if it will always be like this," Avery said, interrupting her thoughts. "If I'll always have to struggle to get by. If I'll never have a house of my own—or a husband or family."

"You'll have a family," Riley assured her, then bit her lip. Who was she to reassure Avery? She could never seem to shake her bad luck—with men, with work, with anything. But out of all the things that had happened to her, nothing left her cringing with humiliation like the memory of the time she'd asked Boone to dance.

She'd been such a child. No one like Boone would have looked twice at her, no matter how friendly he'd been over the years. She could still hear Melissa's sneering words—*No one wants to dance with a Tagalong. Go on home*—and the laughter that followed her when she fled the dance.

She'd returned to Chicago that last summer thinking her heart would never mend, and time had just begun to heal it when her grandparents passed away one after the other in quick succession that winter. Riley had been devastated; doubly so when she left for college the following year and her parents split. It was as if a tidal wave had washed away her childhood in one blow. After that, her parents sold their home and caretakers watched over the ranch. Uncle Russ, who'd inherited it, had found he made a better financier than a cowboy. With his career taking off, he'd moved to Europe soon after.

At his farewell dinner, one of the few occasions she'd seen her parents in the same room since they'd divorced, he'd stood up and raised a glass. "To Riley. You're the only one who loves Westfield now, and I want you to think of it as yours. One day in the future it will be, you know. While I'm away, I hope you'll treat it as your own home. Visit as long as you like. Bring your friends. Enjoy the ranch. My parents would have wanted that." He'd taken her aside later and presented her with a key. His trust in her and his promises had warmed her heart. If she'd own Westfield one day she could stand anything, she'd told herself that night. It was the one thing that had sustained her through life's repeated blows.

"I wish I could run away from my life, even for a little while. Six months would do it," Savannah said, breaking into her thoughts. "If I could clear my mind of everything that has happened in the past few years I know I could make a fresh start."

Riley knew just what she meant. She'd often wished the same thing, but she didn't only want to run away from her life; she wanted to run straight back into her past to a time when her grandparents were still alive. Things had been so simple then.

Until she'd fallen for Boone.

She hadn't seen Uncle Russ since he'd moved away, although she wrote to him a couple of times a year, and received polite, if remote, answers in turn. She had the feeling Russ had found the home of his heart in Munich. She wondered if he'd ever come back to Montana.

In the intervening years she'd visited Westfield whenever she could, more frequently as the sting of Boone's betrayal faded, although in reality that meant a long weekend every three or four months, rather than the expansive summer vacations she'd imagined when she'd received the key. It wasn't quite the same without her grandparents and her old friends, without Boone and the Horsemen, but she still loved the country, and Westfield Manor was the stuff of dreams. Even the name evoked happy memories and she blessed the ancestor whose flight of fancy had bestowed such a distinguished title on a Montana ranch house. She'd always wondered if she'd stumble across Boone someday, home for leave, but their visits had never coincided.

Still, whenever she drove into Chance Creek, her heart rate kicked up a notch and she couldn't help scanning the streets for his familiar face.

"I wish I could run away from my dirty dishes and laundry," Avery said. Riley knew she was attempting to lighten the mood. "I spend my weekends taking care of all my possessions. I bet Jane Austen didn't do laundry."

"In those days servants did it," Nora said, swiping her arm over her cheek to wipe away the traces of her tears. "Maybe we should get servants, too, while we're dreaming."

"Maybe we should, if it means we could concentrate on the things we love," Savannah said.

"Like that's possible. Look at us—we're stuck, all of us. There's no way out." The waver in Nora's voice betrayed her fierceness.

"There has to be," Avery exclaimed.

"How?"

Riley wished she had the answer. She hated seeing the pain and disillusionment on her friends' faces. And she was terrified of having to start over herself.

"What if… what if we lived together?" Savannah said slowly. "I mean, wouldn't that be better than how things are now? If we pooled our resources and figured out how to make them stretch? None of us would have to work so hard."

"I thought you had a good job," Nora said, a little bitterly.

"On paper. The cost of living in Silicon Valley is outrageous, though. You'd be surprised how little is left over when I pay my bills. And inside, I feel... like I'm dying."

A silence stretched out between them. Riley knew just what Savannah meant. At first grown-up life had seemed exciting. Now it felt like she was slipping into a pool of quicksand that she'd never be able to escape. Maybe it would be different if they joined forces. If they pooled their money, they could do all kinds of things.

For the first time in months she felt a hint of possibility.

"We could move where the cost of living is cheaper and get a house together." Savannah warmed to her theme. "With a garden, maybe. We could work part time and share the bills."

"For six months? What good would that do? We'd run through what little money we have and be harder to employ afterward," Nora said.

"How much longer are you willing to wait before you try for the life you actually want, rather than the life that keeps you afloat one more day?" Savannah asked her. "I have to try to be a real pianist. Life isn't worth living if I don't give it a shot. That means practicing for hours every day. I can't do that and work a regular job, too."

"I've had an idea for a screenplay," Avery confessed. "I think it's really good. Six months would be plenty of time for me to write it. Then I could go back to work while I shop it around."

"If I had six months I would paint all day until I had enough canvasses to put on a show. Maybe that would be the start and end of my career as an artist, but at least I'd have done it once," Riley said.

"A house costs money," Nora said.

"Not always," Riley said slowly as an idea took hold in her head. "What about Westfield?" After all, it hadn't been inhabited in years. "Uncle Russ always said I should bring my friends and stay there."

"Long term?" Avery asked.

"Six months would be fine. Russ hasn't set foot in it in over a decade."

"You want us to move to Montana and freeload for six months?" Nora asked.

"I want us to move to Montana and take six months to jumpstart our lives. We'll practice following our passions. We'll brainstorm ideas together for how to make money from them. Who knows? Maybe together we'll come up with a plan that will work."

"Sounds good to me," Avery said.

"I don't know," Nora said. "Do you really think it's work that's kept you from writing or playing or painting? Because if you can't do it now, chances are you won't be able to do it at Westfield either. You'll busy up your days with errands and visits and sightseeing and all that. Wait and see."

"Not if we swore an oath to work on our projects every day," Savannah said.

"Like the oaths you used to swear to do your homework on time? Or not to drink on Saturday night? Or to stop crank-calling the guy who dumped you junior year?"

Savannah flushed. "I was a child back then—"

"I just feel that if we take six months off, we'll end up worse off than when we started."

Savannah leaned forward. "Come on. Six whole months to write. Aren't you dying to try it?" When Nora hesitated, Savannah pounced on her. "I knew it! You want to as badly as we do."

"Of course I want to," Nora said. "But it won't work. None of you will stay at home and hone your craft."

A smile tugged at Savannah's lips. "What if we couldn't leave?"

"Are you going to chain us to the house?"

"No. I'm going to take away your clothes. Your modern clothes," she clarified when the others stared at her. "You're right; we could easily be tempted to treat the time like a vacation, especially with us all together. But if we only have Regency clothes to wear, we'll be stuck because we'll be too embarrassed to go into town. We'll take a six-month long Jane Austen vacation from our lives." She sat back and folded her arms over her chest.

"I love it," Riley said. "Keep talking."

"We'll create a Regency life, as if we'd stepped into one of her novels. A beautiful life, with time for music and literature and poetry and walks. Westfield is rural, right? No one will be there to see us. If we pattern our days after the way Jane's characters spent theirs, we'd have plenty of time for creative pursuits."

Nora rolled her eyes. "What about the neighbors?

What about groceries and dental appointments?"

"Westfield is set back from the road." Riley thought it through. "Savannah's right; we could go for long stretches without seeing anyone. We could have things delivered, probably."

"I'm in," Avery said. "I'll swear to live a Regency life for six months. I'll swear it on penalty of… death."

"The penalty is embarrassment," Savannah said. "If we leave early, we have to travel home in our Regency clothes. I know I'm in. I'd gladly live a Jane Austen life for six months."

"If I get to wear Regency dresses and bonnets, I'm in too," Riley said. What was the alternative? Stay here and mourn the child she'd never have?

"Are you serious?" Nora asked. "Where do we even get those things?"

"We have a seamstress make them, or we sew them ourselves," Avery said. "Come on, Nora. Don't pretend you haven't always wanted to."

The others nodded. After all, it was their mutual love of Jane Austen movies that had brought them together in the first place. Two days into their freshman year at Boston College, Savannah had marched through the halls of their dorm announcing a Jane Austen film festival in her room that night. Riley, Nora and Avery had shown up for it, and the rest was history.

"It'll force us to carry out our plan the way we intend to," Savannah told her. "If we can't leave the ranch, there will be no distractions. Every morning when we put on our clothes we'll be recommitting to our vow to devote six months to our creative pursuits. Think about it, Nora. Six whole months to write."

"Besides, we were so good together back in college," Riley said. "We inspired each other. Why couldn't we do that again?"

"But what will we live on?"

"We'll each liquidate our possessions," Savannah said. "Think about how little most people had in Jane Austen's time. It'll be like when Eleanor and Marianne have to move to a cottage in *Sense and Sensibility* with their mother and little sister. We'll make a shoestring budget and stick to it for food and supplies. If we don't go anywhere, we won't spend any money, right?"

"That's right," Avery said. "Remember what Mrs. John Dashwood said in that novel. 'What on earth can four women want for more than that?—They will live so cheap! Their housekeeping will be nothing at all. They will have no carriage, no horses, and hardly any servants; they will keep no company, and can have no expenses of any kind! Only conceive how comfortable they will be!'"

"We certainly won't have any horses or carriages." Savannah laughed.

"But we will be comfortable, and during the time we're together we can brainstorm what to do next," Riley said. "No one leaves Westfield until we all have a working plan."

"With four of us to split the chores of running the house, it'll be easy," Avery said. "We'll have hours and hours to devote to our craft every day."

Nora hesitated. "You know this is crazy, right?"

"But it's exactly the right kind of crazy," Riley said. "You have to join us, Nora."

Nora shook her head, but just when Riley thought she'd refuse, she shrugged. "Oh, okay. What the hell? I'll do it." Riley's heart soared. "But when our six months are up, I'll be broke," Nora went on. "I'll be homeless, too. I don't see how anything will have improved."

"Everything will have improved," Savannah told her. "I promise. Together we can do anything."

Riley smiled at their old rallying-cry from college. "So, we're going to do it? You'll all come to Westfield with me? And wear funny dresses?"

"And bonnets," Avery said. "Don't forget the bonnets."

"I'm in," Savannah said, sticking out her hand.

"I'm in," Avery said, putting hers down on top of it.

"I guess I'm in," Nora said, and added hers to the pile.

"Well, I'm definitely in." Riley slapped hers down on top of the rest.

Westfield. She was going back to Westfield.

Things were looking up.

End of Excerpt

The Cowboys of Chance Creek Series:

The Cowboy Inherits a Bride (Volume 0)
The Cowboy's E-Mail Order Bride (Volume 1)
The Cowboy Wins a Bride (Volume 2)
The Cowboy Imports a Bride (Volume 3)
The Cowgirl Ropes a Billionaire (Volume 4)
The Sheriff Catches a Bride (Volume 5)
The Cowboy Lassos a Bride (Volume 6)
The Cowboy Rescues a Bride (Volume 7)
The Cowboy Earns a Bride (Volume 8)
The Cowboy's Christmas Bride (Volume 9)

The Heroes of Chance Creek Series:

The Navy SEAL's E-Mail Order Bride (Volume 1)
The Soldier's E-Mail Order Bride (Volume 2)
The Marine's E-Mail Order Bride (Volume 3)
The Navy SEAL's Christmas Bride (Volume 4)
The Airman's E-Mail Order Bride (Volume 5)

The SEALs of Chance Creek Series:

A SEAL's Oath
A SEAL's Vow
A SEAL's Pledge
A SEAL's Consent
A SEAL's Purpose
A SEAL's Resolve
A SEAL's Devotion
A SEAL's Desire
A SEAL's Struggle
A SEAL's Triumph

Brides of Chance Creek Series:

Issued to the Bride One Navy SEAL
Issued to the Bride One Airman
Issued to the Bride One Sniper
Issued to the Bride One Marine
Issued to the Bride One Soldier

About the Author

NYT and USA Today bestselling author Cora Seton loves cowboys, hiking, gardening, bike-riding, and lazing around with a good book. Mother of four, wife to a computer programmer/backyard farmer, she recently moved to Victoria and looks forward to a brand new chapter in her life. Like the characters in her Chance Creek series, Cora enjoys old-fashioned pursuits and modern technology, spending mornings in her garden, and afternoons writing the latest Chance Creek romance novel. Visit **www.coraseton.com** to read about new releases, contests and other cool events!

Blog:

www.coraseton.com

Facebook:

www.facebook.com/coraseton

Twitter:

www.twitter.com/coraseton

Newsletter:

www.coraseton.com/sign-up-for-my-newsletter

56493431R00202

Made in the USA
San Bernardino, CA
12 November 2017